Mission Compromised

by

Graysen Morgen

2018

Mission Compromised © 2018 Graysen Morgen
Triplicity Publishing, LLC

ISBN-13: 978-0999737088
ISBN-10: 0999737082

This is a work of fiction. Names, characters, places, and incidents are the product of the author's imagination and are used fictitiously. Any resemblance to actual persons, living or dead, business establishments, events of any kind, or locales is entirely coincidental.
Printed in the United States of America
First Edition – 2018

Cover Design: Triplicity Publishing, LLC
Interior Design: Triplicity Publishing, LLC
Editor: Megan Brady - Triplicity Publishing, LLC

Also by Graysen Morgen

Boone Creek (Law & Order Series: book 1)

Castor Valley (Law & Order Series: book 2)

Never Let Go (Never Series: book 1)

Never Quit (Never Series: book 2)

Meant to Be

Coming Home

Bridesmaid of Honor (Bridal Series: book 1)

Brides (Bridal Series: book 2)

Mommies (Bridal Series: book 3)

Crashing Waves

Cypress Lake

Falling Snow

Fast Pitch

Fate vs. Destiny

In Love, at War

Just Me

Love, Loss, Revenge

Natural Instinct

Secluded Heart

Submerged

Special thanks to my editor, Megan Brady, who catches all of the minuscule mistakes my eyes overlook! *Muchas gracias!*

For my wife.
Je t'aime et cette vie aventureuse.

PROLOGUE

Natalia Luis de Faria Moreno stood on her tippy toes and wrapped her arms around her father's neck, kissing his bearded cheek. "Are you sure, Papai?" she asked in their native Portuguese.

"Of course, Nita." Sabio Davi de Faria Moreno smiled, looking dearly at his only child. She'd grown up into a beautiful woman. "It is for you. Keep it safe always," he added, turning his eyes to the round pendant lying just below the center of her collarbone. It had a cloudy stone in the middle, with a mixture of black and gray colors. The yellow gold setting and matching chain complemented her olive complexion.

"I will." She grinned, showing off pearly-white teeth before hugging him again. Her father was like a big teddy bear to her. He was a robust, but strong man with a dark-brown mustache and goatee that connected to a jaw line beard. He had a full head of thick, matching hair that he kept short and neatly trimmed. There was barely a time in her life when he wasn't impeccably dressed, and now was no exception as he stood in front of her wearing a grayish-blue, three-piece suit and a striped tie with an off-white shirt.

"It reminds me of your eyes," he said, looking at the color that matched her mother's. Ana Cintia de Luis Moreno was beautiful and could've easily been a model. Her daughter shared her nearly black, wavy hair and gray

1

eyes. Both women were slender built, but Natalia stood three inches taller at five foot seven.

Natalia pulled the stone away from her chest and peered down at it. "I think it looks like moon dust."

Sabio shrugged. "I'm pretty sure it's more valuable," he mumbled.

Natalia raised a brow. Her father had never brought up finances with her. They had always had money, his job working in diplomatic relations for the Portuguese government paid him well and had allowed them to live in other countries around the world for her entire childhood, but finances were something he'd never spoke about with his family. "Is everything okay?" she asked.

"Yes. Why wouldn't it be?" he questioned, puffing out his chest, which lifted his chin slightly.

"I don't know," she answered, smiling before turning to look out the window. The Eiffel Tower glimmered in the distance with colorful tourists gathered around its base. She missed France. It was the last country she'd lived in with her parents before going home to Portugal for college, where she received a bachelor's and then master's degree in Marine Conservation. She stayed when she was offered a position at the Lisbon Oceanarium, a job she'd had for three years. Before France, her family had spent time in Spain, the USA, and UK.

"What time does your flight leave?" Sabio asked, checking his watch.

"Soon," she sighed. Leaving her parents was always hard, even when she was heading back home to pack for her first vacation in almost three years; a two-week trip to Fiji, and birthday present from her father. She'd been overly excited ever since he'd told her about it a month earlier. He bought it so that she could enjoy peace and serenity while she prepared for her upcoming PhD exams, something she'd worked very hard for, and needed if she ever wanted to get somewhere with her career.

"Your mother is jealous. I believe I'm going to have to take her to Tahiti or some other exotic place to make up for it," he teased.

"Isn't she in Madrid with her friends, helping with one of their daughters who is getting married?" she laughed. "I think her hands are full … at least for now."

"You know your mother. I don't think Cintia has said no to anyone in the thirty years that we've been together." He smiled. "It's good for her to go do things. I spend more time in my office than I do at home anyway."

"You work too hard, Papai."

"Bah," he mumbled, brushing her off. "You're going to be late."

"Thank you again," she added, touching her pendant.

"Anything for you, my child. Remember, keep it safe, Nita."

"Always." She kissed his cheek again. "I love you, Papai. Give my love to Mamãe when she returns."

"I will. Don't spend all of your time in that water, my little fish. Study hard," he said.

"You know me so well," Natalia laughed, waving as she walked out the door.

*

Christian Garnier couldn't remember the last time she'd done anything remotely close to vacationing. When the opportunity suddenly arose, a little relaxation had sounded wonderful. Even though she had work to do, what

3

better place to do it than a private resort in Fiji? She uncrossed her ankles, stowed her tray, and watched the turquoise water get closer and closer as the plane descended.

PART
1

CHAPTER ONE

After touching down at Nadi International Airport on the mainland, the plane taxied to a stop at the first of only two gates at the terminal. Christian was one of the first few passengers off the plane. She walked over, leaning her back against the wall, just inside. She had never been to Fiji, but she'd seen a few exotic places in her lifetime. She was thankful for the dark, Rayban sunglasses hiding her eyes as she examined the people exiting the plane and gathering around nearby.

"Welcome to Fiji!" a man said, rushing over with his hands in the air and a huge smile on his face. "The baggage claim area is to your right, at the end of the terminal."

Christian wondered how many times a day he must do that same routine, greeting each incoming plane.

"Your luggage will be available momentarily. If you are transferring to an outer island, please make your way towards the buses to Denaru Island, where you will be able to catch the Malolo Catamaran to the Mamanuca Islands, or book a helicopter or sea plane to any of the other islands."

Christian pushed her sunglasses up on her head and followed the crowd towards the transfer area. A few people went over to the helicopter and sea plane desks, but the majority waited to collect their luggage and board the buses.

Natalia stood on the upper deck of the catamaran, feeling the salty air tinge her face as the boat raced across the turquoise water. It had been so long since she'd had the sun on her back and ocean water on her skin. Working as a Marine Conservationist, you'd think she spent most of her time around marine life and ocean water, but her job was managing the education workshops for teachers, as well as all of their educational tools. The reason she was going for her PhD was to become the Head of Education at the Oceanarium. Her goal in becoming a conservationist was to educate people on marine life and how to preserve it.

As the cat rolled over a wave, Natalia's mind was elsewhere and she was thrown slightly off balance. She barely had time to react before someone steadied her. Natalia didn't have to look twice, to tell the person with short, curly, dark hair and dark sunglasses, was female.

"Careful," the woman said as she passed by, walking towards the port side from the bow without looking back.

Natalia's focus went back to the island in front of them, growing larger as they became closer. She reached up, touching her pendant. "Thank you, Papai," she whispered.

CHAPTER TWO

"What do you mean you double booked?" Natalia growled. "I had an overwater bungalow booked over a month ago."

The man on the other side of the check-in desk at Totoka Wasa Resort sighed. He'd never seen two people booked for the exact same time in the exact same bungalow, and he'd worked for the resort for four years, and the last year as the desk manager. "I'm sorry, Ms. Moreno. I've checked and rechecked our system. There are two parties booked for your bungalow. Perhaps we can reschedule your booking."

Natalia shook her head. She was seething with anger. "Don't you have other bungalows available? Who booked first? Put the second person in a beach bungalow instead of over water."

"Ma'am, we are completely booked for the next two months. My assistant just called around and all the resorts on this island are fully booked."

"What the hell am I supposed to do? Share my room with a stranger?"

*

Christian watched the heated exchange from her position at the other end of the counter, where another desk employee, presumably the assistant manager, was giving her the same speech.

"How is this even possible?" she asked.

"We're unsure, ma'am. But, you have our deepest apologies."

She checked her watch and raised a brow. "What exactly are my options? I've been standing here for nearly half an hour, after flying halfway around the world."

"We have no other accommodations available. We can make a call to another island or the mainland, perhaps there is another resort with a vacancy. Have you met the other guest? Maybe you two wouldn't mind sharing."

"Would you share your vacation with a stranger?" she asked in a monotone voice.

*

"I've flown around the world. I don't even know what day it is right now. I'm not about to turn around and fly home," Natalia sighed. She'd tried to call her father, but her cell service was completely unreliable on the small island.

"Excuse me," Christian said from a few feet away. "We meet again," she added.

Natalia gave her an odd look.

"Bow of the catamaran," Christian said.

"Oh … yeah. Right." Natalia nodded, clearing her throat. "Wait…are you the other person booked in my bungalow?"

Christian nodded. "I believe you're booked in mine."

"Actually," the manager cut in. "We can't see the exact time, but you both booked on the same day."

Natalia squeezed her eyes shut and shook her head. Her quiet vacation in paradise was turning into hell, and it hadn't even begun.

"I'm sure you're as upset as I am about this situation."

"Upset? That's an understatement. How much will it take for you to rebook?" Natalia asked. "If I can get my father on the phone, I can wire you whatever you want…within reason of course."

Christian shook her head. "I haven't been on vacation in three years, and this has been planned for a long time. I don't get time off from my job. I'm sorry, I can't change my plans. What about you, can you rebook?"

"No," Natalia said flatly. "This is a special trip for me."

"Well, where does that leave us?"

"Perhaps you could share the room," the manager interjected with a shrug and sympathetic smile. He was out of options and sure he was going to get fired for this snafu.

Natalia looked at Christian. She seemed harmless, and had a touch of an accent in her English that Natalia couldn't quite place. "Are you from the UK?"

"France … well, both actually. I'm a bit of a European mutt. You?"

"Portugal."

"Beautiful country," Christian mumbled.

"I'll pay for all of your expenses for this trip and pay for first class accommodations for you anywhere in Portugal. My father works for the government."

"That won't be necessary."

"You honestly think we should share the room?" Natalia squeaked.

"We seem to have no other choice. We've been standing here for over an hour, hemming and hawing, and we've gotten nowhere. Do you have a better suggestion, besides trying to buy me off?"

"No," Natalia sighed as she ran a hand through her long, dark hair, pushing it back over her shoulder.

"I apologize. I know that it's not enough, but your meals, drinks, rentals, anything … it's on the house for your entire stay," the manager said.

"I didn't say I was sharing," Natalia mumbled, still unhappy about the situation.

"Look, I'm not thrilled about this either, but I'm tired and hungry. I'm willing to share space if you are," Christian said.

Natalia nodded.

"Wonderful," the manager said, blowing a sigh of relief. "You're on the very end of the dock in number twelve. Here are two keys. I'm going to keep both names on the reservation, but there's no need for a credit card for incidentals. Everything is on Totoka Wasa Resort."

"Great," Natalia said sarcastically as she grabbed her key and signed the paper.

Christian smiled sympathetically at the manager, knowing it wasn't his fault, as she also signed for the reservation. Natalia was already out the door by the time she grabbed her luggage and headed for the exit.

*

Natalia opened the door to number twelve, the last bungalow at the end of the gangway, and pulled her suitcase inside behind her. The room was slightly larger than she'd pictured, with a king-size bed and wicker couch

12

directly in front of it, both facing the sliding glass door that went out to the deck. An oval, glass-topped coffee table sat in front of the couch. A sea of turquoise water added some color to the lightly stained teakwood furniture, floor and sundeck. Creme-colored linens covered the bed, with matching cushions on the couch.

She left her bag near the door as she looked around, opening the first of two closed doors, which was a small closet. She went to the next door, hoping to find another bedroom, but it was the bathroom, complete with an oval tub in the center of the room, and a glass enclosed shower along the back wall. The double sink counter was on the opposite end, with the toilet next to it.

"This just keeps getting better," she growled sarcastically.

"Let me guess, one bed?" Christian said from the doorway of the bungalow.

"Yep."

Christian nodded. This wasn't exactly what she had in mind, but she'd have to make do. "I guess we can alternate nights in the bed with the other person taking the couch," she suggested.

"I didn't fly halfway around the world to sleep on a couch," Natalia huffed.

"You think I did? Look, uh … I'm sorry, I didn't get your name."

"Natalia … Moreno. You?"

"Christian Garnier."

Natalia smiled for the first time and mumbled, "Fifty Shades."

Christian furrowed her brow. "Not exactly. I didn't read the books or see the movies, but I'm pretty sure *that* Christian was a man. Besides, I don't need a sex room to make a woman's legs tremble," she said matter-of-factly, placing her suitcase on the bed and completely ignoring the guffawed look on Natalia's face. "Anyway, we're stuck in this situation, and unless you want to give up and go home, I say we make the best of it."

"Uh huh …" Natalia muttered. *I can't believe this is happening. I've worked so hard and was looking forward to nothing but these two weeks. Now, I have to spend them with a complete stranger…no matter how attractive she is. This is … hell in paradise.* She watched the other woman across the room. She was dressed casually in slacks and a collared shirt. Natalia could tell she exercised often by the way her body filled out her clothing. A pile of curly, dark hair sat on top of her head, barely long enough to run your fingers through, with the sides trimmed up. One stray curl fell forward, lying against her forehead. She wasn't as pasty white as most French or British people, but she certainly wasn't naturally olive-skinned like Natalia.

*

Christian opened the sliding glass door and stepped out onto the deck. A round, wicker chair, big enough for two people to curl up on, sat to the left. Two loungers were directly in front of her. A narrow staircase of four steps took her down to the small swim platform. A ladder was folded up on the side that went down to the water, and two boat cleats were mounted to the edge for tying up kayaks or canoes. She could see through the clear water to the white sandy bottom. A handful of colorful fish swam by, forming a tiny school. *It could be a lot worse,* she thought as she looked around at the sea around her. A smaller island was off in the distance, miles away more than likely. Turning back towards the bungalow, she noticed the mountainous range behind the resort that made up the entire island. "It's not so bad," she called, seeing Natalia looking at her.

Natalia felt her demeanor change completely as she stepped out into the sun and salt air. "This is where I belong," she whispered, walking down to the swim platform, just as Christian had. "Thank you, Papai," she uttered, touching her pendant as she let her eyes take in one of the most beautiful places she'd ever seen.

"It's serene, isn't it?" Christian said quietly from a couple of feet away.

Natalia startled slightly at the sound of the voice nearby. For a split second, she was sure she was alone. "Yes … yes, it is," she replied softly.

CHAPTER THREE

The sun was still an hour away from the beginning of its descent when Christian's stomach rumbled. She hadn't eaten since earlier on the plane, and the mini fridge in the room was stocked with several bottles of spring water and a dozen mini liquor and liqueur bottles. The shelf above the fridge had a coffee pot, two cups, and a handful of coffee packages with sugar and cream packets. A small basket with bananas and oranges sat next to the coffee supplies. Christian eyed the basket but decided against it after looking at the time on her black, square-shaped watch. It looked similar to a sports watch for a runner or athlete. The LED display lit up with blue numbers, revealing the time whenever she moved her arm. A heavy-duty rubber-type strap kept it secured to her left wrist. "Do you want to go up to the restaurant and get dinner?" she asked, hoping the other woman would say yes. She was a stranger, and Christian didn't trust her not to go through her suitcase.

Natalia was lying in one of the loungers, staring out at the water. She'd been fighting off her own hunger ever since they arrived at the resort. She let out a deep breath and stood up. "Sure," she replied, walking back inside.

*

When the waitress stopped at their table out on the lanai, facing the lagoon pool, Natalia ordered a floral sounding, local cocktail. Christian asked for a water with lemon.

"You don't drink?" Natalia asked.

"Yes, I just wasn't in the mood." Christian shrugged as she perused the menu.

"After the day I've had, she could leave a pitcher of whatever I ordered."

Christian laughed softly. "I don't doubt it. My day hasn't been the greatest either. However, the island sea bass sounds delicious, as does the coconut cheesecake. I believe I'll be drowning my bad day in food."

"If your growling stomach is any indication, you're probably right." Natalia smiled. "So, since we're stuck in the same room for the next thirteen days, tell me about yourself. I need to know you're not a serial killer or something worse."

Christian raised a brow. "What exactly would be worse?"

Natalia shrugged and laughed. "I have no idea."

"Well, I assure you, I'm not a serial killer. I work for a company that allows me to travel the world, but it also keeps me too busy to have much of a life. I'm afraid I'm pretty boring."

"Is that what you're doing here ... working?"

Christian nodded. "Yes and no. Work brought me here, but I always like to enjoy a little leisure time. What about you? What brought you to paradise?"

"Surprisingly, work, too. I'm studying to get another degree so that I can be promoted. What better place to have tranquil peace and quiet?"

"That makes sense, but why waste a wonderful vacation?"

"Oh, there won't be any wasting, I promise you. However, I'm not sure how much actual work I'll get done now that I'm not alone."

The waitress broke the conversation long enough to deliver their drinks and take their dinner order.

"I'm sure we'll be doing our own thing and only see each other in passing," Christian added once she walked away.

"I agree. There's no reason why we shouldn't be able to give each other the space we need to work."

"I'll drink to that," Christian replied, holding up her water.

Natalia grabbed her pink drink, clinking her glass to Christian's before taking a sip of the fruity and floral mixed concoction. "Mmm. Yes, she can definitely leave a pitcher of this behind."

Christian chuckled as she pushed her sunglasses up on her head. The bright orange glow of the setting sun covered the island, then quickly vanished beneath the horizon.

*

Natalia had wanted to hate the woman sitting across from her. In a way, she actually did, but their situation was as much her fault as it was Natalia's, and neither of them had control over the computers and registration system of the resort. Still, the inconvenience was enough to make Natalia bitter…at least until the woman turned a pair of beautiful, baby blue eyes on her.

You're not doing it. No way. I don't care if she's a stranger you'll never see again…not happening, she told herself. How the hell could she be attracted to the person who is invading on the private birthday vacation her father bought for her?

I'll just have to keep hating her. It's better this way.

*

As soon as they'd finished their dinner, the evening show began on the lawn near the pool deck. Three men dressed in what looked like grass skirts, lit the ends of their batons on fire and began swirling them around and around. Three women with matching grass skirts and bikini tops joined them, dancing with their hips bouncing from side to side like hula dancers in Hawaii, while another two men pounded a beat on the bongo drums.

Natalia and Christian were lucky to have chosen outdoor seating. They were close to front and center for the show, with only the pool separating them. No words were spoken, only oohs and ahhs were heard from the crowd as the baton twirlers became more and more creative, tossing them in the air and back and forth to each other. One man even lit another baton and twirled two at the same time, one in each hand.

Natalia took pictures and video of the show with her phone, while Christian simply sat back and watched, taking in her surroundings at the same time. The resort seemed to come to life at night. She wondered what it would be like in the middle of the day when everyone was awake and out and about. She also wondered how many people were staying at the private, adult only resort. She knew there were twelve overwater bungalows, but she had no idea how many they had on land. She remembered the brochure she was given after signing the papers for her reservation. The land bungalows faced the beach on one side of the gangway that led to the overwater bungalows. The beach on the opposite side was for sunbathing and water activities. It was also a nude beach.

By the time Christian's mind came back to the show going on in front of her, it was over. Tiki torches were then lit all around the pool area, giving it a soft glow. She tried to stifle a yawn, but that only made it worse.

"That's contagious," Natalia mumbled, yawning herself. "It's been the longest day in my life. I'm going to head back."

"I think I'll join you. I'm afraid they'll find me passed out right here at this table if I don't go now."

Natalia shrugged. "Sure you don't want to stay?" she teased.

"You're not getting rid of me that easy. Enjoy the bed because tomorrow night it's mine."

"Can't wait," she replied sarcastically.

CHAPTER FOUR

Christian watched the first rays of orange, paint the horizon in delicate streaks as she sipped her coffee. She was stretched out on a lounger, which felt like a high-end pillow-top mattress compared to the thin, straw-filled cushions of the couch she'd slept on. She was sure the floor would've given her a better night's sleep.

After sneaking back inside, careful not to wake sleeping beauty in her perfect slumber, she returned to the chair with a full cup of coffee, and a banana. By this time, the sun had begun to make its appearance, covering everything in an orange glow. Sunrise was her favorite time of day. There was something calming about being up to watch a new day dawn.

She tore open the banana, wishing she had some peanut butter to spread on it. On a whim, she dipped the end into her coffee and took a bite. "Not bad," she whispered, doing it again.

*

Christian was about to go change into her running clothes when the glass door opened. Natalia appeared with a cup of coffee in her hand, sipping it carefully. She walked to the railing of the deck, looking out at the water surrounding them. She was dressed in a tiny pair of pink satin shorts with a matching tank top that left little to the

21

imagination. A loosely tied, thigh-high robe completed the ensemble. She'd obviously packed for someone who wouldn't be sharing her room with a stranger.

Christian nearly swallowed her tongue as she pulled her eyes away from the woman standing nearby. She'd seen the way Natalia had looked at her…more than once. It wouldn't take much, but she wasn't there to make friends, and she certainly wasn't there to find a bed companion. Relationships complicated things. She had work to do, and it was about time she got to that work … before she made a mistake she'd never be able to take back. She stood up and tossed the last of her coffee into the water.

"That's bad, you know that, right? Anything that isn't natural to the environment upsets the chemistry. Any fish that were schooling right there are liable to never return to that spot," Natalia chided.

"Thanks. I slept great, too," Christian grumbled as she went inside. *What the hell is she, some kind of environmentalist?* She quickly changed into a pair of running shorts, a sports bra, and a tank top. Then, she pulled on her socks and sneakers, and shoved her phone into the holder on her upper arm. She was gone by the time Natalia turned around to see what she was doing.

"She's such a pain in the ass," Natalia said to no one as she sat down in the same lounger, feeling a touch of warmth leftover from Christian. She thought about opening her laptop to start studying her notes, but she couldn't pull her eyes from the water. She'd wanted nothing more than to take a dip since she'd arrived, but her rumbling tummy told her breakfast was more important. She shook her head when she saw the banana peel on the ground beside the lounger. "I'm surprised she didn't fling this in, too," she growled, grabbing it and throwing it in the trash. "I don't like her," she huffed.

*

Natalia chose an inside, window seat in the restaurant. Breakfast was a full buffet bar consisting of the usual eggs, bacon, sausage, and toast, but it also had several types of fruits, cereals, grains and muffins. She chose a vanilla flavored, Greek yogurt cup and opened the lid. Then, she added a spoonful of blueberries, strawberries, and whole grains. The waitress had brought her a cup of coffee by the time she'd returned to her table. She threw her hair over her shoulder and mixed the yogurt concoction before taking a hearty bite. She glanced at her phone, which seemed to still be struggling between one and two bars. Looking out the window, she noticed people were already in the pool and lounging in the chairs on the deck. She couldn't see the nude beach, but the side of beach in front of the restaurant and land bungalows, was in plain view. A handful of people were out in the sand. She took a few more bites of her breakfast, squinting her eyes to try and zoom in further down the beach. It didn't take long for the object to come into view. She nearly missed her mouth with the spoon as she recognized the odd woman sharing her room. *Christian.*

She wanted to get mad, but how was the woman to know she liked running, too? It wasn't like they'd talked about much. "Does she have to run with no shirt on? Really?" she muttered, trading her yogurt for coffee as she drew her eyes back to the pool. *I hate her.*

*

Christian checked her watch. She'd run four miles, creating a path around the resort and down the beach. Her legs felt good. It had been at least three days since her last run, but that one had been on steadier terrain along the Seine River. And it was nowhere near as hot. She realized the mistake in wearing her tank top a mile and a half in, and removed it, tucking it into the back of her shorts like a tail. She walked further down the beach, past the restaurant and pool area while she cooled her legs down. The sight of a naked man lying on a beach towel, with his hairless penis flopped to the side, nearly made her gag. She turned around and headed back to the bungalow to change and take a quick dip in the pool to finish her cool down.

*

"How was your run?" Natalia asked sarcastically, seeing Christian as soon as she entered the bungalow.

"Eye opening. You should've gone."

"You didn't exactly ask."

"We're not glued at the hip. I figured you might want some space."

Natalia nodded. "Where did you go?"

"Just around the resort and down the beach. There are a few different trails that look like they go up into the mountain, but I stayed close. I'll probably check them out tomorrow. I like exploring new places," Christian answered before popping into the bathroom to change.

"So, that's what was eye-opening?"

"No. I saw a penis," Christian said, stepping back out of the bathroom in a black and white bikini top with short shorts for bottoms. Up close, Natalia could see she wasn't just slender, she had the body of an athlete.

"Wait. What?"

"The nude beach. I suggest you not go over there … unless floppy, wrinkled penises are your thing." Christian winked, walking past her with a beach towel.

Natalia simply stared as she left the bungalow.

*

The lagoon-style pool was quite large and wrapped around a corner. Most of it was shallow at only four feet deep, so there wasn't much swimming. Everyone was either at the swim-up bar, sitting on water stools; or standing against the edge of the bar, with their body in the water. Christian avoided that area as she swam a few laps back and forth in the cool water, all the while, keeping her eyes on the gangway. She sunk down into the water when she saw Natalia walk over to the rental hut. She was wearing a white, nearly see through, string bikini that left little to the imagination. *What are you up to?*

Her thoughts were answered a few minutes later when her roommate passed by with a snorkel set and a paddle board. Christian's curiosity was peaked, but she couldn't remember the last time she'd had a pool at her discretion, so she went back to her laps.

CHAPTER FIVE

The bungalow was empty when Christian returned. It had been nearly an hour since she'd seen Natalia up at the rental hut, but it didn't take long to find her. Christian leaned over the railing, looking down at the crystal-clear water. A nice view of Natalia's round ass and bareback was visible as she snorkeled over a reef twenty yards away. She sighed, glancing around at her surroundings. They seemed to be the only two people, but she knew the resort was at full capacity.

Going back inside, Christian grabbed a bottle of water and checked her phone. The crisp, cool liquid coating her throat felt wonderful as she took a long gulp, swallowing down close to half of the bottle. She put the cap back on and went back outside to relax in a lounger and let the sun dry her water-logged skin and bathing suit.

*

Natalia hadn't noticed Christian until she walked from the swim platform up to the next level. She wished she'd had sunglasses on so she could discreetly examine the toned body before her. There was something about the mysterious woman that both intrigued and infuriated her. She still wondered why the woman hadn't taken the offered money to change her booking. Then again, she wasn't budging either. So, here they were, two strangers sharing a

500sqft space for the next two weeks. *Make the best of it,* she thought as she toweled off her hair.

"Did you see any fish, or have they all vanished forever?" Christian teased. She'd been watching from behind the dark lenses of her sunglasses as Natalia toweled off. She forced herself to pull her eyes away when Natalia bent over, wringing the water out of her long hair, but not before roaming her nearly naked body one last time.

"As a matter of fact, there were no fish where you tainted the water. I had to swim out a ways to see anything," Natalia grumbled.

Christian rolled her eyes behind her shades and ignored her as Natalia walked inside, returning with a bottle of water. She stared out at the water, scanning back and forth. She wished she could see the gangway, but it was located on the front side of the bungalows, with the deck and swim platform on the back. Splashing to the left caught her attention. She quickly turned her head to see a man and woman playfully slapping water at each other as they swam around. By the looks of their affection, they were probably newlyweds on their honeymoon. Christian checked her watch, then lied back, closing her eyes.

*

"Damn it," Natalia huffed. She'd been trying to get on the paddleboard for the last twenty minutes to no avail. "This looks so damn easy on YouTube," she mumbled, climbing out of the water to try again. Each time she attempted to step off the dock onto the board, it moved, tossing her into the water.

"You're doing it wrong," Christian called.

Natalia looked up to see her leaning against the railing. She gritted her teeth and grabbed the board, giving it another try.

Splash!

Natalia spit water out of her mouth and climbed back up the ladder, twice as angry as she was before, because now she had a know-it-all audience.

"I told you, you're doing it wrong," Christian chuckled.

"If you're so damn good at it, let me see you do it!" Natalia snapped.

Christian hadn't meant to piss her off, but she truly was going about it incorrectly. In fact, she was lucky she hadn't cracked her head on the swim platform. Shrugging, she set her water bottle down and walked down the stairs. Natalia handed her the paddle, and Christian walked over to the board floating beside the platform. She climbed down the ladder and stepped right onto the board. Balancing, she put the paddle in the water and began propelling herself around, managing to paddleboard in one try without getting wet.

"Show off," Natalia muttered. "Of course she's perfect." She crossed her arms and shook her head.

Christian paddled close to the platform and grinned like a Cheshire cat as she passed by. "Want a ride?" she called.

"You're an ass," Natalia called.

Christian laughed as she came over to the swim ladder and stepped off the board. She handed the paddle back to Natalia.

Following her example, Natalia stepped down the ladder and placed one foot on the board. As soon as she attempted to place the second one, she was dumped in the water. "Son of a bitch!" she sputtered.

"You have to balance and use your core," Christian said. She was still standing on the swim platform.

Natalia wanted to fling her into the water headfirst. "I'm using my core. I know how to balance. I'm not stupid." She swam the board back over and gave it another failed try.

Unable to watch any longer, Christian walked over, taking the paddle from her. She went down the ladder and sat on the board, straddling it like a surfboard with her feet dangling in the water under her. "Come here," she said.

"What? Where?" Natalia questioned.

Christian slid back slightly. "Here," she added, patting the board in front of her.

Natalia looked at her like she was crazy.

Christian removed her sunglasses and handed them to Natalia, who rushed up the stairs to place them on the table between the loungers. "I promise not to drown you," she said.

"Somehow, I don't think I believe you," Natalia replied, coming back down the stairs.

"Do you trust me?" Christian asked, turning her beautiful, baby blue eyes up to Natalia.

"I ..." Natalia strained for words.

"Come on." Christian held out her hand.

Throwing caution to the wind, Natalia stepped closer. *What's the worst that could happen? I'll just wind up back in the water. Maybe that's a good idea. I could use some cooling off.* Her mind raced as she placed her hand against Christian's.

"Go slow and use your balance. Just sit down like I am," Christian directed.

Natalia did as she was told, climbing down onto the board like a little kid on the monkey bars for the first time. As soon as she was seated with her feet in the water, she slid back to keep from pushing the nose of the board down and backed right into Christian's crotch. She froze.

"It's okay. We have to keep our weight together or we'll tip over," Christian said, gulping down the lump in her throat that rose as soon as she felt the warmth of another body against her. "Here we go," she added, taking a deep breath as she grabbed the paddle and pushed off.

Natalia had nothing to hold onto, except Christian's thighs which were pushed up against hers. She only grabbed them a few times as Christian maneuvered them all around.

"If you keep your core muscles tight, you'll be able to feel every little ripple of the board scooting over the water. This will help you balance while you paddle. It's fairly easy … once you get the hang of it. It's all about feeling the board and making tiny adjustments with your weight using only your core," Christian explained as she tried to calm her racing heart. Natalia's soft hand on her thigh was driving her mind in a direction she didn't need it to go. She paddled them back over to the dock and kept the board steady while Natalia climbed off. Then, she got off the board, holding the paddle an extra second while looking into Natalia's smoky gray eyes. "Give it a try," she said, clearing her throat.

Natalia was sure she saw the hesitation in Christian's eyes, but unsure what to do about it, she ignored the burning in her gut and stepped down onto the board. With a gentle push off the dock, she tightened her core to balance herself and placed the paddle in the water. Using one slow stroke after another, she paddled around like a beginner, but she'd finally done it.

"Not bad," Christian called. "Let me know when you want to race," she teased.

"Funny!" Natalia said sarcastically.

Christian watched her move around like a turtle for a few minutes before going back up to the deck. Locating her sunglasses, she slid them back on but kept a vigil on the new paddle boarder a few yards away.

*

Christian listened to the shower running as she lay on the lounger, looking out at the water. She hated having to wait her turn to wash off the saltwater and sweat from the day, but she wasn't about to do a tandem shower, and Natalia had been the first to go inside. She'd chosen to stay outside and wait her turn. The little stunt on the paddleboard had been too close. She couldn't remember the last time she'd actually looked at someone. For that split second, it was like time had stood still. She'd forgotten where she was; what she was doing. She'd nearly lost herself in the person looking back at her, and it startled her. For so long, nothing had had any meaning. She'd poured herself completely into her job ... becoming soulless and numb. It had only taken one moment for her to feel again. Hearing the shower stop, she tamped down the psychoanalysis. *It's not going to happen.*

*

Natalia dressed in her thigh length, rose-colored satin robe and towel dried her long, dark hair. She needed

31

to study. She'd been settled in Fiji for a few days and had managed to do anything but work. This trip was for her to relax and study but also spend a little bit of time for herself, enjoying her birthday. She glanced at the clock on the wall. In just over five hours, she'd turn another year older. Another year that she'd poured into her career. Another year spent alone. *Hard work pays off, Nita,* she heard her father say. "Yeah, but at what cost, Papai?" she asked the room.

*

The sun had set before Natalia's claim on the shower, but the sky hadn't completely darkened. Christian watched the last of the orange embers fade to black. A million tiny sparkles dotted the sky, making it look like someone had poked countless dots in a black piece of fabric then shined a flashlight on it from the other side. The half-moon was merely a larger tear in that same fabric, allowing more light to protrude. Traveling the globe, waking up in a different country, on a different continent, was nothing new. In fact, she'd grown accustomed to it over the years, but no matter how many nights she'd spent staring up at the moon and stars, or wherever she happened to be, the sky was always the same, but what she saw never was.

The sliding door made a soft whoosh sound as it slid open. Christian smelled Natalia before she laid eyes on her. The gardenia and coconut scented shampoo she used was subtle, but whenever the wind blew, Christian got a whiff of the light, tropical fragrance.

"The shower is all yours," Natalia said.

Christian lulled her head to the side, taking in the sight of the woman standing a couple of feet away. Her

32

damp hair fell in loose waves around her shoulder. The satin robe outlined the sexy curve of her waist and hips, as well as the swell of her breasts. Hard nipples pushed against the smooth fabric, creating tiny peaks. Christian took a steady breath and rose out of the chair, walking past Natalia as if she wasn't sexually aroused just by looking at her.

"Were you stargazing?" Natalia asked, noticing the dotted sky.

"Something like that. You should try it sometime," Christian replied, walking into the bungalow.

I do, every chance I get, she thought, leaning against the rail. She heard the ripple of the water, but it appeared silky black without the bright sunlight.

CHAPTER SIX

Christian was up before the sun. It was her night on the couch, and she would've much rather taken her chances with the night bugs out on the deck, although she'd slept in worse conditions. There was something about curling up on a paper-thin cushion, just to make your whole body fit, when there was a perfectly fine, comfortable bed with plenty of room, less than a foot away. She glanced at Natalia, who seemed to be sound asleep, and shook her head. She didn't care about being quiet. She'd just slept on the couch. She had every right to wake up as early as she wanted and get her day going. So, when she stepped across the room to change into her running clothes, she purposely didn't avoid the creak in the floor. The spine-tingling squeak it made as she stepped on it, made her smile.

The slumbering woman stirred before prying her eyes open. "What time is it?" she mumbled.

"Five-thirty," Christian replied, walking into the bathroom to splash some water on her face and brush her teeth.

"Seriously? Where are you going at this hour?"

"For a run. Want to join me?"

"Running?"

"You said you like to run," Christian chuckled, leaning over to spit out the toothpaste and rinse her mouth. "If you think the sunset is pretty, the sunrise will blow your mind."

"Is that why you've been running before dawn every morning? To see the sunrise? I can see it just fine from the deck outside."

"Suit yourself." Christian shrugged.

"Fine. I'll go. Give me five minutes to get my ducks in a row."

Christian looked oddly at her.

"You know. Wake up, get dressed, brush the fuzz off my teeth."

Christian nodded. She checked her phone, then shoved it into the holder that was strapped to her upper arm.

*

When the sun finally began to paint the sky, Christian and Natalia were headed up the mountain behind the resort, running along one of the trails. Natalia had no idea what heaven looked like, but she liked to think it was something like the scene unfolding in front of her. A mixture of orange and yellow hues swirled around, gradually painting everything in bright shades as it crept closer and closer to the island. The water slowly faded from black to turquoise to clear.

"It's …" Natalia tried to speak, but she was breathless.

"Yeah," Christian whispered.

Once the sun was completely visible, they ran a little further up the trail to a switchback, keeping an easy gait with a steady pace.

"I assume you're not married," Natalia said, making small talk.

"Correct."

"No kids?"

"Correct again."

"Where did you say you live again? France, was it?"

"Paris," Christian replied.

"My family is living in France at the moment. They've been there about five years now. My father works at the Portuguese Embassy in Paris."

"Really?" Christian asked.

"Yes. He's been in Democratic Relations since I was a little girl. We lived in the UK for most of my childhood, then the States and Spain. Now they're in France. What about your parents … are they in France, too?"

"No."

"I live in Portugal, so I know what it's like having to travel to another country to see my parents. When Papai retires in a few years, they plan to return to Portugal and live by the sea. That's their dream, to own a beach house."

Christian nodded.

"What do you do?" Natalia questioned, wiping the beginning of a sheen of sweat from her brow. "I mean, I know you said you travel around, but what is it that you actually do?"

"I work in operations. You?" Christian said, putting the subject back on Natalia.

"I'm a Marine Conservationist at the Lisbon Oceanarium. I work in education, making sure teachers have the right tools to teach the children about marine life and what conservation is all about."

"I see," Christian uttered.

"What?"

"Nothing really. It just makes sense now. The whole coffee thing."

"It's bad for the ecosystem. You can't just toss whatever the hell you want into the water," Natalia growled, obviously still angry about the incident.

"You have my word; I won't do it again."

"Good." She looked back towards the resort, trying to get her bearings. "I heard there is a waterfall up here somewhere … on one of the trails."

"I've been up here a few times and haven't seen anything, but I also haven't been on this trail," Christian replied. She was about to suggest they turn back when she saw a small sign up ahead. "I think we're headed right for it."

"I hear it!" Natalia exclaimed as they made their way through the thick rainforest-style plants and brush.

The other side of the thicket opened up into a small clearing. A waterfall poured crystal clear water down into a natural lagoon, less than twenty feet away. It didn't roar as loud as Niagra Falls, but it was noisy enough to be heard if you were nearby.

"Let's go in," Natalia said, pulling off her sneakers.

"As in swim?"

"Sure, why not? How often do you swim in natural lagoons with waterfalls?" Natalia ripped off her tank top, revealing a white and black sports bra. Then, she tucked her socks into her shoes and pulled her shorts down.

Christian quickly turned her head.

"I'm wearing panties, silly," Natalia laughed. "Come on!" she squealed, rushing over to the water.

Christian watched her dive in.

"Oh my God, it's really cold!"

"Well, it's probably spring fed," Christian said as she began removing her shoes and outer clothes, stripping down to her sports bra and underwear, which were both black. "You're going to regret this," she mumbled to herself as she walked over, diving headfirst into the deep water.

Natalia playfully splashed her with water as soon as she broke the surface. "See! It's not so bad," she teased. "It's kind of refreshing, actually," she added, attempting to float on her back.

Christian ignored her as she swam around, letting the water cool her heated skin.

"I'm pretty sure I need one of these at home," Natalia said, swimming closer.

"I'm more of a hot tub person," Christian stated.

"I love any kind of water, especially when I'm in it, but I prefer natural water like the ocean or something like this."

"Is that why you haven't been in the pool this week?"

"Exactly. Why go in chemically enhanced water when you have all this beautiful ocean around you, teeming with marine life?"

"You must have to be an environmental nerd to not like pools and hot tubs," Christian teased.

Natalia laughed and splashed her.

Christian gave her a stern look, then grinned as she returned the favor. For the first time in a long time, she smiled from pure joy. The feeling was invigorating…for a split second. Then, a small animal rustling in the bushes nearby, brought her crashing back to reality. She began pushing her emotions back down. "We should probably go before we turn into prunes," she said, turning back towards the rocky edge.

"Do you think that leads behind the waterfall?" Natalia asked, pointing at a narrow trail as she pulled her clothes back on.

"Probably," Christian mumbled while trying to get her wet feet back into her sweaty socks.

"Come on," Natalia called, already heading up the path.

Shaking her head, Christian tied her shoes and started after her.

*

"It's beautiful," Natalia murmured, captivated by the sensation of the water rushing over her hand as she stuck it through the spray of clear water. It felt just as cool as the lagoon water.

Christian watched her swirl her hand around like a vision impaired person touching something new for the first time.

"You have to try this," Natalia said, grabbing her hand and shoving it into the flowing stream.

Christian's palm felt like it was burning where their hands were joined as the cool water rushed over them. Sensing what she knew she should avoid, she turned her head anyway, seeing Natalia's eyes locked on her. She tried to move away, but her feet were rooted to the ground. She willed her hand to pull back, but it didn't budge. The air in the little bit of space between them was intoxicating. Losing sight of reality, Christian focused only on the gray eyes boring into her. She had no idea she'd leaned closer until her lips grazed Natalia's softly.

Natalia's lips parted, allowing Christian's warm, velvety tongue to brush against her own in a slow, sensual kiss that left them nearly breathless. The waterfall was forgotten as Christian grabbed the front of her tank top, pulling her in closer as their bodies came together. Natalia's arms wrapped loosely around Christian's neck, and Christian's hands moved to her waist. They nipped and suckled each other's lips while their tongues danced the devil's dance.

Breaking the embrace, Christian pulled away, taking a step back. Hot blood raced through her veins, awakening senses she'd long forgotten as her mind reeled. She took a deep breath. "I'm sorry," she sighed, "we can't do this. I … can't do this."

"I never asked you to," Natalia whispered before walking away.

Christian thought about going after her. Natalia had headed back in the direction of the resort, but Christian went the opposite way on the trail, moving further up the mountain. "Damn it!" she spat as her mind went through a million reasons why she shouldn't get involved with Natalia.

She'd gone three or four switchbacks above the waterfall, not really paying much attention to her surroundings, until she stopped moving and took a look around. She noticed a piece of concrete jutting from the face of the mountain, a little more than a hundred yards away. It was square-shaped, like a box, but there was an open square cut into it. It definitely looked like it didn't belong, but at the same time, it looked like it was part of the mountain. Curiosity took over as Christian moved closer. There was no direct path to the box, and in running shoes, she didn't have stable enough footing to go any further. The last thing she wanted to do was fall off the side of the mountain. However, she did get close enough to see the box from a better angle. "I'll be damned," she murmured in awe. It was a WWII gunner's station, more than likely left behind after the Allies had pulled out. She knew Fiji had played a part in the war, especially for the British. They'd used the island as a training base because of its central location. Japanese seaplanes had flown over it quite often during the war.

*

Natalia was on a lounger when Christian returned to the bungalow. She walked outside, leaning against the deck rail, dangling a water bottle between her fingers as she looked out at the turquoise water.

"I thought maybe you'd gotten lost," Natalia muttered.

"I hiked up a little further," Christian replied, taking a sip of water before turning and sitting down opposite her on the other lounger. The fire was gone, but embers still burned hot between them. She'd felt it as soon as she stepped out onto the deck.

"Some birthday, huh?" Natalia muttered.

"I didn't know," Christian said, feeling even lower. "Hap—"

"Don't," Natalia said, cutting her off.

"I'm sorry. You and I both know it wouldn't be fair to either of us. We live different lives … in different countries. We could never have a real relationship," Christian sighed, "we'd be chasing ghosts."

Natalia nodded slowly. "I know."

CHAPTER SEVEN

Christian spent most of the next afternoon sitting on the beach, staring out at the last bungalow in the row. She couldn't see Natalia, even if she were out on the deck, because the back of it faced the water, but she stared anyway. She'd barely known the woman a week, however the physical attraction between them was magnetic, pushing and pulling her. It wasn't like anything she'd ever felt. It was wrong on so many levels. *This isn't why you're here. Just do your job, enjoy the mini vacation, and go home. You'll never see her again.*

She craved a glass of whiskey, but that wasn't the answer. "She's just another woman … another stranger," she said to herself, knowing that wasn't true.

Thinking a walk may clear the fog from her head, Christian stood and brushed the sand from her shorts. She walked around the resort to the path that ran behind the property. It wasn't one of the mountain trails with switchbacks and elevation, so there were more people out and about. She followed the trail all the way to the end, which led to the far side of the nude beach. Looking out at the water to avoid the dozen or so people lounging on towels in the sand, she shoved her hands in her pockets and strolled along the water's edge.

Halfway across the beachfront, she glanced up ahead, noticing a dark-haired woman. Her eyes became transfixed as she moved closer. Hoping to find a distraction, only led to her finding Natalia, propped up on her elbows on a towel, and wearing a white, thigh-length, net dress with nothing under it. She was actually the most clothed person lounging on the beach, but the wide holes left nothing to the imagination. Christian kept her distance and held her head straight, pretending not to look as she passed by, but her eyes strained until they felt like they would pop out of their sockets. Natalia was far enough away that very little was revealed, but it left Christian's chest aching.

*

When Natalia finally returned to the bungalow, she didn't bother changing. Christian had a full view as she walked in front of her lounger, on the way down to the swim platform. Small, dark areolas with taut nipples peeked through the thumb-sized netting holes. She was thankful her eyes were behind dark sunglasses as she scanned the beautiful, lithe body. She tried desperately to pull her eyes away. *You're only hurting yourself. It's not going to happen. It can't happen.*

Natalia glanced back for a split second before walking down the stairs.

Christian opened her mouth to speak, but words failed her, just as her eyes had. Her stomach growled, reminding her that she'd missed most of her meals that day. Food had been the absolute last thing on her mind. Needing to get away before she lost control of herself, she stood up and moved to walk back into the bungalow. "I'm going up to the restaurant. Do you want to go? Or can I bring you something back?" she asked.

"I ordered room service," Natalia called.

Christian blew out a deep breath as she went inside the bungalow. Her eyes drifted to the closet where her suitcase was located. It would be so easy to remove herself. She could make a call and have someone else come do the job she was sent to do. The job she'd nearly forgotten all about in the last twenty-four hours. Shaking her head at the thought of quitting, she pulled the door shut behind her and headed up the gangway.

*

Natalia sighed when she heard the click of the door. "Some vacation," she uttered. "I wish I could just focus on what I came here for. I've barely opened my books. She's been in my damn head since I first laid eyes on her. What am I going to do?" she said, asking the fish swimming beneath her. *Papai would be so mad at me for forgetting my studies. He probably wouldn't care for her either. He'd call her a distraction. Maybe he's right. Maybe I am using her as a distraction. I know that material inside and out, yet I let him fly me halfway around the world on a birthday vacation so that I could have a serene place to relax and learn everything in those books. If you only knew what kind of predicament I wound up in, Papai, you might understand.* "He and Mamãe have always called on my birthday. Maybe they can't get through because of the horrible cell service on the island," she continued aloud, watching a school of tiny, yellow-striped cardinal fish.

*

After dinner, Christian stayed for the poolside fire show, hoping to avoid any kind of small talk or conversation with Natalia, and praying she'd finally put some clothes on. She wasn't sure what to say, and was sure she'd said all that she *could* say.

Specks of white dusted the night sky, outlining different constellations in twinkling lights as she made her way back to the bungalow. When she moved her wrist, blue LED numbers lit up on her watch, indicating 10:15PM.

She couldn't see the deck from the gangway, but it was dark inside the bungalow when she entered. Seeing the dark hair sprawled out on the pillow, made her sigh in relief. Natalia was fast asleep. She quietly slipped off her shoes and avoided the squeaky spot on the floor as she crept into the bathroom to get ready for bed. Within minutes, she was on the couch, tossing and turning, while trying to find comfort in the thin, lumpy couch cushions was impossible.

Not looking forward to another night with no sleep, Christian grabbed her pillow and thin blanket, and went out onto the deck, hoping the circular double lounger in the corner, felt as comfortable as it appeared. She hadn't sat on it at all during the week, but as soon as she stretched out, she grinned. *I should've done this days ago.*

*

The sound of the sliding glass door woke Natalia. She sat up, looking around for Christian. The couch was empty. She hadn't heard her come in, but she was sure she'd heard the doors leading to the deck. Reaching for her robe, she slipped out of bed and pulled it on over the crème colored, satin tank top and matching shorts she'd been sleeping in.

"The bugs are going to eat you," she said, noticing Christian on the double lounger when she stepped outside.

Christian woke immediately when she heard the sound of the door. "I'll take my chances," she replied, pushing the blanket to the side to let the cool air flow over her. "Anything is better than that damn couch."

"Can we talk?" Natalia asked, sitting down on the edge of the lounger.

"I'd really like to sleep. So, unless you're giving up the bed ..."

"We could share," Natalia said, biting the side of her lower lip.

"You think that's a good idea?"

"I don't know. I ..." she paused, reaching out in the near darkness, making contact with Christian's arm.

"Don't start something we can't finish," Christian whispered.

"Why can't we do what we know we both want? I know we'll never see each other again."

"It's more complicated than that," Christian sighed, willing herself not to give in, but the warm hand on her arm was like a match, setting her blood on fire.

"You felt the same thing I did at the waterfall. You can't deny it. I saw it in your eyes. If it wasn't dark, I bet I'd see it again right now."

"What is it that you see?" Christian asked softly.

"Desire," Natalia murmured.

Christian reached out, running her hand along Natalia's smooth thigh, inching higher and higher until she brushed her fingers over the tiny, silky shorts. She looked up, catching a glimmer of the moon in Natalia's eyes just before she grabbed the tank top covering her torso, tugging Natalia closer as their lips met in haste. Natalia's dark hair fell to the side of Christian's face as she moved further onto the lounger. They continued chasing tongues and nipping each other's lips, never parting their mouths.

Christian moved her hands under Natalia's tank top, sliding them up her sides to her shoulders, removing the garment in one swift motion. Natalia moaned into her mouth when Christian's hands covered her breasts, kneading and teasing her nipples between her fingers and thumbs. She tugged Christian's t-shirt up, parting their burning lips long enough to get it over her head.

Both women finally broke the kiss as they removed their shorts.

"Come here," Christian whispered, pulling Natalia over to straddle her lap.

Natalia licked Christian's bottom lip seductively before wrapping her arms around Christian's shoulders, pressing their bare chests together. Their lips, still moist and swollen from the fervent kissing, met once more while their hands explored soft skin.

Christian moved her hands down to Natalia's butt, squeezing before moving one hand down between their bodies. Warm wetness coated her fingers as she ran them between her wide-open legs. Natalia hissed, breaking the kiss as she leaned her head back. Christian moved her mouth to the delicate, olive skin of her neck, placing tiny kisses from her chin to her collar bone, then up to her ear, all the while, rubbing her fingers back and forth in lazy strokes.

Natalia's hips began moving in rhythm with the fingers teasing her. Leaning forward, she kissed Christian hard, tugging on the short curls on top of her head. "Go inside," she groaned, "fuck me."

Christian felt her own crotch drench the cushion under her as she slid two fingers deep inside of Natalia.

Hot, wet muscles squeezed as she pressed further, before pulling nearly all the way out and pushing back in again.

"Yes," Natalia breathed against Christian's mouth, kissing her languidly as she moved up and down, riding the fingers sliding in and out of her in slow, steady strokes.

When Natalia broke the kiss to lean back once more, Christian ran her tongue down her chest to her breasts, suckling and biting each nipple back and forth.

"I'm so close," Natalia whimpered, moving faster as Christian pressed harder into her.

"Let go. I've got you," Christian murmured, kissing her tender lips just before she felt Natalia begin to tremble against her. She held her tightly with one arm until her body stilled. Then, she carefully pulled her fingers free.

"Oh my God," Natalia gasped breathlessly. She opened her eyes, seeing slivers of moonlight in the baby blue ones staring back at her. She couldn't remember ever being so wild and raw with anyone, but she'd also wanted the woman looking back at her, more than anything in a long time … and she wanted more.

"We should go inside before the bugs carry us off," Christian uttered.

Natalia nodded before climbing off of her and standing up.

"Are you okay?" Christian asked, running her clean hand over Natalia's cheek when she got to her feet.

"Yes." She smiled, taking Christian's hand in hers as she led her into the bungalow. As soon as Christian pulled the glass door closed, Natalia backed her up against it with a heady kiss. She ran her hands up and down the front of Christian's body, squeezing her breasts and dragging her short nails over her firm stomach. Reaching lower, she passed her fingers through the soaked folds between Christian's legs.

Christian broke the kiss and ran her lips along Natalia's jaw to her ear. "You did that. Now, what are you going to do about it?" she asked, her voice dripping with seduction.

"What I've been wanting to do since the first day I saw you," Natalia said confidently before running her palms down Christian's body as she lowered herself to her knees. Christian had no time to say anything as Natalia took her into her mouth, licking and sucking like a baby animal drinking from its mother.

"Ohhh," Christian moaned a deep guttural sound. She spread her legs further and placed one hand on the back of Natalia's head, guiding her mouth where she needed it most as she moved her hips in unison. "Just like that," she whimpered, clenching her teeth.

Natalia slowed her pace and adjusted her strokes to slide the tip of her tongue inside of Christian, teasing her opening on every other pass. She didn't have to look up to see how close Christian was. She could feel her getting hotter and wetter against her face.

"Don't stop …" Christian mumbled almost incoherently, nearly riding the mouth assuaging her.

Natalia picked up the pace once more, licking back and forth and sucking her harder … until Christian's thighs shuddered. Then, she softened her strokes.

As soon as she could breathe again, Christian reached down, pulling Natalia to her feet. Their lips met in a searing kiss. Tasting herself on Natalia's tongue made her want the Portuguese beauty all over again. Grabbing Natalia's hand, she broke the kiss and pulled her over to the bed.

Natalia watched as Christian put the two pillows together up against the headboard before getting on the bed and sitting back against them with her legs open. She raised a brow in confusion, but Christian patted the space between her legs. Natalia climbed onto the bed, sitting down in the spot. Christian pulled Natalia back against her chest and ran her hands from her waist up to her breasts and back down from her position behind her.

"Watch," Christian whispered in her ear, tracing it with her tongue as she pointed towards the glass doors.

Natalia ran her hand up into Christian's short curls as Christian's fingers made their way down between her legs. "Mmmm," she murmured, moving her hips slowly, matching the leisurely pace of the fingers rubbing circles around her swollen center.

Christian moved her other hand to Natalia's breast, kneading the full weight before pinching the hard nipple between her fingers. She kept her mouth near her neck and ear, kissing the soft spot delicately.

"That feels so good," Natalia moaned, melding further into the woman behind her.

Each deliberately slow movement gradually pushed Natalia closer and closer to climax as dawn began to break, painting the sky in breathtaking yellow and orange hues. Natalia felt completely intoxicated by the most passionate sexual experience she'd ever had in her entire life. Her eyes were transfixed on the rising sun as her body gave way. Her hips pumped against Christian's hand, trying to get every last ounce of the mental and physical orgasm that tore through her, leaving a limp shell in its wake.

Christian carefully pulled her hand free and wrapped her arms around the trembling woman.

"Wow," Natalia whispered, barely able to catch a breath. She rolled her head to the side, meeting Christian's lips in a soft kiss, before turning them back to the beautiful sunrise, lighting the turquoise water one section at a time.

CHAPTER EIGHT

Natalia opened her eyes to the sun-filled room. A smile crept across her face as her gaze landed on the slumbering woman next to her. She eased out of bed, checking the time on her phone. *One bar ... no wonder I haven't spoken to my family since I arrived. This place has the worst cell service I've ever seen,* she silently huffed as her stomach roared loudly. She glanced quickly at the bed.

"I've been up," Christian said, opening the most beautiful baby blue eyes Natalia had ever seen. "You looked so peaceful, I couldn't wake you," she added.

"I'm pretty sure my empty belly is what did it." Natalia smiled. "It's too late for breakfast, but they're serving brunch."

"That sounds good ... after a shower, of course. I'm pretty sure I smell like a wet mule," Christian replied, climbing out of the bed.

"A shower sounds good," Natalia murmured, running her eyes over the naked woman.

Christian moved closer, leaving less than a foot between them. "You and I both know if we take a shower together, we'll never leave this room."

"What's wrong with that? They have room service, you know."

Christian grinned and shook her head before moving around her and into the bathroom. She turned the spray all the way to hot and stepped in, standing directly underneath it. There was no sense in mentally chastising herself. What was done ... was done. There was no going back. She wasn't angry with herself for spending one of the most passionate nights of her life with a beautiful woman. No. She was furious because she had let herself feel.

Hot water nearly scalded her as she stood there, letting her mind race in a hundred directions. She was going to break Natalia's heart ... and if she wasn't careful, her own as well. "Damn it," she muttered.

"Don't use all the hot water, or I *will* get in there with you," Natalia called from the door.

Christian let out a deep sigh and quickly washed her body and hair. She was barely out and toweling off, when Natalia jumped in. She put a little bit of gel in her hair and ran her hand through the short, bouncy curls on the top of her head. One fell forward, touching her forehead.

The water shut off just as she walked out of the room, indicating Natalia had finished. She put on her black, two-piece bathing suit that had short, board shorts for bottoms and threw on a tank top. She slipped her feet into a pair of Teva sandals as Natalia appeared, freshly showered and nude. Her long, dark hair was pasted to her back, and tiny water droplets that she'd missed with the towel, ran down the middle of her torso, between her breasts, pooling in her belly button.

Her stomach growled loudly, breaking the fixation Christian's eyes had on her. She placed her hand over it, slightly embarrassed.

"Let's go before that thing eats us both," Christian teased. She shoved her cell phone into her pocket and went out the door, preferring to wait out on the gangway while Natalia dressed.

When she opened the door, wearing an emerald-green bikini with a matching sarong tied around her waist, Christian raised a brow.

"What's wrong?"

"Don't tell me you brought a different bathing suit for every day."

"No," she laughed, "but I wasn't sure I'd be able to do laundry, so I did pack a few."

Christian simply nodded.

Natalia slipped into her flip flops and fell in step next to her as they made their way up to the resort.

*

Both women had let their empty stomachs order for them, leaving the table with an array of food. Everything was on the house because of the room mix up, so it didn't matter how much food they ate, alcohol they drank, room service they ordered … they paid for none of it during the entire stay.

"I don't think I could eat another bite," Natalia sighed, pushing her plate away.

"Me neither," Christian replied, scanning the people in the pool area on the other side of the window. She was sure she'd just seen a guy walk by wearing jeans. She shook her head, thinking maybe she was mistaken.

"Are you going running today?"

"Probably not. I like to go first thing in the morning. What are your plans for the day?"

"I was thinking of snorkeling again … away from your tainted area, of course," she teased.

Christian's laughter was cut short when she saw a man with a backpack and jeans, walk through the pool area.

This time, she knew she wasn't dreaming. He certainly didn't look like a tourist visiting a tropical island. At least, not in jeans, a dark shirt, and boots. "Come on," she said, a little more sternly than she'd meant to. "I'm sorry. I'm just finished looking at this food. Let's get out of here."

Natalia nodded in agreement as she stood and walked out of the restaurant with her. She wasn't sure what was bothering her, but Christian's demeanor had abruptly changed. "Is everything okay?"

"Yeah," she said, smiling at her, but she was lying. No, she wasn't okay. All of her senses were on high alert. She slowed her breathing, a technique she'd learned years earlier, to keep her heart rate and adrenaline level from spiking.

They made their way through the pool area and turned the corner, starting up the gangway. Christian spotted another man coming out of their bungalow seconds before Natalia.

"What the—"

"Come on," Christian whispered loudly, grabbing her hand. She snatched Natalia off the gangway and walked as quickly as she could without bringing attention to them. As soon as they were on the other side of the resort, she began running. "Keep up with me!"

"What's going on? Who was that?" Natalia called, trying not to get dragged as they raced down the trail, towards the paths that led up the mountain.

Christian turned her head, keeping one eye on the ground as they ran. "They will be on us within two minutes. Just be quiet and stay close to me. We have to move faster," she said, tugging Natalia's hand.

*

Just as Christian had said, the men had spotted them running up the mountain. Three gun shots sounded in the air, with one of the bullets shaving bark off a nearby tree.

"Oh, my God!" Natalia screamed.

"Come on!" Christian yelled, pulling her harder.

"I can't go any faster!"

"If you don't, we're dead!" Christian growled, angry at herself for leaving her duffle bag behind. Her passports, gun … everything, was in that bag. *We have to keep going up. We're sitting ducks if we go back down.* Changing course, she took one of the switchbacks. Then, she left that trail and headed through a thicket, towards a path she knew was in the area, but she'd only been on it once. She turned around, trying to spot the resort so she could get her bearings. She had no idea where the men had gone, and she had no clue how many there were. She'd spotted at least three, maybe four, but it could easily be as many as ten. "Get into these bushes and duck down."

"Where are you going?"

"To see where they are. Just go!" Christian hissed.

Natalia went into the thicket and squatted down. Scared out of her mind with her heart nearly pounding out of her chest, she looked around. Christian had disappeared, but a minute later, she heard footsteps and what sounded like the squawk of a walkie-talkie. She parted the bushes just far enough apart to see with one eye.

Christian jumped out of the brush, hitting the man in the back of the head with a large stick. He stumbled and spun around, dropping his gun as he lunged for her. She squared off, hitting the dazed man in the jaw with the stick like Babe Ruth swinging a bat. He fell back against a tree and slid to the ground. Christian jumped on top of him, sitting on his chest as she lifted his head and broke his neck in one swift motion. Then, she quickly got up, grabbed his wrists, and pulled him off the trail, into the thick brush. She checked his pockets, but nothing was in them except a picture of Natalia. She searched around for the gun but knew there wasn't much time. The others would be coming up the trail. They'd obviously split up, so she had no way of knowing where anyone was.

"I don't know where the others are. We have to keep going," Christian whispered, pulling Natalia back out of the thicket.

"What the hell is going on, Christian? Did you just kill him?"

"I need you to trust me."

"Trust you? I don't know what's happening! What are you? Some kind of special forces?"

"MI6," Christian said, peering down the trail.

"Isn't espionage their thing? You look like a lot more than a spy. I'm pretty sure you killed that man."

"Damn it," Christian sighed in frustration. "I'm an operative, and unlike James Bond, I don't have fancy guns and invisible cars, so come on before the rest of them find us!"

Natalia's brain was on overload as she let Christian drag her further up the side of the mountain. She didn't know what to believe, and she certainly had no idea who the woman next to her was … not at all.

Seeing a tiny fleck of white in the distance, Christian knew she was on the right track. "I'll explain everything, just keep running," she said, finally finding the slightly hidden path that would take her where she wanted to go.

Natalia looked back but saw nothing but mountain. The resort was completely out of sight, as were whoever it was that was chasing them. When she glanced out at the water, she realized they'd moved around to the front of the island. She'd never been this high up and wondered if Christian knew what she was doing. There was no way off the island, except for the catamaran, which was on the other side of the resort.

When they came up on a concrete box that looked like it was part of the mountain, Christian instructed Natalia to get down inside of it.

"Wait! What? You want me to get in there? What the hell is it?"

"It's a World War Two bunker. Just get in the damn thing and be quiet!" she hissed between clinched teeth. "There has to be another way off this damn island," she mumbled to herself. "I'll be back. Stay here. Don't say anything. If you see one of the men, don't move."

"How do we know they're not gone? Why are they after you?"

"It's not me, Natalia." Christian shook her head. "They're looking for you."

"Me? Why? My father can help us. Do you have your phone? Maybe you have a signal up here. I can call him."

Christian shook her head softly. "I know who you are Miss Moreno, and so do they."

The color drained from Natalia's face.

"Your father can't help you. Sabio Moreno was murdered six days ago."

"Wait. What? Murdered. Papai? No," she cried. "No! No!"

"I'm sorry."

"Who the hell are you?" she tried to scream, but Christian covered her mouth with her hand. She tried to bite her, but Christian pulled back, raising her hand to slap her.

"Don't make me do it ... please, Natalia. I'm trying to save you."

"Save me? Why? What the fuck is going on, Christian? Is that even your name? I don't know who you are. You were lying to me this whole time," she cried as tears flowed down her cheeks. She desperately needed a phone. She needed to call Papai. If it was true, if he was gone, then Mamãe needed her.

"I never lied to you. My name is Christian Garnier. I live in France. I'm a dual citizen of France and the UK. That is all true. I'm also an MI6 operative, and my mission is to protect you. When your father was killed, I was sent here to make sure they didn't come after you."

"Why? Why was he killed? Who would do such a thing? My father was a good man."

Christian wanted to hold her and wipe the tears away, but that was because she'd made a mistake, crossed a line by sleeping with her and feeling for her. "I don't know the details."

"I'm going to die out here on this mountain, and my mother is all alone right now, probably scared and wondering where I am."

"Your mother is fine. MI6 grabbed her in Spain. She's safe in London."

"Oh, thank God."

"And you're not going to die. I'm going to get us out of here. I need you to trust me ... please, Natalia."

"I can't, but I have no other choice," she muttered, still wiping tears that slid down her cheeks.

"I'll be back. Stay down and be quiet. Don't come out unless you hear me calling for you."

Natalia nodded and turned away. Her entire life had been ruined in less than twenty minutes. Not knowing what or who to believe absolutely terrified her. She felt sick but swallowed hard to keep it down.

*

Christian kept moving along the mountain face towards the side opposite the resort. She knew from talk around the resort that there was a local village somewhere in that vicinity. As she moved further, searching for signs of the village down by the water, she noticed a large house with a floatplane docked in a lagoon, obviously belonging to some rich person who had a vacation home on the island. *Yes*, she thought, *a way out of here!*

Turning around, she hurried back towards the bunker, hoping the men hadn't spotted it. She grabbed her phone, trusting the one to two bar signal would be able to send a message. She quickly texted: BEEN MADE. PACKAGE SECURE. HEADING EAST.

*

Natalia was sitting in the corner with her knees tucked up under her chin when Christian jumped inside next to her in the tight spot.

"We're leaving."

"They're gone?"

"No. I have no idea where they are, but I'm sure they're close."

"The catamaran is the other way."

"I found us a quicker ride. I need you to move fast though."

"I can't go any faster in flip flops."

"Then take them off," Christian said, poking her head out of the bunker to look around. "Come on. We have to move now!" She grabbed Natalia's hand, tugging her along as they ran along the side of the mountain.

Natalia clutched her flip flops to her chest with her free hand and prayed she didn't trip on a rock or root and break her neck. The turquoise water in the distance looked so serene and peaceful. There wasn't a cloud in the bright blue sky. When she'd woken that morning, feeling a level of happiness that was akin to a natural high, she had no idea that within a couple of hours she'd be running for her life around the mountain in the middle of the island…with a complete stranger who made her feel alive and terrified at the same time. All while trying to process the death of her father. She wished she could go back to bed and start the day again. It had begun so beautifully.

*

Christian guided Natalia through the maze of switchbacks. They weren't kept up like the ones near the resort and were also quite a bit steeper. She'd slipped a couple of times on loose ground. She needed to follow an odd path to make sure the men didn't spot the plane and try to sabotage their only chance of getting away. Letting herself get involved with Natalia, and treating this mission like a vacation had caused her to let her guard down. She was being flirty, overly friendly, and having fun…when she should've been working around the clock. "It's up ahead," she said, pointing towards the large house.

"A house! We can call for help!"

"Not the house," Christian said, pointing to the white float plane with a blue stripe down the side and a blue belly.

"You've got to be kidding me!"

"Nope."

"Can you even fly a plane? Wait, why bother answering," she said, shaking her head as they ran down the dock.

Christian was thankful, albeit surprised that the door was unlocked. She helped Natalia climb inside, then she untied the dock lines and joined her. It had been a while since she last flew, but every cockpit was virtually the same. She pulled the engine choke knob and flipped on the electronic switches that brought the gauges to life. The panel in front of her lit up like a Christmas tree. Then, she put the radio headset over her ears. With the push of a switch, the engine sputtered to life. She stepped on the tail rudder pedals, getting a feel for them, before pushing the choke back in and nudging the throttle forward.

Gun shots rang out, hitting the dock behind them as they pulled away. Christian turned to see two men running down the dock. She pushed the throttle forward, causing the plane to basically ski on top of the clear water. Then, she pulled the yolk back gently, lifting the nose.

"What if they hit the plane?" Natalia screeched.

"They won't."

Natalia gripped the seat until her knuckles were stiff as the plane rose into the air. "Holy shit," she whispered.

Once they were leveled out around 4,000 feet, Christian checked the fuel gauge and began fiddling with the GPS to get a feel for how far they could go. She wanted to steer clear of the mainland in case there were more men waiting for them. The closest island was New Caledonia. It was located about halfway between Fiji and Australia. Based on the fuel calculation on the GPS, they would make it with less than a couple of gallons of fuel remaining.

She turned up the volume on the radio, waiting to hear a tower calling her tail number, but she'd tried to stay between three and four thousand feet, which was under the radar range. No one needed to know who they were or where they were headed.

Satisfied that air traffic control had no idea they were in the air, she removed the headset.

"What do we do now?" Natalia asked.

"Fly," Christian replied. "We have about four hours."

Natalia shook her head in disbelief. Her perfect morning had turned into a nightmare. She turned around, looking at the interior of the plane. She'd jumped in so fast, she hadn't noticed the extra seats behind them. The Piper Aztec plane was a six-seater float plane with a pair of side by side seats directly behind the cockpit seats, and another set of seats behind them that were slightly wider and up against the back wall. The interior was all blue, including the floor carpeting, and the seats were gray.

"You can curl up in those seats and go to sleep," Christian stated. "We'll be fine up here."

"I'm okay," Natalia sighed. "Are you really with MI6?"

"Yes," Christian replied with a nod as she checked the GPS to make sure they were still on course. *Here comes four hours of twenty questions*, she thought.

"How do you know my father was murdered?" Natalia asked. It took everything she had to say that last word.

"You know I can't talk about any of that. It's classified information."

"Are you serious right now? We're in the middle of nowhere … in a stolen plane! I deserve to know the truth...if there even is any at this point."

"Natalia, I've never lied to you. I just didn't give you all of the details about why I was here. I'm sorry. Last night should've never happened."

"It's a little too late now," she mumbled, crossing her arms and looking out the side window.

"If I knew what happened, I would tell you," Christian sighed. "I know what it's like to lose your parents, but this is classified information and my security clearance doesn't go that high. I was given a mission and that was to protect you so that it didn't happen to you, too. I'm afraid that's all I have."

Natalia wiped a couple of stray tears. Thinking about her father made her angry. She just wanted to know why. Why did someone take him away from her and her mother? Who could do such a thing? Thinking about her mother made her sad. She wished she was there with her. "Were those men MI6, too?" she asked, needing a change of subject from her parents.

"No," Christian laughed. "More than likely, they were paid mercenaries. If they were any kind of operative, I would've had to kill them all, not just the one who was the closest."

"So, you did kill that guy!"

"Of course. Did you want him to kill us?"

"Who the hell are you?" Natalia questioned, scooting a little closer to the wall of the fuselage.

Christian let out a deep breath. "We've been over this. I'm not the bad one here, and I'm not going to spend the rest of our time together trying to prove that to you."

"How long will that be? All of my stuff is back on that island. My passport, my clothes, my phone … everything."

"I left stuff behind, too."

"Are we going back?"

"No."

"Why not? I can't go home without my passport!"

"Do you have some kind of death wish or something?" Christian shook her head.

Natalia ignored her.

Christian turned on the autopilot but kept a close eye on the GPS as she turned on her cell phone. She pressed a combination of numbers and listened to three short beeps, before a male voice said one word: Lancelot.

"Excalibur-CG48510 calling from a secure line," she said. "I was ambushed in Fiji. I've taken a seaplane and am heading west, towards New Caledonia."

"Where is the package?" Lancelot asked.

"Safe and sound with me, Sir."

"Good. Look for Koumac. It's a town on the edge of the island. Refuel and get back in the air. Continue east towards Fraser Island off the coast of Australia. The cleanup crew is en route. I'll text you the coordinates for the extraction point."

"Roger."

"And Garnier, keep the package secure."

The line went dead before she could say anything.

CHAPTER NINE

Christian glanced at the fuel gauge just as the tiny island strip of New Caledonia came into view in the distance. She slowed her speed and adjusted the wing flaps to lower her altitude slightly.

"We're landing in about ten minutes," she called.

"What?" Natalia mumbled, sitting up and looking out the window. She'd been curled up in the back row of seats. The low, steady rumble of the plane's engine had lulled her right to sleep.

Christian pointed to the island in front of them.

"Land!" Natalia cheered as she climbed back up to the co-pilot's seat in the cockpit. The island had large, green-grass covered mountains and was surrounded by beautiful turquoise blue water. "Where are we?"

"New Caledonia," Christian replied, putting on the headset and changing the channel on the radio until she picked up the marina chatter. "Koumac Marina … this call is coming from an inbound seaplane, tail number: F310T. We are flying on reserve and need to refuel. Over."

"F310T … Koumac Marina. We see you. Our refueling dock is on the north end. Put it down about thirty yards out, and we'll have a boat tow you in. Over."

"Roger," Christian pushed the microphone away and said, "strap in."

"Please tell me you know how to land this thing," Natalia said as the small coastal area came further into view

66

the closer they got to the island. She noticed a large bay with boats lining long docks, and a town or village just behind it.

"I hope so," Christian muttered, checking the gauges as she lowered the flaps as far as they would go. Then, she backed off the throttle and pulled back on the yolk to raise the nose up.

The white and blue plane skidded across the clear water of the bay like a water skier and came to a stop. Christian cut the engine off.

"Look through all the compartments. We need something to barter for fuel. Hurry, I see the boat coming to tow us in," she said as she stowed the map she'd been using and shut down all the electronics. It had been a few years since she'd flown, and so far, she'd done everything right.

Natalia checked the compartments but found nothing. She ran her finger over the necklace she wore. It was the last thing her father had given her. *No*, she thought, removing her hand.

The boat arrived quickly, and two men hooked a line to the front of the plane where the skids were connected, similar to what they would do when towing a boat. They waved to Christian, who waved back. Then, they put the boat in gear and pulled the plane further into the bay where the marina was located. As soon as they pushed the plane up against the dock, the men tied it off so that it wouldn't float away.

Christian bumped her elbow when she climbed out of her seat and the stowed maps fell out of the compartment, revealing an antique gold watch. She quickly shoved it into her pocket. "Stay here," she said.

"I really need to find something to wear, other than a bathing suit."

"I don't have any underwear on," Christian retorted.

"Are you seriously trying to make a comparison?" Natalia huffed.

"Just stay put," Christian sighed, "I'll see what I can find."

"What about them?" Natalia asked, looking at the men who were waiting on the dock.

"Lock the door behind me," Christian said, climbing out.

"No shit," Natalia mumbled. She glanced around, noticing how much larger the mountains were now that they were at ground level. "Everything's so green," she whispered to herself.

"Fill it as full as you can get it," Christian said to one of the men, as she closed the door and headed up the dock towards the marina office.

*

"No trades," the manager said.

"Where can I sell it?" she asked.

"Market, half a mile away that way. They trade things."

"Fill up the plane. I'll be back."

Christian shoved the watch back into her pocket and headed off in the direction the man had pointed in. New Caledonia was predominantly French speaking, which was fine because she was fluent, but the men at the marina had spoken English, probably because of the yachts and sailboats that stopped for provisions or fuel.

When she reached the village, Christian easily found the market. Just like the man had told her, there were tents and tables set up everywhere. People had everything you could think of for sale from food to handmade jewelry and everything in between. She perused the tables, looking for the right person, before offering up her merchandise.

Seeing an elderly woman with an array of odds and ends made of silver, Christian stepped over, asking if she wanted to buy a gold watch. She shook her head no but pointed to a man a few tables down. Christian went straight to the bald man with a thin, scraggly gray beard, and pulled the watch from her pocket.

"How much?" he asked.

"One thousand," she said, undervaluing the heirloom by nearly twenty-five percent.

"Two hundred," he countered.

"Eight."

"Four."

"Seven."

"Five hundred. My last number. No higher," he said, shaking his head.

"Let me have a t-shirt to go with it, and you have a deal."

He nodded and pulled an old, metal tackle box out from under the table. He counted out the money, handing her a stack of bills as she handed him the watch. Then he grabbed a white, tourist type t-shirt with a map of the island on it and gave it to her. She didn't bother checking the size as she rushed out of the market, practically running towards the marina.

*

Natalia sunk down into the seat. She wished she could call home, but if Christian was right, there was nothing she could do but try to get back as soon as possible.

She watched the men eyeing the plane as they pumped it full of fuel. She avoided eye contact and kept the doors locked.

A sudden pounding on the door scared the hell out of her. She jumped six inches in her seat before looking over and seeing Christian. She leaned over and quickly flipped the lock up. Christian climbed in and closed the door. She tossed the t-shirt at Natalia as she eased into the tight cockpit space.

The two men got back into their boat and tugged the plane away from the marina, towards the open ocean on the other side of the lagoon. Christian knew she needed at least fifty feet to get the plane off the ground, so she'd given them a spot to tow her to.

"What is this?" Natalia asked as Christian began powering on the gauges and checking the map for the new GPS coordinates. She pulled the choke and prepared to start the plane.

"It's a shirt."

"I can see that. What am I supposed to do with it? I asked for clothes, not a tent!"

"That was all they had."

Natalia mumbled incoherently in Portuguese as she put it on.

Christian watched as the men drove away in their boat, clearing a path for her to take off. She started the plane's engine and had them taxiing across the lagoon in no time. "Here, I got this, too," she said, reaching for the bag of locally grown fruit and nuts once she had the plane leveled out at the altitude she'd chosen.

"Where are we headed? I assume you're taking me home to my mother," Natalia said, satisfying her stomach with a banana and a handful of nuts.

70

"I told you she's at a safe house in the UK."

"Okay, is that where we're going?"

"Yes and no."

"What the hell does that mean?"

"Natalia, my job is to keep you safe. The less you know … the safer you are."

"That sounds like a load of crap. Is that what you say to all of your protectees … or whatever you call us?"

Christian gave her the side eye, then she shook her head and laughed. "I'm not in the Protection Command," she said, referring to the UK's version of the USA's Secret Service. "I'm with MI6, and as you put it, we're into espionage … not protection."

"Then, why did you take me on the run? What is all of this?"

"I can't give you the details of my mission."

Natalia pinned her with a stare and crossed her arms.

"I've told you all that I can … all that I know, really. More than I should have. The people who killed your father are obviously after you. Until MI6 figures out why and what is going on, my job is to keep you safe," Christian stated. "This will go a lot smoother if you stop questioning everything."

"Try being in my shoes. Five days ago, my perfect vacation was turned upside down, leaving me to share my space with a complete stranger. Six and a half hours ago, I woke up feeling happier than I have in I don't know how long, and that stranger was in the bed next to me … albeit she was no longer a stranger. No, not at all. She was mysterious, but that was part of what attracted me to her. I thought we'd made a connection. It had certainly felt like we did anyway. Five hours ago, my world turned upside down once again when I discovered that stranger, whom I'd given myself to like no other, betrayed me in so many ways. She wasn't who I thought she was. In fact, nothing in the past five days was real." She paused, wiping a tear that had escaped her eyes. "I could barely wrap my head around all of that, when suddenly we're being shot at and she informs me that my father has been murdered; the men shooting at us are after me; and she's the only person I can trust. This person who had been deceiving me since the moment we met. This person who let me give myself to her. The last person on Earth that I want to trust ... now, or ever again. So, forgive me if I have some fucking questions," she said.

"It wasn't fake," Christian sighed, knowing she should just leave it alone ... leave Natalia to hate her, but she'd felt something too. *Don't do this. You know you can't have any kind of a relationship.*

"What does that mean?"

Christian's racing thoughts finally came together in one direction ... reality. "Nothing," she muttered, checking the GPS. "You're right. I was just doing my job."

"I want to hate you," Natalia murmured, wiping a few more tears.

"Why don't you?"

"Because if I don't find a way to trust you, I may never get out of this nightmare."

*

The rest of the long plane ride was silent. Fighting back the urge to look over at the woman sitting a foot away, Christian kept her eyes bouncing from the horizon, to the gauges and the GPS, then back again. *Let it go*, she told herself as she concentrated on flying the plane while trying not to run out of fuel before they reached Fraser Island. According to her calculations, they were going to be cutting it close.

"Land!" Natalia exclaimed, staring straight ahead.

Christian saw the eastern coast of Australia come fully into view, with a stick-shaped island jutting out from the side, just as the engine began to spit and sputter.

"What's wrong?" Natalia questioned, scanning the gauges when an alarm began to sound. "What's happening?"

"We're out of gas," Christian replied, adjusting the wing flaps.

They were still a few miles out and closing in quickly. There was no lagoon or bay area. Christian had no choice but to put the plane down near the edge of the island and let the waves beach it. She had never glided a plane before. Her palms were sweaty and her back was stiff as a rod, but other than that, she remained calm, calculating every move.

"We're going to crash," Natalia said under her breath.

"No, we're not. Put your seatbelt on."

"It is on."

As they crept closer and closer to the water, Christian opened the flaps completely and pulled the nose up. The engine stalled out, leaving them drifting like a bird.

"Brace for impact," Christian said, doing everything she could to manually control the tail rudder with the pedals, but everything on the plane was hydraulic. She literally had no control.

The skids bounced off a wave, tossing them up into the air before fully connecting with the water, forcefully jarring the plane to a stop as the skids sunk down deeper than they were supposed to go. Christian's forehead smacked the side window frame above her left brow, causing an intense throb behind her eye. She ignored the pain and checked her surroundings. They were above water, and the casual rise every couple of seconds meant the waves were indeed pushing them to shore.

"Are you okay?" she asked, looking at Natalia.

"Yeah," she replied shakily. "Oh, my God, you're bleeding!" she shrieked, seeing the red line running down the side of Christian's face.

"It's nothing. The waves are bringing us in. We need to be ready to go."

"Christian, you're hurt."

"I'm fine," she said, sounding harsher than she'd meant while wiping her face on her shirt. "Come on, we're almost on shore. I'm sure people heard the plane. We need to get out of here."

Natalia shook her head and gritted her teeth angrily at the stubborn woman. She could have a concussion and all she was worried about was someone seeing them. What did it matter? They were hundreds of miles away from Fiji and the men who were after her.

CHAPTER TEN

The thick sand was hot on Natalia's feet as they raced across it towards the woods that covered the island. She stopped in her tracks as a skinny, medium-sized dog came towards them. Wishing she had something to feed the scrawny mutt, she reached out to pet him.

"Don't touch it! That's a dingo. He'll bite your hand off!" Christian yelled, clutching her hand. "Come on, we have to get away from that plane."

"What the hell is a dingo? I thought that was a stray dog."

"Have you ever been to Australia?"

"No."

"Well, welcome. They have a lot of interesting wild animals here. Dingoes happen to be one of them. They're sort of like dogs and wolves mixed together, and they're vicious," Christian explained, still holding her hand as she led her into the thick brush of the woods.

*

Once they were a good ways away from the area where they'd beached the plane, they found a vehicle trail. Christian checked the GPS on her phone. The extraction point was over twenty-five miles away.

"Son of a bitch," she muttered.

"What's—"

Christian grabbed Natalia, snatching her back into the woods, causing them to tumble to the ground in a heap, just as a park ranger Ute came around the corner. Their eyes met and for a brief second, they were back in Fiji under the stars. Her lips parted, anticipating the softness of Natalia's mouth.

Natalia's heart pounded in her chest from a mixture of adrenaline and sudden arousal.

Christian turned away first, getting to her feet and inching out to see if the vehicle had stopped. She looked back, offering her hand to Natalia, who refused it as she got up on her own. "Wait here," she said.

"Great. What are you going to do, steal the truck?" Natalia replied sarcastically.

"Yes," Christian stated matter-of-factly. "Stay down, and don't move. I'll be back in a few minutes."

"Are you serious?" Natalia squeaked.

"How else do you expect us to go twenty-five miles in less than an hour?" Christian stood still, waiting for an answer. "I thought so. Now, for the last time, trust me to do my damn job. I'll be back," she growled as she took off running, deeper into the woods as she followed the direction of the vehicle trail.

Natalia watched her disappear, then she sat down, pulling her knees up to her chest and wrapping her arms around them. She felt extremely uncomfortable in only a bikini with a giant t-shirt over it. She'd ditched the sarong when it got stuck in a tree branch back in Fiji.

*

Christian saw the Ute a half mile away, parked on the side of the trail where a path led to several camp shacks.

She rushed across the trail and nearly fell over when she saw the keys in the ignition. "Oh, thank God," she whispered, quietly pulling the door open. She glanced towards the camp area as she pushed the clutch in and turned the key. The Ute came to life, she slammed it into first, and popped the clutch, winding the gear all the way out before changing to get as much speed as she could. She was long gone by the time the ranger realized he'd heard a vehicle and went to check on his.

Dirt and dust flew up as the Ute skidded to a stop on the trail. Christian rolled the window down and stuck her head out. "Natalia!" she yelled, looking for any sign of her white t-shirt.

"I'm here," Natalia called, running towards the single cab vehicle. She snatched the door open and jumped inside, barely making it onto the seat before they were speeding down the trail, bouncing all over. She gave Christian a stern look when she finally got her door closed and buckled her seat belt. "I can't believe you stole this."

"Should I have just asked him for a ride?" she asked sarcastically. "Do you have your passport? Or perhaps any form of identification at all? How would you explain how you arrived on the island ... in a stolen plane?"

"Fine," Natalia grumbled, grabbing a hold of the dash as the vehicle jolted. "At least slow down before you kill us!"

Christian ignored her, checking the GPS again as she turned off the trail and headed through the uncut woods, hoping there were no other rangers looking for them. She glanced at the time on her watch. They had fifteen minutes and five miles to go. She shifted gears again, pushing the Ute faster. The ranger's paperwork, soda cup, and other personal items flew around the cab as they bounced side to side. The glove compartment suddenly opened, scaring Natalia so badly, she screamed.

"We're here!" Christian said, careening to a stop with the edge of an open clearing less than twenty feet away. She cut the engine. "Roll your window down," she added, checking her watch. *Five minutes.*

"What now?" Natalia asked.

"Listen for any noise."

Natalia heard nothing but the sound of her breathing, and the occasional rumble of her empty stomach. She was hungrier than she'd ever been in her life, but even thirstier. The water and snacks Christian had brought to her when they were leaving new Caledonia, were long gone. She took her seatbelt off and bent down, rustling through the ranger's personal items that had wound up on the floor. She found nothing but an empty soda bottle and a candy bar wrapper.

"Goddamn it!" she growled, sitting up when she heard the low buzz of a plane. She stared in disbelief as a red, single engine bush plane flew over the top of the trees and touched down in the clearing. Its large tires bounced along the old, dirt and rock runway, then rolled to a stop. "What the hell?"

"Stay here," Christian said. She got out of the Ute and walked towards the clearing, seeing a man dressed in black fatigues climb out. "Jousting only because of the king's pleas," she called.

"Lanced once too often feeling apathy," the man yelled in reply.

Christian sighed in relief as he dropped his gun and ran over. She rushed back to the truck. "Our ride is here," she said, pulling Natalia's door open. She grasped her hand and tugged her towards the plane.

"Excalibur?" the man asked, using her codename as he held his handgun out, covering them.

Christian nodded.

"Lionheart," he said, using his codename.

"Let's get the hell out of here," she replied, as they ran towards the plane.

*

The bush plane was nothing like the sea plane they'd flown from Fiji. There were two front cockpit doors, and two rear doors behind them, similar to a four door car. The pilot was in his seat, readying the plane for another takeoff, when Christian and Natalia climbed in, taking the two seats behind the cockpit seats. The carpet and worn leather seats were red and the gauge panel in front of the pilot was black.

The man calling himself Lionheart, entered the cockpit at the co-pilot door and took his seat. The pilot started the engine and within seconds they were bouncing along the makeshift runway towards the trees.

"Who are these men?" Natalia asked, leaning close to Christian. She didn't want to let on how scared she felt in their presence.

"They're with me," Christian replied.

"MI6?"

Christian nodded.

Natalia closed her eyes. *Please don't let us crash. Please don't let us crash. Please don't let us crash.*

"We are two hours out from your drop," Lionheart said loudly over the plane's engine as soon as they were airborne and over the tree line.

"Roger," Christian replied.

"Thank God," Natalia whispered to herself as she watched the sun set in the distance through the window.

"You'll find your pack under your seat, along with your provisions bag," Lionheart added.

Christian bent down, pulling out a black duffle bag. She quickly opened it, checking the contents: six passports, a stack of money in four different currencies, two handguns with ammo, two black jumpsuits, two pairs of black boots, two pairs of clear goggles, two cold bottles of water, and a handful of granola protein bars. She pulled out the water and snacks and zipped it back up. Then, she handed half of the food to Natalia.

"Eat and drink slowly. Otherwise, you'll puke," she said, "it's been a while since we've eaten or drank anything."

Natalia wanted to scarf the food down, package and all, and drown in the water bottle. However, the idea of being covered in puke changed her mind. She ate tiny bites and took little sips, savoring the cardboard-tasting granola bar. *If this is what military rations taste like, I would've never made it,* she thought, feeling like she was chewing on a crunchy shoe.

Christian ate and drank slowly as she watched the day begin to fade to night through the window. It had been a day from hell, and it certainly wasn't over. She knew the goons in Fiji more than likely hadn't followed them, but whoever had sent them, could still be tracing their every move. She had to follow protocol. Her phone vibrated with an incoming text message. She pulled it from her pocket and read off the coordinates, which was a set of latitude and longitude numbers, nothing else was in the message. She quickly programmed them into the GPS on her watch.

"One hour out," Lionheart yelled.

Christian pulled the duffle bag back out from under her seat and retrieved the two black jumpsuits. "Here," she said, handing one to Natalia. "Put this on."

"What? Why?"

"Just do it," Christian stated firmly as she began to pull on the other one.

Natalia removed the giant t-shirt and put her feet into the one-piece pantsuit. She wiggled around, pulling it up over her bathing suit in the small space. It fit like a wetsuit but wasn't skintight. She noticed Christian was wearing the same thing and had started pulling on a pair of boots. An identical pair was on the floor by her feet.

"Sorry we don't have any socks, but we won't be in this for long," Christian said.

Natalia was happy to have something besides flip flops, especially if they were about to go running around somewhere in the dark. She pulled on the half a size too big boots and leaned her head back. She was completely exhausted and wasn't sure how much more she could endure. She'd only been awake for 14 hours, yet it had felt more like 41.

"Thirty minutes out," Lionheart called.

Christian slid the backpack out and began checking the straps. The color drained from Natalia's face in the darkened plane when she noticed it had some kind of harness and clips attached to it.

"Please tell me we're not jumping out of this plane," she said.

Christian's eyes met hers in the darkness. "You'll be fine."

"Oh, dear God," she whispered.

"Have you ever been skydiving?"

"No."

"Well, you're about to. Take your seatbelt off and put this on," Christian said, holding up the tandem harness. "Stick your legs through these openings, then pull it up to your crotch. Your arms go through the top two openings."

"I can't jump out of a plane!"

"You're not jumping … I am. You'll be attached to me. Now, come on. We have to be ready or we'll miss our mark," she said, helping Natalia into the webbing of the harness. Her hands brushed Natalia's inner thighs as she slid the straps up between her legs. Once she had her arms through the upper straps, Christian connected everything and cinched it tight.

"Fifteen minutes out," Lionheart announced.

Christian put on her own harness and pulled the attached backpack up on her shoulders. Then, she checked all the heavy-duty clips one last time before fastening the duffle bag to her leg. Satisfied that it wasn't going anywhere, she put her goggles over her head, leaving them dangling around her neck and helped Natalia with her pair. She was glad Natalia had always worn a hair tie around her wrist to put her hair up in a ponytail whenever she felt like it. Her hair had been up ever since they first went on the run in Fiji and Christian left her in the bunker. When she'd returned, Natalia had a ponytail. She brought up the GPS on her watch, which popped up with a bright LED map picture. There was a blinking red dot and a solid blue dot. Red was her current position, and blue was her destination.

"Five minutes out," Lancelot yelled, rattling Natalia's already nervous brain.

She took a couple of deep breaths, letting them out slowly.

Christian moved her position, hiking her left leg up into the seat behind Natalia. She pulled Natalia back against her. Then, she connected her harness clips to the D rings on Natalia's, cinching the straps as tightly as she could. "Put your goggles over your eyes and tug the straps until they are suctioned to your face," she said into her ear so she would hear her.

Feeling Christian's breath on her skin and her voice in her ear made Natalia tingle from head to toe. She wanted to hate her so much, but her own body continued to deceive her. She did as instructed and counted to one hundred in her head, hoping it would help keep her calm. *We're jumping from a plane in the middle of the night, in the middle of nowhere. What can go wrong?*

CHAPTER ELEVEN

It was loud. So loud Natalia felt like a freight train was moving at breakneck speed between her ears. An extreme rush of heavy wind pushed against her face, peeling her cheeks back to her ears. She was thankful for the suit that protected the rest of her body, otherwise she was sure she would end up with loose, floppy skin like a basset hound. The immense dose of adrenaline coursing through her veins overrode her fear. In her mind, she was flying through the darkness towards the stars, when in reality, she was careening towards the dimly lit ground at over 100MPH. She'd tried to scream at first, but her mouth wouldn't open.

Christian kept her eyes on her watch, constantly checking the altimeter and GPS as she moved her arms like wings, adjusting their course. At 4500 feet, she reached back and pulled the rip cord. The backpack burst open and a solid black parachute blew out, unfolding itself in the air. The tandem women came to what felt like a sudden halt, snatching them back as the chute filled with air and expanded.

The unexpected jolt made Natalia queasy. Her stomach flip flopped around. They were moving much slower now that the parachute was dragging behind them, giving her a much better view of her surroundings. It took a few deep breaths to get her nausea under control, but once she did, she was able to look around at the town below. The lights were spread out with a lot of dark patches that seemed to be getting larger and larger. She no longer felt like she was flying with her head outside the window of a jet. The new sensation was more like a bird, gliding through the air.

Christian tugged on the left and right straps, guiding them towards their landing location, which was coming up faster and faster. "Natalia, if you can hear me, pull your legs up, tucking your knees to your chest, when we land," she yelled.

*

Natalia stiffened when she realized the dark patches were clusters of trees as they flew over top of one of them. Her heart pounded like a horse galloping in a derby, thumping hard against the wall of her chest. She wanted to close her eyes, but she couldn't. They seemed glued as wide open as they would go without her eyeballs falling out of the sockets. She wasn't sure if Christian was talking or not. She couldn't hear anything but the wind whooshing past her ears.

Christian spotted a tree clearing that looked like it was their location according to the GPS. It wasn't completely open, as there were still trees in the area, but they weren't grouped together. She pulled the steering lines, directing them towards the open back yard behind a house that had a large, two or three-acre lot like most of the surrounding homes in the rural neighborhood. The exterior light was on, giving her a better view as she steered them closer and closer.

Natalia reacted, seeing a building coming straight for them. She pulled her knees in, curling into a ball as she braced for impact.

"Here we go!" Christian yelled to deaf ears as she yanked the steering lines. Her feet hit the ground with her legs running a few yards from the momentum. The extra weight in front of her caused her to topple over with Christian on top of Natalia as the chute collapsed on the ground beside them.

Everything had happened so fast, Natalia didn't realize they were on the ground until she noticed it was silent. The loud noise piercing her ears was gone instantly. She reached her hand out, touching the Earth. "Oh, thank God," she whispered.

Christian rolled to the side and unhooked the clips that had them strapped together. Their bodies instantaneously separated. She moved to her knees, threw off her goggles, and rolled Natalia to her back to make sure she was conscious.

"Are you awake? Can you see me?" she said, shaking Natalia's chest.

"Yes," Natalia replied, stilling her hand as she sat up. "You're not very good at this, are you?"

Christian stood and pulled Natalia to her feet. "If you were more cooperative, we wouldn't have so many problems." She paused, listening for noise. "I don't think anyone heard us, but we need to get this chute rolled up." She looked around for somewhere to get rid of it. "We can stuff it into that shed."

"Where are we?"

"A safe house," Christian mumbled, removing her harness and the duffle bag attached to her leg. Then, she quickly helped Natalia out of hers before gathering up the silky material.

Once they had the evidence of their arrival hidden, they walked towards the house that sat close to twenty yards away. The lot was quite large and had a wooden privacy fence around it. Christian rummaged through the bag for her cell phone. The latest text message had a five-digit numerical code. She grabbed one of the handguns from the backpack and cocked it, moving a bullet into the firing chamber, before walking over and punching the numbers into the keypad for the lock.

"Stay here," she said quietly.

Natalia watched as she turned the knob and entered the dark house with the gun pointed out in front of her.

*

Christian spanned the house, checking every room, every closet, every space someone could be hiding in. The house was dark and empty. She called for Natalia to come inside as she turned on the living room light. The two-bedroom, one-bathroom house was small, but quaint and cozy, despite the electronic equipment taking up the dining area and part of the living room. She was sure the house was used for a lot more than simply as a safe house, but it didn't matter at this point.

"What is this place?" Natalia asked, looking at the three large, flat screen TV's and computer station with four flat screen monitors.

"It's an MI6 safe house."

"What exactly is a safe house?"

"Operatives live and work out of places like these all over the world. They're basically places no one can be traced to. We use them to hide people, gather intel … and other things. It's okay. No one can find you here."

"Why do you need all of this equipment?"

"I don't … and it's not for us. There's a bathroom down the hall, and two bedrooms. The dressers should have clothing in them. I'm sure you could use a shower and some real clothes," Christian replied, getting her phone from the duffle bag.

"Please tell me you are ordering food."

Christian glanced at her. "I don't even know where we are."

"Wonderful," Natalia sighed.

"I'll find us something to eat after I make a call," Christian said, walking out the same door they'd come in.

Natalia explored the house on her way to the bathroom. There wasn't much to it. The living room was sparsely furnished with a simple couch and coffee table. The bathroom had a corner shower, toilet, and sink … no tub. *So much for soaking in a hot bath.* She noticed both bedrooms had double beds and small dressers with various sized men's and women's clothing. She rummaged around and settled on a white tank top with some kind of surf and sun logo on the front, and a pair of dark blue sweatpants. Unsure how many days she would be there, she was happy to find a package of panties in her size and a halfway decent bra. Everything still had store tags attached to it.

She set the pile of clothing on the sink and searched for the necessities in the cabinet below. Similar to a hotel, she found mini shampoo and conditioner bottles, as well as packaged toothbrushes, deodorant, and toothpaste. *It's not the Four Seasons, but it'll do.* She turned on the spray and began to remove her jumpsuit and boots. Catching a glimpse of her disheveled self in the mirror caused her to gasp. She ran her hand through her messy hair and sighed, "Natalia Luis de Faria Moreno, what the hell have you gotten yourself into?"

*

"The package has been put away," Christian said.

"The dogs have been put down," Lancelot replied, meaning the men who were chasing them in Fiji had been taken care of. "In twenty-four hours, you and the package are to board a commercial flight from Cairns to Chengdu, Sichuan. You're booked as a newlywed couple, headed to China for your honeymoon, under the names Leigh and Mariah Michaels. You'll receive further instruction upon arrival."

"Roger."

The line went dead before she could say anything else. Christian leaned her head back, stretching the sore muscles of her body, surprised to see how many stars were in the sky. She checked the GPS on her phone. They were in a rural part of Queensland, Australia, about two hours outside of Cairns. She was hungry and smelled like a mule, but she wasn't sure she was strong enough to go back in. The woman inside that house had a hold on Christian like nothing she'd ever felt before, and it scared the hell out of her. "Pull yourself together, Garnier. It's just a mission. *She's* just a mission," she said to herself.

*

"I thought you were cooking," Natalia said, walking into the living area in her newfound clothing, freshly

89

showered and towel-drying her long locks. "Were you on the phone this whole time?"

Christian nodded and walked over to the kitchen.

The refrigerator had a loaf of bread in it and nothing else, but the freezer was full of frozen breakfast, lunch, and dinner foods. She read the back of several boxes before deciding on which ones to throw together to create a real meal.

Fifteen minutes later, she set two plates on the counter in front of the bar stools. They were full of seasoned chicken with fettuccine alfredo and an array of vegetables, which had taken six different frozen dinners to make.

"We don't have any pepper or anything, so I hope it tastes as good as it smells," Christian said, throwing the boxes into the trash before sitting down.

"It could be cardboard smeared with sauce, and I'd eat it at this point," Natalia replied, happy to have anything remotely similar to food.

*

After filling her stomach, Christian had excused herself to the shower. Standing under the spray, the last twenty-four hours replayed through her head. She'd never made such a huge mistake. *Getting involved with Natalia ...* "Should've never happened," she murmured, shaking her head. She needed to get her head on straight. The mission wasn't over, and she had no idea how far it was going to go. She had a feeling she was bringing Natalia to the UK, but she wasn't sure. Lancelot, the senior agent in charge of the overall mission, was her handler. He set everything up; told her where to be and when. Everything was on a need to know basis. She never got the whole picture up front. MI6 didn't operate like that … certainly not with their field operatives. She was told if information pertained to her current situation, otherwise, she was in the dark. She went when she was called upon, and did what was asked of her. This had been her life for the last ten years. Never once had she come across someone she couldn't ignore … not until Natalia Moreno.

The hot water had slowly turned cold. Christian still stood under it, letting the spray hit the back of her bent head and run down her body. She lifted her face to the water and held her breath.

CHAPTER TWELVE

Dressed in dark gray sweatpants and a navy-blue t-shirt, Christian walked into the living room and sat down on the couch, leaving two feet of space between her and Natalia. The TV was on, but she wasn't interested.

Natalia lulled her head to the side. "I take it this isn't your first time in one of these."

"No," she muttered.

"That looks bad," Natalia said, reaching out to touch Christian's forehead, but she pulled away.

"It's fine."

"It won't be if it needs stitches. At least let me see how deep it is."

Christian blew out a deep breath and leaned over, allowing Natalia's soft hands to touch her face.

Natalia tried to avoid the light blue eyes as she palpated the cut, but she couldn't. They drew her in like a moth to a flame. *Damn your eyes. Damn them for taking my breath away. Damn them for making me want you.* She backed away, turning her eyes back to the TV. "It's not very deep," she mumbled.

Christian knew that. She'd looked at it in the mirror. But she'd given in … as much for herself as for Natalia.

"This person you keep talking to, does he or she know more about my father?"

"No. I'm sorry. I wish I could tell you more." *I've been there. I know how much it hurts.*

"How long will we be here?" Natalia asked.

Christian checked her watch. "Forty-three hours."

"Am I going home?"

"Not necessarily."

"What do you mean?"

"I'll fill you in tomorrow."

Natalia was too tired to play cat and mouse or try to decipher what Christian was covering up. She wanted to be mad at her, but despite how crazy the day had gotten, she had kept Natalia safe… risking her own life in the process. No, she wasn't mad … she was sad. Sad that she couldn't talk to her mother or get any information about her father, but she was also scared. The people who had killed her father were after her.

She looked over at Christian, who appeared to be sleeping awake … if that was even possible. She felt safe with her, despite the distance that had grown between them in the past twelve hours. She was amazed at how quickly life could change in twenty-four hours. She felt like she'd been on a rollercoaster with incredible highs and terrible lows.

"I'm going to bed," Christian murmured, rolling her head to the side to face the woman looking back at her.

"Me too," Natalia replied, reaching over and squeezing her hand. "Thank you."

"For what?" Christian's brow furrowed.

"Everything," she sighed, "keeping me safe. I know—"

"No one is going to hurt you. I'm not going to let that happen," Christian said, softly cutting her off.

*

Natalia wrestled with one bad dream after another. She was exhausted, yet her body wouldn't lay claim to the rest it so desperately needed. Her mind kept replaying the events of the horrendous day, filling her head with nightmares much deeper than a few guys chasing her. She woke up several times, just before she was raped or beaten, or shot in the head. Each time she fell asleep, it was a new scenario. Nothing remotely similar had happened to her, but fear of the unknown could make anyone feel paranoid. She had no idea how her father had died, only that he'd been murdered. Did he suffer? Was he tortured? Did it happen quickly? Was she in for the same fate? What about her mother, were they after her, too? Whenever she tried to quell the dark thoughts, images of Christian replaced them, making her feel somewhat safer.

*

Christian's body sunk into a deep slumber as soon as her head hit the pillow, but the first little noise she heard woke her to full alertness. Reaching for the 9MM under the spare pillow, she listened to footsteps that paused outside of her door. She trained the gun on the door and quietly got out of bed, easing along the wall as the knob clicked and began to turn.

When the door opened, Christian grabbed the person, slamming them against the wall with the gun pressing into their forehead in one swift move.

Natalia screamed at the top of her lungs, causing Christian to let go of her.

"Oh my God," Christian gasped. "What the hell are you doing sneaking around in the middle of the night?"

"I … I …" Natalia tried to talk, but her heart raced, her breathing was shallow, and tears stung her eyes.

Christian set the gun on the nearby dresser and pulled the trembling woman into her arms. "I'm sorry."

Natalia relaxed into her and began sobbing uncontrollably.

Damn it, Christian mentally chastised herself. They were in a safe house. There literally was no other place safer than a safe house, yet she'd kept her senses on high alert. Natalia had been through so much already that day, and now she'd probably traumatized her for life.

This was why she didn't do relationships. When life was black and white, she lived in the gray area, a place where intimacy didn't exist. She had no idea how to console the woman in her arms, so she simply held her until she'd cried it all out.

"I'm sorry," Natalia whispered, as she pulled away to wipe her face on her shirt.

Christian caught a glimpse of her in the sliver of moonlight peeking through the blinds. Natalia had on the same tank top she'd dressed in after her shower, with her dark hair hanging forward over one shoulder, and a pair of white panties that contrasted against her olive skin … nothing else. She quickly turned her head, suppressing the arousal that had begun to build low in her belly. "You have no reason to be sorry," she said, clearing her throat.

"I should've knocked on the door," Natalia sighed, still trying to calm her frazzled nerves.

"Well, yes." Christian nodded. "Sneaking up on an MI6 operative in the middle of the night isn't the best idea."

"I wasn't sneaking. I just … I guess I didn't want to wake you."

"Then, why come into my room?"

"I don't know. I keep having nightmares." She pushed her hair back over her shoulder. "I thought maybe … I don't know … I might feel safer in here with you," she muttered, chancing a look at Christian's eyes.

"I'm sorry," Christian breathed heavily, feeling horrible for man-handling her, then added, "I didn't mean to scare you. I've probably made things worse, huh?"

"I'm okay."

"Are you sure? I didn't hurt you, did I?"

"No," she murmured, shaking her head. "You did scare the hell out of me, though."

"I could've killed you. I almost killed you. Damn it."

"I should probably get back to my room. I don't think I've slept more than an hour."

"No," Christian said, grabbing her hand and stopping her. "You came in here for a reason. It's okay. Let's get some sleep."

CHAPTER THIRTEEN

Christian awoke to the sound of pouring rain pelting the windows. The sun had risen but was masked by the darkened clouds. She kept still, taking even breaths, careful not to wake the woman curled up against her. Natalia's head rested on her chest, just below her shoulder, and her hand was sprawled across her stomach. Christian had her arm around Natalia with her hand casually lying on her hip over the waistband of her panties.

She tried to remember the last time she'd woken up in such an affectionate position, besides twenty-four hours earlier when she and Natalia had spent hours pleasuring each other. Even then, they'd woken on separate sides of the bed. She hadn't actually *cuddled* with anyone in so long, she couldn't remember the last time ... or the person for that matter.

Wanting to get lost in a moment she would more than likely never have again ... in a feeling so warm and intimate ... she closed her eyes, breathing in the light floral scent of Natalia's hair.

*

Natalia felt like she'd had the best sleep of her life, despite it being only a handful of hours ... until the nightmares of the day before flooded her head. She stirred lightly, trying to make herself go back to the fantasy dream she was having before she came back to reality. Christian was running her hands up her thighs … closer and closer. Yes, that's where she'd left off before waking.

The hand on her hip grasped her a little tighter.

How is there a hand on my hip and two on my thighs? Shaking herself out of the dream once more, she opened her eyes. *Oh, dear God, I'm lying on top of her.* She held her breath, unsure of what to do. Should she ease herself away? Roll over and pretend she had no idea? She hoped Christian was still asleep.

"Everything okay?" Christian murmured, sensing her body go rigid.

"Yeah," Natalia whispered, "uh, good morning." She pulled away, removing her hand from Christian's body as her hand fell away from Natalia's hip. Their eyes met in the soft light.

Christian sighed, turning her head as she sat up and got out of the bed. She'd slept in her t-shirt, but her sweatpants were on the floor nearby. She reached down, pulling them on before stepping over to the window.

Huge drops of water splashed the glass as lightning flickered across the sky and thunder rumbled in the distance. She needed to get out of there, get some air … put some distance between her and Natalia. *Damn the rain!* She raised her fist to smack it on the wall in frustration, but a pair of hands starting at her abdomen and sliding to her chest from behind, got her attention, breaking her train of thought. She felt Natalia's warm breath on the back of her neck. "We can't," she whispered, mostly to herself.

"Whatever this … is … between us …" Natalia murmured between light kisses against Christian's skin, "we can't … control it."

Christian swallowed the lump in her throat, hearing the loud thump in her ears. She tried desperately not to give in…not to make the same mistake twice, but she couldn't quell the desire burning deep down inside of her. There was no strings attached sex … she'd done it many of times … but with Natalia it was so much more, and it was something she didn't need; something she didn't want; something she couldn't have. "You're going to get hurt," she muttered.

"Then, hurt me," Natalia said, pushing her hands under Christian's t-shirt, squeezing her breasts and pinching her nipples. "I need you, Christian. Make me feel alive."

Christian squeezed her eyes closed as blood rushed through her veins, heating every inch of her body. She knew better than to give in to desire, but nothing in her training or ten years of operative work had prepared her for Natalia Moreno.

Stilling her hands, Christian pulled them from her shirt and in one swift move, she pulled Natalia in front of her, backing her up against the wall. She moved closer, pressing their bodies together as her hands held Natalia's face. Their lips met in a ferocious kiss that left them both breathless. Christian backed away slightly, putting enough space between them to run her hands down the front of Natalia's body, from her aching breasts to her wet panties. She grabbed the waistband and lowered herself to her knees, pulling the material down with her.

The heady scent of desire burned her nostrils, beckoning her like a moth to a flame. She slid her hands up Natalia's legs, pushing them apart. Then, she ran her tongue up the inside of one thigh, blowing a gentle breath on the pulsating mound in the middle, before continuing down the other leg.

Natalia's breathing filled her ears as she moved her mouth once more, gliding her tongue over the glistening folds in front of her, careful not to press too hard.

Natalia's hips jerked and bucked on their own accord, wanting more contact. She reached down, tugging softly on Christian's short curls, silently begging her not to tease.

Christian swirled her tongue in circles, making delicate passes over the swollen, throbbing center.

"Yes, baby ... just like that," Natalia moaned, "I'm so close." She moved against the wall, holding Christian's head where she needed her most.

Feeling Natalia's body begin to go rigid, Christian backed away, running her hands up Natalia's body, removing her tank too as she stood. Natalia's eyes were heavy-lidded. Her chest rose and fell quickly. Christian's face came into focus as the fog began to leave her brain, but tasting herself on Christian's lips sent her right back into overdrive. Her body felt like it was teetering on the edge of a cliff. The kiss was soft, but passionate; velvety tongues passed over each other; lips were gently bitten; languid breaths were shared.

Christian broke the kiss. "Turn around," she whispered.

Natalia faced the opposite direction, bracing herself with her hands on the wall and spreading her legs like someone under arrest. Christian moved up behind her and slid one hand around to the front of her body, kneading her breast while her other hand pushed the long, dark locks forward, revealing her full back.

Natalia's body trembled as Christian's mouth skimmed over skin, placing kisses over her shoulders and the back of her neck, then down her spine. As she moved back up, Christian dragged her hand along one of Natalia's inner thighs.

"Oh, God," Natalia cried out as two fingers glided easily inside of her from behind. Her hips pushed down, trying to fill herself with every thrust.

Christian's hand moved back and forth between her breasts, kneading and playing with her nipples, while the other slid in and out of her, working deeper with every stroke.

Natalia's body was on fire, burning from the inside out. Thousands of colorful flecks fluttered behind her closed eyelids. Blood pulsed through her veins at breakneck speed with every thumping beat of her heart. She literally felt like she was about to explode into a million pieces.

Groaning loudly, Natalia mumbled something incoherently as her body tightened around Christian's fingers. She thrust into her one more time as deep as she could, then stilled her fingers as Natalia rode out the last of her powerful orgasm. Her other hand went around her mid-section, holding the limp woman against her so she didn't crumble to the ground, as she softly eased her fingers out.

Natalia leaned back against the solid body behind her as she slowly came down from the euphoric high. Her mind was fuzzy and her legs were wobbly like she'd just run a marathon. A few deep breaths helped her collect herself while her heart rate gradually returned to normal. The morning sun fought to peek through the rain clouds, adding a little more light to the room as the showers continued.

"Are you okay?" Christian whispered in her ear, feeling the woman regain her strength while she held her.

"Yes," Natalia replied, reaching her hand back between them and under the waistband of Christian's sweatpants.

Christian put space between them when Natalia's fingers skimmed her wet center over the top of her underwear.

Natalia spun in her arms and looked at the baby blue eyes staring back at her. Christian opened her mouth to speak, and Natalia's lips covered hers in a sensuous kiss. Velvety tongues softly prodded, and breaths were shared. Natalia put her hand in the center of Christian's chest and pushed back, breaking the kiss as she bit her lower lip.

Christian let herself be led as she walked backwards until her legs bumped the bed. Natalia shoved a little harder, pushing her back onto the bed. Then, she tugged her sweatpants and underwear down around her ankles, before running her hands back up Christian's thighs and spreading them apart. Glistening, dark pink folds of skin awaited her as she lowered her mouth, teasing with leisurely strokes.

Christian sat up on her elbows, watching the red tongue swirl around everywhere except where she needed it most. She reached out for Natalia's head, hoping to ease her into position, when two soft hands grasped her wrists, holding her in place. She was physically capable of getting out of the hold, but her brain was beginning to turn to mush from the torturing caresses. Her labored breathing and thrusting hips were completely out of her control.

"Oh God," she groaned as the pressure built deeper and deeper.

Natalia had yet to graze the swollen mound in the center, focusing instead on making delicate circles around it in both directions, over and over. She kept hold of the writhing woman under her, feeling her getting wetter and wetter in her mouth.

Christian's heart pounded like a thoroughbred in her chest. Her legs trembled. She wanted to throw her head back, but she couldn't take her eyes off what was going on between her legs. The site of Natalia's mouth on her made her twice as aroused.

Suddenly, Natalia let go of one of Christian's wrists. She slid two fingers deep inside of her as her tongue made a hard pass directly over the pulsating spot she'd been avoiding. Christian's body bucked like a bull.

"Mmmmm," Christian moaned deeply, making a raspy, guttural sound as Natalia's fingers and tongue worked in unison. She was barely able to keep her half-lidded eyes trained on the woman pleasuring her.

Feeling on fire from the inside out like she was about to spontaneously combust, Christian grabbed Natalia's head with her free hand, holding it where she wanted it. She thrust her hips, riding her tongue and fingers harder and faster until she imploded. A kaleidoscope of shiny slivers danced behind her closed eyelids. She held her breath as her body stilled. Her head and shoulders fell back against the bed. For a handful of seconds, she appeared lifeless.

Natalia watched her chest heave up and down until her rapid breathing began to slow to a more normal pace. She moved up next to her, kissing her cheek softly as she curled into her side.

CHAPTER FOURTEEN

Christian sat on a rickety wooden chair on the back patio; a warm cup of coffee in her hand. The rain had finally stopped, leaving a bright, sunny sky and steamy heat in its wake. A mini forest of tall trees surrounded the two-acre property, which was closed off by a privacy fence.

She sipped her coffee and let out a long sigh. "This has to stop," she uttered, chastising herself. She'd made so many mistakes in the past three days, and this morning was no exception. She wasn't sure what it was about Natalia Moreno, but she'd been drawn to the Portuguese beauty since the moment she saw her. Having an attraction to someone had never caused Christian to lose focus. She'd never gone against the number one rule … until now. After all hell broke loose, and Natalia had found out who she was and why she was there, she figured that would quell the heat between them. Obviously, she was wrong. Whatever this was between them, it was wild and raw … and very powerful. She needed to put an end to it, but deep down she wondered if she was too late.

The heavy click of the door handle grabbed her attention. Natalia had awakened, and if she felt anything like Christian, she'd be famished. She tossed the last of her cold coffee into the grass and stood up.

"I was wondering where you were," Natalia said, stepping outside with her own cup of coffee. She was wearing a man's long-sleeved, white dress shirt and a pair of black panties. All the buttons were undone on the shirt except the one in the very center, revealing a wide gap of olive skin above and below it. The shirt was cinched just enough to cover her breasts, and the sleeves were rolled up three-quarters of the way. Her dark hair fell forward in loose waves over one shoulder as she leaned against a roof post and brought the mug to her lips with both hands.

"Getting some fresh air," Christian replied softly, taking her in. "The rain has stopped."

Natalia studied her eyes, hoping the enigmatic operative would give her some kind of sign. She'd woken alone, which only added to the confusion filling her mind. There were no words for whatever this was between them. She hated the situation she was in; hated the lies; hated feeling trapped ... all of which Christian had control over. She should've hated her, but she couldn't. Christian eased the pain and sadness of losing her father, and the anger of not being with her mother. She lessened the fear in their nightmarish situation. Most of all, she made her *feel*.

"We can't do this again," Christian sighed.

"I know," Natalia said, her voice barely above a whisper.

Christian stepped forward, reaching for her hand, but thought better of it. "Come on. I'm sure you're as hungry as I am," she uttered, walking past her and into the house.

*

"Pack a light bag with whatever clothes you want to take with you from here. You'll need enough for at least three days, maybe four," Christian said, clearing the throw-away plates she'd used for their breakfast of frozen pancakes and sausage links.

"Where are we going?" Natalia asked.

"China ... on our honeymoon."

"What?"

"We're a newly married couple. Your name is Mariah Michaels and I'm Leigh Michaels. How's your Australian accent, by the way?"

Natalia stood with her arms crossed over her chest and her eyes pinned on Christian. "You can't be serious."

Christian returned the stare. "Do you want to see your mother? Perhaps go home?"

"Of course."

"Well, we have to go through China to do it, and we can't travel using our real names, so this is it. Go pack a bag. Our flight leaves in three hours, and we have an hour-long drive."

"I guess it makes sense with Australia legalizing gay marriage." She shrugged. *Is this some kind of test? When is this nightmare going to end?* "By the way, I'm not good with accents of any kind," she added, walking down the hallway.

"Let me do most of the talking and remember to drop your R's," Christian called.

"This ought to be interesting," she whispered.

*

Christian sat on the couch, checking her watch diligently. A small bag packed with miscellaneous clothing was on the floor near her feet. The array of clothing options in the house wasn't exactly like going to a boutique. It was more like the outlet mall where this piece or that piece is in your size, but nothing fits perfectly. She was lucky to snag a pair of jeans, which she had on, a sweater, a sweatshirt, two t-shirts including the one from the night before, a pair of shorts, and a pair of sweatpants, also from the night before. She wondered how Natalia had fared since she was a size smaller and an inch or two shorter. Judging by the amount of time it was taking, Christian figured she too had struggled in the wardrobe department. She glanced up when a small bag, similar to her own, flopped on the floor in front of her.

"I hope we're not going sight-seeing or doing any other honeymoon stuff … outside of our safe house. With what's in that bag, I'll certainly be making a fashion statement … and not a very good one."

"Actually, we'll be in a hotel, like a proper honeymooning couple."

"Wonderful," Natalia muttered sarcastically.

"Hey, at least we don't have to jump out of the plane this time. We get to ride all the way to the airport, land, and taxi to the terminal like normal people," Christian replied.

Natalia rolled her eyes, although Christian was right. *If we have another hair-raising experience involving a plane, I might shoot you myself.* "How are we getting to the airport? I don't suppose you called an Uber?"

Christian grinned and shook her head. She grabbed her bag and walked through the kitchen to a side door Natalia hadn't noticed the night before. She snatched her bag from the floor and hurried after her.

A medium-sized, black SUV was backed into the garage. Christian took Natalia's bag and placed it on the back floorboard, along with hers. Then, she pulled the passenger door open and waved for Natalia to get in.

"So, now we're stealing another vehicle?" Natalia questioned, "or is it borrowing? I forgot."

"Borrow. Always borrow. We haven't stolen anything. As for this vehicle, it's MI6 property. Technically, we're borrowing it, too," she replied, starting the engine and pushing the button to raise the garage door.

"I see," Natalia mumbled under her breath while looking at the rural neighborhood for the first time as they drove through the area. It was unlike any place she'd ever lived. Each house was situated well off the main road, with large spreads of property and thick trees around it. No wonder MI6 had chosen it for a safe house. It was remote and secluded but still considered residential.

*

Christian kept her comments and thoughts mostly to herself during the drive. She needed to focus. Natalia had caused her to break concentration so many times already, she wondered if she was growing close to retirement. As an operative, the absolute last thing you should ever do is compromise yourself … in any way. That includes sleeping with someone while on a mission. In over ten years as an MI6 operative, she rarely made a mistake … certainly not one of this magnitude.

The more she tried not to think about Natalia, the more she thought about her. It wasn't hard, especially with her sitting a foot away, watching the surroundings of Queensland, Australia pass by through the window. In the last thirty-six hours, she'd been through a hell of an ordeal. Most people would be at their wits end, or perhaps a basket case all-together, at this point. But, not Natalia Moreno. She was different ... unlike anyone Christian had ever met. That was part of the reason Christian found her so compelling.

*

Natalia avoided looking at anything in Christian's direction. She knew sleeping with her was a bad idea. She'd known it from the very beginning. There could be no relationship between them, not now ... not ever. When this ordeal was over and she finally made it home ... *if* she made it home, she'd never see Christian Garnier again. That was both a welcoming thought and a disappointment. Choosing not to dwell on uncertainty, she reached over and turned the radio on.

"Any particular genre?" she asked, pressing the button to scan the stations.

"No." Christian shook her head, keeping her eyes trained on the road. She had on dark sunglasses that she'd found in the visor but was sure Natalia could see right through them. "I'm good with whatever you choose," she added.

Natalia quickly passed over the couple of easy-listening, love songs, as well as the rap music she couldn't understand, finally settling on a top 40s pop channel. The song didn't matter; she just wanted noise in the quiet vehicle.

The closer they got to the airport, the more nervous she became. What if she forgot to use the Australian accent, or her poorly botched version of it? What if she forgot the fake names they were traveling under? What if ... *Stop with the what ifs. You can do this. You want to get home, don't you? This is the only way.*

"Everything okay?" Christian asked, noticing her mumbling under her breath.

"Yeah. Pretending to be someone else isn't exactly my forte."

"Oh, and it's mine?" Christian said harshly.

"Well, you fooled me pretty good."

"Fooled you? How so? I never said I was anything. You know my real name, for God's sake. Most people at MI6 don't even know that."

"You kept my father's death a secret. You obviously rigged things so that we'd be in the same bungalow. That whole time I thought you were a stranded traveler just like me," Natalia snapped angrily.

"I have no control over what MI6 plans. I had no idea we'd be sharing the bungalow, so get that idea out of your head. I was as confused as you were, but I was there to do a job. In fact, I'm still doing that job right now. You're safe, aren't you? Those guys didn't get to you because of me."

"You almost shot me!"

"Great. We're back to that! You snuck into my room in the middle of the night! Shall I remind you that I am a highly trained operative?" Christian growled, pulling the vehicle over on the side of the road.

"What are you doing?"

"I'm certainly not going up there," Christian said, nodding towards the entrance to the Cairns Airport, which was visible a mile and a half away. "We can't go in there arguing. We're supposed to be newlyweds."

"I know that," Natalia grumbled.

"What's going on? Whatever it is, we need to hash it out right here and now."

"There's nothing to hash out," she sighed, "I didn't mean to … I don't even know how it started."

"I know what it's like to not know what's going on with your parents or find out they're dead. You feel lost; out of control. The things that have happened between us are confusing and have only complicated the situation. It was a huge mistake that never should've happened. We both know that. It's better if there is nothing physical between us, and definitely no more sex. Do you agree?"

"Yes," Natalia replied softly.

"Good. Now, Mrs. Michaels, let's go on our honeymoon!" Christian said, putting the SUV back in gear and pulling out onto the road.

Natalia shook her head and laughed. *She makes me crazy.*

CHAPTER FIFTEEN

The black SUV pulled into one of the parking lots closest to Cairns Airport. Christian rolled her window down and pressed the button for a parking ticket, which she placed in the cup holder in the center console. Then, she drove around to an empty space.

"What's going to happen to this thing?" Natalia asked, referring to the vehicle they'd been driving.

"It'll get picked up within twenty-four hours," Christian replied, digging through the small duffle bag she was using as a suitcase. She pulled out a passport and a gold wedding band, both of which she handed to Natalia. "Put the ring on and keep the passport in your pocket."

Natalia watched Christian slide a matching ring onto her finger, before opening the passport. Her picture was inside, along with her same date of birth, but the name and address were not hers. She wondered if they were real. Did Mariah Michaels exist, and was this her address? The ring on her finger felt foreign and looked out of place.

"We were married yesterday in a small ceremony in front of friends and family at our home because we were saving for this trip," Christian stated, shoving some Australian dollars into her pocket before closing the bag.

"I don't know if I can do this. What if I mess up?"

"You'll be fine. We won't be here long," Christian said, trying out her Australian accent.

Natalia raised a brow.

"We need to get moving. That plane can't leave without us," she added, sounding like she'd lived down under all of her life.

Natalia had no idea who was after her or why. It was frightening not knowing who to trust. Having to pretend to be someone else only added to her uneasiness. *Go to the place you use when you talk to large groups. Find that comfort zone*, she told herself as they began walking towards the airport entrance. *Of course, talking about the ocean and sea life is easy. This is different ... very different.* She took a deep breath and pulled herself together.

"Are you okay?" Christian whispered, taking her hand.

"I'll be alright," Natalia said, trying out her best Australian accent.

Christian grimaced. "That needs more work than we have time for. I'll do most of the talking."

"I'm nervous."

"Think of it like this, you're one step closer to your mother."

Natalia nodded and squeezed her hand.

*

As they sat at Gate 12 in terminal B, Christian carried on a polite conversation with an older couple who was seated nearby. Natalia flipped through a magazine, listening as they discussed the weather and traveling. Christian's thick Australian accent sounded identical to the man and woman she was speaking with. Natalia glanced at the woman sitting next to her. She found it almost disturbing how Christian could change her persona in the blink of an eye and pretend to be a local, leaving on a vacation trip. She wondered who the real Christian Garnier was, and if there really was such a thing. Was she the woman who 'borrowed' modes of transportation and parachuted out of planes? Was she the master of disguise in the airport? Was she the charming, albeit arrogant, paddle boarder in Fiji? Whoever she really was, didn't exactly matter. Still, Natalia wondered how she could be so drawn to someone she knew nothing about. That thought was more unsettling than Christian's newest act.

Checking her watch, Christian said a polite goodbye to the couple and grabbed Natalia's hand. "We need to go," she whispered, smiling as they grabbed their bags and walked away from Gate 12.

"Where are we going?" Natalia asked.

"Our plane is boarding."

"Wait, that wasn't our gate?"

"No. We're at Gate B 21, which is boarding, so pick up the pace."

Natalia blew out a breath of frustration. She nearly had to jog to keep up with Christian.

*

The Airbus A330 was nearly full by the time Christian and Natalia boarded. Two seats awaited them on the left side of the business class section.

"Don't stow your bag. Just shove it under the seat in front of you," Christian whispered.

Natalia did as she was told, before taking the seat closest to the window.

"Welcome aboard. Beverages will be served as soon as we take off," the flight attendant said, giving Christian the once over.

Natalia rolled her eyes and looked around the cabin before leaning back against the seat. She lulled her head to the side, watching the grounds crew hard at work, preparing the plane for takeoff while Christian rummaged through her bag, prior to setting it down by her feet and buckling her seatbelt.

The plane jerked slightly as it was pushed back from the gate. Then, it swayed around as it maneuvered towards the runway. The captain came over the speaker, announcing they were next for departure. Natalia gripped the armrests of her seat.

"After everything we've done in the past few days, don't tell me you're scared of flying?"

"I don't like takeoffs, especially in these big planes," Natalia replied as the engines roared to life, sending the plane careening down the asphalt strip at one hundred and eighty miles per hour. The large plane bounced and bobbed, then felt weightless as it entered the blue sky, nose first.

Christian looked through the window at the cloudless sky. The nasty rain early that morning had turned into a beautiful day.

"How long is the flight?" Natalia asked, feeling calmer now that the plane had settled.

"Seven hours for this one. We have an hour-long layover in Hong Kong, then a three-hour flight."

"Where are we going?"

"China."

"No shit."

Christian glanced at the woman next to her. "Sichuan," she sighed, glad they weren't in first class. It would've been much more comfortable, but with an aisle between them, they wouldn't be able to talk much, and

Natalia's butchering of the Australian accent wasn't helping matters.

"Have you ever been?"

"Yes. You?"

"No." Natalia shook her head. "It's on my list of places to go. How ironic," she muttered.

Christian didn't say anything else as she stretched her legs as best she could, then pulled out her cell phone, texting two words: CLEAN EXIT.

Natalia had seen enough covert secret agent crap to last a lifetime. She shook her head at the odd message and pulled down the window cover on her other side. Closing her eyes, she hoped to get some much needed sleep after a fitful night and exhausting morning.

*

The plane hit turbulence halfway through the flight. Natalia opened her eyes to the dimly lit interior of the plane. She'd almost forgotten where she was until she realized she was lying against Christian with her head on her shoulder. She quickly sat up and readjusted her position so that she was back in her own seat.

"It's a good thing you don't snore."

Natalia furrowed her brow as she looked at the woman next to her. "Why is that?"

"I would've ordered you the vegetarian dish," Christian said, nodding towards the flight attendant who was passing out the dinner trays.

Natalia shrugged. "It would've probably tasted better than whatever else they're serving."

"Nope." Christian pursed her lips. "I upgraded us."

"What? How?"

"I paid for it, of course. But we're having pork dumplings with noodles in a sweet and sour sauce. That's what they're serving in first class. Everyone else back here had a choice of vegetable lo mein or pork fried rice."

"Here you are, two first class pork dumpling meals," the flight attendant said, stopping at their row. "Can I get you anything else?" she asked, placing her hand on Christian's shoulder.

Natalia grabbed Christian's hand. "How about a couple glasses of champagne?" she asked, remembering to use the accent as she looked at the woman. "We're on our honeymoon."

"Oh, uh … congratulations" the flight attendant uttered, removing her hand. Clearing her throat, she added, "I'll see what we have in the back."

Christian raised a brow. "What was that all about?"

"She's been eyeing you like a diabetic kid staring at a candy bar, since we boarded the plane," Natalia growled, letting go of her hand.

Christian laughed. 'That's …"

"We aren't really married, so if an airline floozy is what you want…go right ahead."

"Huh? I'm not interested in her. I told you I don't date. I don't do relationships."

"No, you just have sex."

Christian sighed in frustration. "Nat—Mariah, we've been over this, and we both agreed to stop doing what we were doing." *She's going to make me blow this whole cover.*

"I know," Natalia said softly.

Christian was glad most of the people around them were asleep. She reached over, grabbing Natalia's hand, stilling her as she began to open the covering on her food.

117

"Here you are, ladies. Courtesy of Hong Kong Air. Congratulations, again," the flight attendant said, handing them two glasses of cheap champagne.

"Thanks," they replied simultaneously.

"Were you about to say something?" Natalia asked, looking at Christian.

No, I was about to kiss you because I'm stupid. "Uh, no. I thought you needed help opening that. If you're not careful, you'll be wearing your food. I hate those damn things," she said, avoiding the odd look on Natalia's face as she went back to her own dish, easily opening the lid.

*

The rest of the plane ride was uneventful. The jumbo jet bounced softly over the runway as it taxied to the gate in Hong Kong. Natalia wished it hadn't been dark as they flew in over the city, but the array of multicolored lights below was beautiful.

Christian stood as soon as the plane came to a stop. She nodded for Natalia to follow as they made their way up the aisle. It always seemed to take twice as long to get off a plane as it did to get on. She never understood that concept. Checking her watch, she waited almost impatiently for the door to open. Once it did, passengers began to file out.

"We don't have much time before our next flight leaves. It'll probably be boarding by the time we get to the gate," she said, scanning the screens for their next flight once they entered the terminal.

Natalia gripped her bag and fell in step next to Christian as they maneuvered through the airport, literally walking from one end of the long terminal to the other. She looked around at the people gathered at each gate as they quickly walked by. Most of the passengers were Asian, men and women, with some children. They passed a food kiosk that smelled delectably good, like opening a bag of hot Chinese takeout, and her stomach made note of it, growling loudly.

"Is this our actual gate?" she asked, following Christian to a pair of open seats.

Christian nodded as she scanned the crowd.

"Wait, we're not lying to people and pretending to be going on their flight this time?"

Christian leaned closer. "We were early for our flight. It was best not to give away the actual flight we were taking in case we were being followed. You can't trust anyone. We're sitting here now because this plane is boarding in two minutes."

"Do you think someone is following us? Are those men back?" Natalia's voice cracked as she quickly looked around.

"No," Christian grabbed her hand, whispering, "those men are dead, and no one should know where we are. I can't say that I'm sorry for all the secrecy, though. I have a job to do."

"I know," Natalia sighed as the gate attendant announced the first call for boarding.

*

Natalia stepped inside the jumbo jet that appeared identical to the one they'd flown in less than an hour ago. The only difference was this time, their seats were near the door, giving them a bit of advantage when exiting. She shoved her bag under the seat in front of her and closed the window cover. A sliver of depression crossed her mind at not being able to go explore Hong Kong, a place so rich in history and culture. Instead, she'd had to view it from above in the darkness. The feeling of being trapped in a nightmare surfaced again. *Once was enough.*

Christian noticed the shadow cross Natalia's in the dim lighting of the planes interior and grabbed her hand as they taxied down the runway at breakneck speed. She let go as soon as they were in the air and the plane leveled out. "We'll be in Sichuan in about three hours," she said.

Natalia simply nodded. She reached for the airline magazine sticking out of the pocket on the seatback in front of her, but everything was written in Chinese, a language she didn't speak. She was fluent in Portuguese, English, and Spanish, and knew enough French to get by, but she didn't speak any of the Asian languages.

*

Natalia had dozed off. Hearing Christian's voice, she opened her eyes to see her having a conversation with the man across the aisle … in Chinese. *That figures!* She shook her head, wondering if anyone had ever been able to unravel the mystery of Christian Garnier.

She was about to close her eyes again when the plane began to suddenly rattle and shake. Natalia gripped the arms of the seat. A few people screamed as the plane made a violent drop of about two feet. Items people had in their laps flew up in the air. One baggage compartment popped open, scaring the life out of the people in that row. The pilot quickly came over the intercom, speaking in Chinese, and English, stating that they were flying through a patch of bad weather, but would be clear of it shortly.

Christian leaned over Natalia, pushing the window cover open. It was pitch black outside with only the blinking of the wing lights visible, but the outside of the window glass appeared wet. She shoved it closed and leaned back in her seat just as the plane rattled once more.

"This is bad. This is really bad," Natalia mumbled, still holding the armrests with a white-knuckled grip.

"It'll be fine," Christian reassured. She turned on the aeronautical app on her phone and looked at the plane's coordinates, altitude, and the weather in the area.

"Are you allowed to be doing that? What if it interferes with the pilots?" Natalia questioned, her voice laced with fear.

"It's harmless. I was just checking to see how much further we had," Christian replied, closing the app and stuffing the phone back into her pocket. She pried Natalia's fingers from the armrest between them and pushed it up out of the way. Then, she loosened her seatbelt and slid over, wrapping her arm around the scared woman. "It's just a bit of bad weather. The plane is not in any danger," she whispered.

Natalia let go of the other armrest and clung to Christian as if her life depended on it. The dim cabin lights flickered as the jet shook violently from the turbulence. Natalia closed her eyes and silently prayed that they landed safely. She had no idea how much longer the flight was, but if they had to attempt to land in these conditions, she wasn't sure they would be successful.

Within a few more hair-raising minutes, the plane cleared the storm and returned to the smooth flight they started with. Natalia pulled away from Christian.

"Thanks," she murmured.

Christian smiled thinly.

CHAPTER SIXTEEN

Chengdu, a sub-provincial city and the capital of China's Sichuan Providence, was one of the most important hubs in Western China. Its culture dated all the way back before Imperial China. Of course, coming into the airport at nine o'clock at night left a lot to the imagination, hiding all of the surrounding Chengdu Plain.

Christian looked through the window, shaking her head at the disappointment. All that was visible was at least a million tiny lights. She had no idea how long they were staying, but she hoped she had at least one day to show Natalia the beauty that she'd seen the first time she'd visited the providence.

"Where to now?" Natalia questioned as they made their way off the plane.

Christian dialed a number on her phone as she searched the signs for baggage claim, which would take them to the exit.

"On the ground. Package is secure," she said when Lancelot answered.

"You have reservations at the Temple Hotel. Rendezvous in twenty-four hours for further instruction," he stated before the line went dead.

Christian tucked the phone away and headed to the nearest taxi, ushering Natalia inside. "*Wo qu Temple Hotel,*" she said in Chinese. She knew the language good enough to get around and converse with the locals, but she was by no means fluent like she was in several other languages.

"I assume we're going to eat at some point," Natalia uttered as she searched for the seatbelt.

Christian nodded.

Natalia barely had her seatbelt buckled when the driver took off, nearly mowing people down as he exited the busy airport. She grabbed the handle above the door, holding on for dear life as the tiny car raced through the streets of Chengdu, zipping in and out of lanes like it was nothing. "Holy shit," she whispered.

Christian laughed.

"You American?" the driver asked.

"Australian," Christian corrected.

"Welcome China," he said smiling and nodding.

"*Xie xie*," she replied, saying thank you.

"He's going to kill us," Natalia whispered. "I've made it this far, and I'm going to die in a Chinese taxi."

Christian laughed and shook her head.

When the driver swerved into the drop off for a large, brightly lit hotel, he blew the horn at a pair of pedestrians who looked as if they'd had the right of way. The small car careened to a stop.

"Oh, thank God," Natalia mumbled.

Christian pulled out a few renminbi banknotes from her bag, paying him twenty Yuan. Then, she opened the door and exited the car with Natalia eagerly following suit. The driver sped off before they were up on the curb.

"Welcome to China," Christian chuckled.

"It's worse than New York City!"

"I wouldn't go that far."

"I sure as hell would," Natalia grumbled, following her inside the large hotel.

A full restaurant and bar were on one end of the atrium, and the check-in desk and concierge were on the other. Christian pulled her passport from her pocket, along with a Visa credit card, and handed them to the man at the desk. The smell of fresh Chinese cuisine wafted through the lobby.

"Welcome Chengdu," he said with a nod and a smile.

"Xie xie," Christian replied in the same manor.

He typed on the computer and checked her passport. Then, he swiped the credit card and handed both back to her. Christian listened intently as he gave her the room instructions in Chinese. It translated to: One room. Eighth floor. Number twenty-seven. She nodded and signed the paper as Leigh Michaels.

"Shall we?" She nodded towards the elevator, getting Natalia's attention.

Once they entered the elevator, Natalia's stomach rumbled.

Christian raised a brow and pushed the number eight. The doors closed and the elevator lifted smoothly off the ground. They opened again to a brightly lit hallway painted in shades of dark gold with garnet-colored trim, and matching dark red carpet. Abstract artwork hung on the walls. Natalia followed Christian as she made her way to door twenty-seven and slid the keycard. The small room resembled that of most hotels with two double beds, a set of chairs with a round table in the middle, and a small desk against the wall. Just beyond the chairs was a large sliding glass door that led to a balcony. The room matched the same dominant color scheme as the hallway.

"Home sweet home … for now anyway," Christian said, setting her bag on the bed closest to the door, ultimately claiming it for herself.

"Wonderful," Natalia muttered, tossing her bag down on the other bed.

Christian checked her watch and shoved her passport into her pocket, along with several renminbi banknotes in various Fen and Yuan denominations. Then, she removed the hairspray can and extra deodorant from her bag, unscrewed the bottom of both, and dumped the contents onto the desk. The metal piece that fell out of the hairspray container was actually a folded, four-shot mini .22 caliber, hammerless revolver. Christian unfolded the mini gun and grabbed the cotton encased bullets that had been inside of the other container. She loaded the weapon and tucked it into an ankle strap under her sock. "Are you ready?" she asked Natalia, who was staring at herself in the mirror.

"I look like I stepped out of 1992," Natalia sighed, taking in the oversized sweater, odd-fitting, dark jeans, and sneakers that were a half-size too big.

"Come on. We need to get going."

"Says the woman who looks good in anything," Natalia mumbled.

"Give me your passport," Christian said, putting the room key in her front pocket.

"Why?"

"So it doesn't get lost."

"I'm a grown woman. I think I can keep up with my passport," Natalia huffed.

"Fine." Christian flung the door open and entered the hallway.

Natalia walked out behind her, pulling the door shut. She reached forward, handing her passport to Christian.

"You're going to make me crazy," Christian grumbled, shoving the booklet into her back pocket.

*

The Chengdu Metro had several stops all over the city, with a few interchange stations and a few major stations. Having been to Chengdu before, Christian was familiar with the metro system. She checked the map located outside of the station nearest to their hotel. They needed to take Line One and change to Line Two to get to Chunxi Road, a huge shopping street with over 700 places to shop. There were department stores, boutiques, cafes, street stalls, and everything in between.

Christian paid for two weeklong metro passes, unsure of how long they'd be there. Then, she and Natalia made their way over to the platform. The next train came quickly, whisking them away. After two stops, they changed lines and rode again for another two stops. The sign for Chunxi Road was visible when the door opened.

"This is our stop," Christian said, taking her hand and tugging her from the metro car before it took off again. They rushed up the stairs and straight into the middle of the Chunxi Road. Crowds of people lined the pedestrian street in front of stores and shops.

"It looks like Time Square," Natalia uttered, taking in the long, brightly lit stretch of road. It was closed off to vehicles just like Times Square in New York and had shopping along both sides as far as the eye could see.

"I thought the same thing the first time I saw it," Christian replied, watching her light up. "Come on, the markets just up here."

Natalia had no idea what the market was until they stepped inside. Rows and rows of street vendors with food stations were clustered together. Everything you could think of was available on a stick ... raw or cooked. She wasn't sure if her rumbling stomach wanted to eat or puke. She passed a table with roaches, scorpions, and skinned rats, all on kabob style wooden sticks.

"What is this place?"

"This is the market, and that food you're turning your nose up at, is a delicacy around here. You should try it."

"Why don't you try it?"

"I already have. The squid isn't bad raw." She reached into her pocket and pulled out one Fen and held one finger up, pointing to the squid. The man took the note and handed her a stick full of fresh, raw squid. "Xie xie," she said with a nod, then she grabbed the bottle of duck sauce and doused the meat. "Here, try it."

Natalia shook her head.

"It's your loss." She shrugged, taking a big bite. Yellow sauce dripped down her chin, which she wiped away with a napkin. She made a face like she'd just bitten into the best tasting food in the world.

"Oh, fine. Give it here." Natalia took a sizeable bite, chewing the slimy, slightly rubbery, delicacy, before swallowing. The raw fish taste was mostly masked by the duck sauce, which made it go down much easier, but it wasn't something she wanted to eat again. "It's not completely gross, but it's on the 'tried it once, never again' list though," she grimaced, wishing she had something to drink to wash away the taste.

The further they walked through the market, the more blown away Natalia was. She kept waiting to see a cat or small dog on a stick, and even then, she wasn't sure all the rats on sticks really were rats. Some looked much larger. She refused to try a fried scorpion when Christian bought a stick full of them. She watched her eat two, then give the rest of the stick to a small boy, who ran off, happily eating.

"How about some real food?" Christian asked as they made their way back out to the street. "There are restaurants down here."

"I was beginning to think I was going to starve to death if this was all there was to eat," Natalia said.

"Nah, they have traditional Sichuanese cuisine in all the restaurants. Anyway, I like to go to the market to experience the local culture when I come here."

"How often is that?"

"I try to come back every couple of years. I lived here for about a year, early on in my career. I fell in love with the Tibetan culture. The Wenshu Monastery has been here over 1,300 years and dates back to the Tang Dynasty."

"Oh, wow. I'd love to see something like that."

"It's not far. We can go tomorrow. There's also another place I want to show you, if we have time."

"How long are we here for?"

"I don't know. I'll find out in the morning. I'm sure we will keep moving," she replied as they walked into one of the restaurants.

Natalia looked around the interior of the small room. It was barely larger than their hotel room but packed with tables. The walls were all black, with red and gold

Chinese designs painted on them. Paper lanterns covered the lights above the tables.

When the waitress walked over, Christian gave their order in Chinese. She nodded and disappeared.

"Do we get menus?"

"I ordered for us. Hot pot is a local soup. Everyone makes it differently, but it usually has vegetables and meat or fish. It's spicy, but good. I also ordered pork dumplings and wantons."

"Anything is better than that mess in the market. I can't believe you ate there."

Christian laughed.

"I unravel the mystery of Christian Garnier a little bit each day," Natalia said.

"Oh, really?"

"Yep. I learned today that you eat bugs on a stick."

Christian chuckled. "They're quite good, once you get past the crunchiness."

"Gross!"

Christian shrugged.

The waitress interrupted their banter when she brought all of their food at once.

"Wow, so it's all one course, huh?"

"Pretty much. They don't want you hanging around. Eat and be gone."

Natalia nodded as she started on her soup.

*

"You're definitely French," Natalia said as Christian stopped their stroll along the road. "I'm full to my eyeballs from dinner, yet you seem to have room for pastry."

"There is always room for a pastry," Christian teased, paying the man for her dessert.

"Uh huh. So, you said your parents aren't in France. Where do they live?"

"They don't."

"Right … they don't live in France," Natalia said oddly.

"They don't live at all. They're deceased," Christian stated, taking a large bite of the flaky dessert.

"Oh, Christian … I—I'm sorry."

"Don't be. It's fine. Shall we?" she said, nodding towards the department stores and boutiques. "All the clothes shops a girl could ask for. You have to hurry though. They close in an hour."

Natalia watched her finish the tart and toss the wax paper in the nearby trash. She wanted to know more. When did they die? How did they die? She felt awful. The subject was clearly off limits.

"Well, are you going to shop for clothes that actually fit you, or stand here all night?" Christian questioned.

"Shop … of course." She smiled and entered the first store.

*

Natalia deposited the bags on the floor near the chairs and flopped down on top of the bed nearest the balcony. "I feel like I haven't slept in days."

"Remind me to never go shopping with you again," Christian mumbled.

Natalia laughed and sat up on one elbow, watching Christian remove her shoes, then rummage through her bag for a t-shirt and sweatpants. "No," she complained as Christian moved to the bathroom to change her clothes.

"I don't know why you're complaining. Nothing is happening. We've been over this," Christian said as she walked back into the room, ready for bed.

"I know," Natalia sighed. In all honesty, sex was the farthest thing from her mind. The closer she got to home, the more she missed her mother and mourned the loss of her father. Wanting to see Christian's naked body was her way of finding a distraction. She kicked her shoes to the floor, slipped off her jeans, and crawled under the covers.

CHAPTER SEVENTEEN

The next morning started with an array of menacing clouds that quickly dissipated as Christian and Natalia sat outside of a café, consuming a traditional breakfast of crullers, which were twisted strips of fried dough, and a bowl of warm, sweet congee, something similar to a watery rice pudding.

"This is pretty good," Natalia said, dipping her crullers into her congee. "At least it's not bugs."

"Or is it?" Christian raised a brow.

"Funny," Natalia said sarcastically, playfully smacking her arm.

The phone in Christian's pocket vibrated. She quickly stepped out of earshot of Natalia, but close enough to keep her in view.

"Without faith, without belief in something ..." Lancelot said.

"What are we?" she answered, finishing the quote.

"Line secure?" he questioned.

Christian glanced at the phone, then looked around. "Go."

"You are booked on a flight to Edinburg in twenty-four hours, leaving from Chengdu. From there, you will take the train to Glasgow and rendezvous with Hamlet. He'll escort the package the rest of the way," Lancelot said.

"Roger," she replied.

"Keep the package secure. I'll send you the rendezvous point when you arrive in Edinburg," Lancelot added before the line went dead.

Great. Christian sighed and shoved her phone into her pocket.

"I take it that was our marching orders," Natalia uttered.

"Directly from the queen herself," Christian answered.

"Lovely. And how does she take her tea?"

"With milk and sugar, I presume. I don't know. I've never met her." Christian ate the last bite of cruller. "Shall we?"

"Are you always this forthcoming?"

"Quite the contrary actually."

"Wonderful. I feel privileged," Natalia bit back sarcastically. She hated not knowing what was going on. She wasn't at all interested in being a game pawn, and she certainly wasn't a fan of secrecy. Reluctantly, she fell in step with Christian as they walked towards the metro station. "Are you going to fill me in at all?"

"We leave in the morning." That was all Christian said as she checked the board to see which metro line they needed to be on.

*

The two women took the One line north for three stops, then exited. Natalia took in her surroundings as they walked out of the station. Wenshu Yuan Street was nothing like Chunxi Road had been. The shopping district was modern, where Wenshu was traditional Chinese architecture. She felt like she'd stepped back in time two hundred years, or onto the set of a movie starring Jackie Chan. The entire monastery complex was made of stone and wood.

Christian led the way as they walked under the arch at the entrance gate, then through the vestibule that took them to the five halls which connected to the main hall on the other end. Each hall had several rooms full of beautiful Buddha statues made of jade, mud, and other materials, as well as ancient Chinese artwork and other cultural relics from several Chinese dynasties dating back to 618 B.C., when it was first being built during the Tang Dynasty.

Outside, people were gathered around the tables and chairs, drinking tea and eating snacks at the tea house and food stalls in the pavilion. Several tourists were milling about in the rooms of the halls and around the gardens on their own accord. One tour group passed by, clicking cameras and rambling on in another language.

The wide pavilion in the middle of all the halls, had large, polished stone statues and polished columns with sculptured column tops. There was also an array of small, potted trees, and planted trees that rose up from the stone floor. Natalia ran her hand over one of the statues that was carved into the shape of an elephant. Inside the main hall, there were large golden Chinese dragon statues flanking a huge golden Buddha.

"The gardens are back here," Christian said, leading Natalia to another area full of beautiful trees and lush grass. A large building where people were walking up and kneeling, was in the middle. "This is the holy pagoda," she added, stepping away from Natalia and kneeling.

Natalia watched in awe as Christian paid her respects along with several others, before returning to her side.

"That tall tower over there is the peace pagoda, and the rest of the gardens are this way," Christian stated as they walked along the concrete path that crossed over several ponds. Lush greenery and dense brush created a natural arch over the walkway. They came to a stop under a hut that overlooked one of the ponds with a huge stone statue in the shape of a circle coming up out of the water. "In the late 1600s, a Buddhist monk named Cidu built this hut and lived his life here. When he was cremated, supposedly the statue of Wenshu was in the flames. So, he was believed to be the reincarnation of Wenshu, and thus the temple was renamed Wenshu Monastery."

"Wow, that's beautiful. This place is ... it just feels peaceful."

Christian nodded in agreement.

"Are you Buddhist?"

Christian shrugged. "I'm not religious at all. Well, I wasn't raised in any particular religion, anyway. But I did spend a lot of time walking these grounds and learning about the Buddhist culture when I lived here." She paused, looking out at the water running over the bottom of the statue. "This place helped me find inner peace. I believe in the power of these sacred grounds. I don't get back here often, but, when I do, I always pay my respects as a way of saying thank you. That minute of prayer gives me serenity that I don't give myself. Does that make me a Buddhist? I don't know."

"I think it makes you human. We all have to have something to believe in. That belief is where we find peace," Natalia said softly as she grabbed Christian's hand. "I know you're a very reserved person, so thank you for sharing this place with me."

Christian looked into the smoky gray eyes staring back at her. "You remind me of here," she whispered. "The first time I came here, the physical, emotional, and spiritual calmness overwhelmed me. I felt for the first time in my life."

"That's powerful," Natalia murmured, stepping closer.

Christian paused, their mouths an inch apart as they shared a breath. She could back away, there was still time.

Shivers rolled down Natalia's spine as her heart began to race.

A fraction of a second passed.

A light breeze blew across the back of Christian's neck, urging her forward. Slowly, she closed the gap, pressing her lips to Natalia's. The kiss was gentle and slow. What felt like minutes lasted mere seconds.

Christian took an extra step back, adding more space between them. Unsure of what to say, she cleared her throat and glanced around. Two men standing on the opposite side of the pond were facing her direction. They began walking when they saw her looking at them. She watched them, mentally noting the odd way they were moving around other people in the area. Her instincts told her they weren't tourists. "Let's go back to the pavilion. The rest of this just keeps winding around and comes back out over there," she said, grabbing Natalia's hand and ushering her along. They would be safer in an open area full of tourists than in an alcove on a wooded path.

Natalia wasn't sure what was going on with Christian. She simply shrugged and went with it. They both knew a relationship would never work, but there was no mistaking the intimate moment they'd shared next to the pond.

When they walked by the peace pagoda, Christian stopped and pulled Natalia in for a hug so that she could peer over her shoulder and see if the men followed them out of the gardens. Natalia relished in the casual gesture, holding her close with her arms wrapped around Christian's midsection. Suddenly, she felt her stiffen and pull away.

Christian watched the men come out of the gardens and follow the walkway, their heads swiveling around. *They're looking for something.* She grabbed Natalia's hand and moved further into the crowd as they made their way past the holy pagoda and into the pavilion. She glanced back. The men were less than fifty yards and closing in as they fought to get through the larger, afternoon crowd that had come into the monastery.

"What's going on?" Natalia questioned, feeling something wasn't right.

Christian ducked into one of the corridors and slipped into a room, hoping the men hadn't followed. She let go of Natalia's hand and pulled her cell phone from her pocket. She held a finger to her mouth, indicating the be quiet signal and she dialed a number.

"Excalibur-CG48510, calling from a secure line," she said.

"Line secure. Go," Lancelot replied.

"I have a tail. Two unknowns, possibly more. I'm going to need extraction now."

"Location?"

"Inside Wenshu Monastery."

"Take them out. Then, retrieve your bag from the hotel. Your flight leaves in two hours."

"Roger," she said as the line went dead.

"Christian?" Natalia murmured.

"Two men are following us," she whispered as she tucked her phone away. "We need to get out of the monastery and double back to the hotel."

"What about the men?"

"I'll take care of them once we get out of here. Stay right next to me and move at my speed." She cracked the door to the room and peered down the hall. If they stayed within the corridors, they would be away from the main crowd but still blend with the tourists who were walking the halls. However, if the men made them, it would be much easier to follow. Taking a chance, she grabbed Natalia's hand and headed up the hallway, stopping every so often to look around.

Natalia's blood raced with adrenaline. The horror of running up the mountain in Fiji with gunshots whizzing by, came flooding back to her. How had they found her again? Why in the hell were they after her to begin with? A hundred questions went through her head. She thought the men from Fiji were dead. Were these different men? A new pair out to get her.

As they made their way to the front corridor, Christian ducked out into the crowd, searching for the men. She finally found them, still stuck in the crowd, but closing the distance quickly. She couldn't kill them on the street. She'd have to lead them down a side alley near the metro station. She needed to make sure the men saw them exit the monastery. Once they were outside, they'd need to stay in sight until she found an alley to veer off.

Natalia stayed glued to her side as they walked down the stairs and through the main gate, leaving the beautiful Wenshu Monastery behind.

"Laugh like I said something funny," Christian muttered.

"What? Why?"

"Just do it. We have to look like we don't know they are behind us."

Natalia fake laughed and smiled, bumping shoulders with Christian. Then, she pointed out a few buildings along the street.

Just before the entrance to the metro, they turned off, heading in the direction of a few shops. Christian tucked Natalia behind a car. "Crawl underneath it if you can. I'll be back."

Natalia could only see her feet as she watched her walk away. Her heart pounding in her chest sounded like thunder in her ears. She trembled with fear when she saw two sets of dark boots walk near the car and stop. She held her breath. *Don't look under the car. Don't look under the car.* Her mind kept repeating.

Christian laughed, drawing their attention further down the alley. Natalia watched their feet as they headed off in the direction of the sound. Suddenly, she heard a smash. Then a man yelled, "Hey!"

*

Christian was tucked beside another car twenty yards away. She jumped out, careening into the first guy like a linebacker. He crashed into the side of the car and fell to the ground. The other one yelled and he reached for his gun. She grabbed his arm, pulling his hand in the direction of the guy on the ground as the gun went off. The silencer made a quiet pop noise as the bullet exited. She barely had time to see the blood splatter as it entered the skull of the man on the ground.

The guy holding the gun wrestled with her, finally getting her into a chokehold. She elbowed him in the ribs, causing him to cough and loosen his hold. She spun in his arms and rammed her fist into his nose, causing him to drop the gun and fall to his knees. She bent down, retrieving the gun and quickly fired a shot into his forehead, before pushing his limp body to the side. She checked them both for ID but found nothing. She also took pictures with her phone, sending them to Lancelot. Then, she rushed back to Natalia.

"It's okay. Come out," she said, bending down and looking at the frightened woman.

Natalia slid out and stood up, brushing the dirt and grime from her clothing. "Where are they?" she asked, peering down the alley.

"Not chasing us anymore. Let's go!" Christian stated, grabbing her hand and hurrying away from the alley. Luckily, the gun had had a silencer. The two pops were almost too faint for anyone inside the nearby businesses to hear them. If she'd drawn and shot her own gun, everyone would've heard it, and gunfire isn't a sound often heard in China, especially that area.

"Did you kill them?" Natalia questioned.

"Does it matter?" Christian replied, leading her into the metro station.

Natalia didn't say anything as they swiped their pass cards and headed to the boarding platform. Did it matter? She wasn't sure. She hated that so much violence had happened around her, but if these men were part of whoever was responsible for her father's murder, then she couldn't feel sorry for their deaths. Fear still plagued her mind and she looked around. Were there any more of them? "How did they know where we were?" she asked.

Christian kept silent. She didn't have the answer. Although, knowing that at some point Natalia would be heading home, she'd have to pass through China. How they knew she'd been in Sichuan, or Chengdu, she had no idea. It didn't matter at this point. Her job was to keep the package safe and keep moving.

*

Back at the hotel, Christian removed the gun from her ankle and took it apart, storing it in the original containers to go through airport security. Then, she pulled two new passports from her bag, handing one to Natalia. "It looks like the honeymoon is over. We're now Erin Byron and Isabella Douglas," she added.

"Wonderful," Natalia replied with a hint of sarcasm in her voice. "Where are we going?"

"The airport. Our flight leaves in an hour and a half."

"I figured as much. Where are we flying to?"

"Ever been to Scotland?"

"No. You?"

"Yes."

"I take it that's where we are going."

"Yes."

Natalia nodded and quickly packed what little she'd unpacked and added her new clothing purchases from their shopping excursion the night before. She was going to miss Sichuan. There was so much she wanted to see. "This is definitely a place I want to come back to one day," she murmured.

Hearing her, Christian looked over and smiled. "Alright," she said, zipping her bag closed. "Are you ready?"

"As I'll ever be, I guess," Natalia replied.

"It won't be long before you're home." Christian patted her shoulder. "Let's go. The taxi is probably waiting for us."

"Is that what you were talking with the concierge about?" she asked as they entered the elevator. Christian had carried on a quick conversation in Chinese with the man at the desk.

"Yes."

CHAPTER EIGHTEEN

The ride to the airport had been as eventful as the first time around. Natalia was sure she would never ever ride in a taxi in China again and nearly kissed the terminal sidewalk when she got out of the car.

"That wasn't so bad," Christian said.

"Uh … were you in the same car?" Natalia grumbled.

Christian laughed. "You get used to it. It's kind of like New York City. At first, you're scared to death to ride in any type of vehicle and walk across the street. After a while, you do it like clockwork."

"Yeah, if you think so," Natalia huffed.

Christian checked her watch. "Come on. We need to get through security. We're American this time, so the accent should be easier."

"Great," she muttered, walking next to her as they entered the airport less than twenty-four hours after their arrival.

They were already checked in, so they went to the kiosk to print their boarding passes, then headed straight to the security line.

"This should go quickly," Christian said, checking her watch. They had about forty-five minutes before the flight was scheduled to leave, which meant they had no more than thirty minutes to go through security.

"How long is the flight?" Natalia asked.

143

"Uh, around fourteen hours total, plus a layover in Amsterdam. Edinburg is seven hours behind Chengdu, so it'll be about eleven tonight when we get in."

"It felt like it took forever flying from Portugal to Fiji, and in truth, it took over thirty hours, but this seems so much longer."

"That's because it's been broken up. We're also taking the long way around."

"You enjoy China?" the security officer asked, checking their passports.

"Yes. I can't wait to come back and see more," Natalia said.

He smiled, checked off their boarding passes, and ushered them through to the gates.

"I'm sure you're as hungry as I am. They'll be serving food on the plane, but I'm going to grab a coffee and a pastry."

"You're so French," Natalia laughed.

"Oui," Christian answered in French. "Do you want anything?"

"I don't know. I'll see what they have," she said, following her into the food court for Terminal 2.

*

Natalia finished a bagel and a green tea while Christian worked on her blueberry scone and coffee as they waited to board their flight. The terminal was busy with people hustling to and from the gates. Chengdu Shuangliu Airport was the busiest airport in western and central China, handling over 40 million passengers a year. Natalia glanced around wondering if they were sitting at the right gate, or if this was another of Christian's mysterious chess-type moves.

"Do you think anyone else is following us?" she asked.

"I can't be sure," Christian answered honestly. She'd kept her eyes peeled for anyone who may be standing out in the crowd or paying too much attention to them. So far, she'd seen nothing out of the ordinary. "Let's go. Our plane is boarding," she added, checking her watch.

Natalia smiled and shook her head as she stood up.

The two women walked from near the middle of the terminal all the way to the very end. Christian was about to board the plane when her phone rang. She quickly pulled Natalia out of line as she answered.

"No man fears to kneel ..." Lancelot said.

"Before a God he trusts," Christian stated, "line secure."

"The men in the photos are Moroccan nationals ... same as the men in Fiji. That's all I have."

"How did they know where we were?" she asked.

"Facial recognition, more than likely," he answered, adding, "you are clear to travel. I'll text you the rendezvous point when you land. Keep the package secure."

Christian stuffed her phone back into her pocket and ushered Natalia back into the line. They boarded with the last five passengers before the doors were closed. As she took her seat and stowed her bag, Christian wondered why Moroccans were after Natalia. Had they been the ones who'd also killed her father? If whoever was after her was using facial recognition to track them, they were a lot more than simply thugs. Facial recognition was global software used only by international agencies. She had a hundred questions and no answers. She hated being in the dark, but it wasn't her job to solve the mystery. She was an operative. They did the dirty work out in the field, often risking their lives for reasons they didn't know.

Natalia looked out the window, watching the ground crew for the large Boeing 787 get ready to push it back from the gate. *Goodbye China. Until next time ... hopefully on better terms.*

The co-pilot came across the PA system announcing they were next to depart. At the same time the pilot turned the corner, lined the plane up, and thrust the throttle forward, launching them down the runway at 200mph. The plane bounced around, swaying slightly as it raced. Natalia grabbed Christian's hand in a death grip.

Within seconds, the plane lifted into the air and began a smooth climb towards 27,000 feet. Natalia let go of Christian as she began to relax. She'd flown all around the world for most of her life, but the takeoffs and landings never got any easier. At least not for her.

Christian, on the other hand, seemed fine with the maneuvers as she perused the magazine she'd purchased at the coffee stand without a care in the world. "You might as well get comfortable. We have about eleven hours."

Natalia sighed. At least they were in first class this time, in comfortable leather seats that were similar to recliners in appearance and function. They stretched out almost completely flat and were two to a row on either side of the aisle, and four rows deep. They certainly weren't the cheapest, but if MI6 hadn't spared the expense, Natalia was sure she would've made Christian go into that Mary Poppins duffle bag and pull out enough money to upgrade them.

*

A third of the way into the flight, the attendants walked down the aisle with the lunch cart. They were serving complimentary turkey sandwiches, roast beef sandwiches, and veggie pitas with a bag of chips, but they had other meals available for purchase.

"What would you like for lunch?" the attendant asked with a fake smile plastered across her face.

"Turkey," Natalia said.

"Make that two," Christian added, "and a fruit and cheese tray."

The flight attendant handed the sandwiches and chips over to them, as well as the additional platter, which Christian had paid for.

"I can't wait to see what's for dinner," Natalia muttered.

"It's probably chicken or noodles of some kind. I'll upgrade us if something better is available," Christian said without looking over as she fiddled with her sandwich.

Natalia didn't say anything as she ate her lunch. The last two weeks had been a complete rollercoaster. Part of her wished she was still in Fiji, fighting that damn paddleboard, but part of her wished she was home, back at work, and back to some kind of normalcy. She wondered if her life would ever be *normal* again, but softly, she shook her head, knowing it wouldn't. Her father, the person she admired most, was gone. Taken from her family for a reason she still didn't know, but whatever had happened was extremely serious. The MI6 operative sitting next to her was proof of that. The more she looked at Christian, the less she saw the operative on the outside. The little bit of person on the inside that Christian had let her see, was starting to shine through.

"What?" Christian questioned.

Natalia shrugged and shook her head.

Christian raised a brow and set her sandwich down. "You were staring at me and deep in thought from the look in your eyes. What's going on?"

"Just thinking," she muttered, turning her attention to the bright blue sky.

"About?"

"My family; my life; what I can't have ... I don't know. A lot of shit has happened in the last two weeks. I'm stuck on a plane for the next seven hours. I have nothing else to do *but* think about all of it."

Christian nodded, unsure of what to say to her. Thinking about the last two weeks was the absolute last thing she wanted to be doing. Instead, she'd read a couple of magazines and watched a movie that made no sense.

"You've traveled the world, am I right?" Natalia asked.

"Sure. Not all of it, of course. Why?"

"Name a place that you've been to and have always wanted to go back."

"I don't know," she muttered. "Are you planning your next vacation?"

"No," Natalia laughed. "After this, I'm pretty sure I'm not vacationing for a very long time."

"I enjoyed some parts of South America and South Africa. I've lived all over Europe and in China." Christian thought for a moment. "I guess if there were one place I've thought about going back to ... it would probably be Iceland."

"Wow."

"Not what you expected?" Christian smiled.

"Uh ... no, not at all."

"What about you? Is there somewhere you want to go back to?"

"Fiji was my dream vacation, and you know how that nightmare turned out. I really enjoyed what little I did get to see of China, so maybe I'll get back there one day."

Christian nodded. "What about a place you've never been to, but want to go?"

"You mean like from a bucket list?"

"Sure, if that's what you call it."

"I don't know. I'd love to dive the Great Barrier Reef. I love water, so anything around water and marine life are always my first picks. I'm also partial to warm weather, so count me out on Iceland." She grinned.

"Dually noted. Water and warm."

"I'm not going to ever see you again when this is all over ... am I?"

"Not unless you go to Iceland," Christian teased. "They have a hotel built out of ice."

"I'm serious."

"So am I."

"Chri—"

"Erin," Christian corrected, cutting her off and shaking her head.

Natalia clenched her jaw. She couldn't remember the stupid fake names they were using and she didn't care anymore. Ignoring the questioning look from Christian, she put her headphones on and began scrolling through the movies and shows available in the TV on the seatback in front of her.

Christian sighed. What was she to say? Yes, let's run off and get married? No, she would never see her again. No, she would never hear from her again. No. No. No. Operatives didn't fall in love or lust or whatever it was that

149

was happening between them, and especially not on a mission. Operatives didn't have relationships. They didn't have accountability other than their next mission. Even if she *could* see Natalia again…she was sure she wouldn't. She would only wind up breaking her heart anyway. Her life was very cut and dry. She did her job, and she did it well…using any means possible. That's what she was trained to do. Natalia deserved someone who was capable of always being there…physically, mentally, and emotionally. She deserved someone who could and would make her their top priority…their everything. Christian simply couldn't do that. Even if she weren't an operative, she'd never been that person…not for anyone.

*

When the flight attendant came back around with dinner, both Natalia and Christian were asleep and cuddled together in their connecting seats. She reached down, gently shaking Christian's shoulder. She hated waking the women, but it was policy to always wake the sleeping passengers when full meals were being served.

Christian jerked back, holding Natalia protectively as her eyes came into focus on the woman standing a foot away.

"I'm sorry," the flight attendant said, looking over at Natalia apologetically.

"It's okay. I forgot I was on a plane apparently," Christian replied with a half laugh, letting go of the confused woman lying against her. "What are our options?"

"We have chicken or vegetable lo mein, or these are our upgrades. The price is listed next to them," she said, handing a small, laminated sheet to Christian.

Natalia perused the little menu. Their choices were filet mignon or lobster tail with mashed potatoes and fresh vegetables, or linguine with clam sauce and a side of garlic bread.

"Linguine," both women said at the same time.

Christian pulled enough Yuan from her pocket to pay for the meal and handed it to the flight attendant.

"Upgraded meals take an extra fifteen minutes. They'll be served as soon as they are ready," she said before moving on to the next row.

"Is everything okay?" Natalia questioned.

"Yeah. Fine. You?"

"Uh huh." She nodded, unsure Christian was telling the truth. She was sound asleep until she felt a sudden movement and bear hug that pinned her between the plane's wall and Christian.

"Four more hours to go," Christian said, standing to stretch and use the restroom.

"Yep," Natalia mumbled.

When Christian returned, Natalia was watching another movie. She kept the picture going and pulled her headphones down. "What are your plans after this?" she asked. "When we part ways."

Christian hesitated to answer. The truth was, she had no idea. "I don't know," she finally said. Generally, she would head back to her home in Paris and do a video call to debrief the mission, on rare occasions she'd go to headquarters in London to do it. Lancelot called the shots. It was his team. She simply did what she was told: keep a low profile and be on the ready. When he called, she did as instructed, no questions asked. She was one of the best operatives he'd ever worked with, and she trusted him with her life. "I'll probably go home," she added, hoping that was the case.

"To Paris?"

"Yes."

"I'm sure you don't have pets with all of the travel you do, but I bet you have a bunch of plants," Natalia stated.

"Why do you say that?"

Natalia shrugged.

"Do you have plants?"

"Nope. No plants and no pets."

"Then, why assume what I have?"

"I don't know. I was making small talk."

"I don't like small talk."

"I'm well aware of that," Natalia muttered, sorry she'd brought it up. She slipped her headphones back on and focused on the movie playing in front of her.

Christian sighed and reached over, pulling the headphones off of Natalia's ears. "I used to have a cat. His name is Pierre. I also used to have a house plant, too ... until he ate it."

Natalia laughed. "You really had a cat?"

Christian nodded.

"What did he look like?"

"He is skinny with a thin coat of black fur. He has a patch of white on his chest and belly and the tip of his tail."

"He's alive?"

"Yes."

"Why don't you still have him, then?"

"He decided he liked living with the neighbor better, so I packed his things."

"Are you serious?" Natalia laughed. "That's ... sad."

Christian shrugged. "I'm hard to live with. I told you, I don't do relationships."

"No kidding," she said, putting her headphones back on. As much as Christian captivated her, the eccentricity of the woman drove her nuts.

*

The plane touched down three hours later, skidding across the wet runway and causing mass panic within the cabin. The oxygen masked popped out, swinging in everyone's face as the pilots fought to control the plane.

Terrified, Natalia grabbed Christian's hand, squeezing the blood out of it.

Someone yelled, "We're going to die!"

Please God ... not here. Not like this. Natalia silently prayed as adrenaline raced through her veins.

The pilots finally got control, bringing the plane to a stop in the grass on the side of a completely different runway. Thankfully, they'd slowed enough that entering the grass hadn't caused a catastrophic crash.

"We apologize for the harsh landing. The airport received a massive rainstorm not long ago and we were not informed of the puddles on the runway. Again, we apologize and thank you for flying Air China," the pilot said over the intercom.

Natalia let go of Christian's hand and crossed herself.

"I didn't know you were religious."

"I'm not. I'd kiss the damn ground if I could get off of this thing," Natalia stated, still trying to slow her heartbeat.

There were no reported injuries, so the plane was towed to the terminal building and parked in front of their arrival gate. Nearly every passenger stood up in a mad rush to exit the plane, but as it is with every flight, it took several minutes for the gangway to be attached and the doors to finally open.

"If you tell me we have to fly again, I'm liable to slap you across the face," Natalia muttered as they entered the airport terminal.

"No, from here we take the train."

"Thank God."

"You do know you'll have to fly when you head back to Portugal, right?"

"Should I slap you now or later?"

Christian grinned. "Come on. We don't have any bags to claim," she said, leading them towards the exit signs. Her phone rang just before they flagged a taxi. She stepped aside and answered.

CHAPTER NINETEEN

The taxi ride had been uneventful compared to the death race driving in Chengdu. The old building they arrived at looked more like a castle than a hotel and had certainly felt that way once they'd stepped inside.

Natalia waited patiently as Christian checked them in. She was surprised when she heard the desk clerk say they were only there for one night. Christian had yet to inform her they were booked on the early train to Glasgow the next day to make contact with another operative. From there, he would escort Natalia to the safe house in England where her mother was located.

"This place has an odd feeling," Natalia said.

"It's probably haunted," Christian muttered.

"Funny."

"I'm serious. A lot of these old hotels were castles at one time. They are over a hundred years old; some are even two-hundred years old."

Natalia didn't reply as she followed Christian into their room, allowing the door to swing closed behind her. She dropped her duffle bag on the floor and folded her arms. *One bed? Someone is punishing me,* she thought, glancing around at the small, sparsely furnished room.

The double bed seemed to go unnoticed to Christian as she concentrated on checking the adjoining door lock, followed by the windows.

"I guess it's a good thing we're sleeping together tonight. I'm not interested in getting visited by a ghost."

"What?" Christian questioned, turning towards her. Natalia pointed to the bed.

"Damn it," she mumbled. "I thought he meant two beds when he said a double bedroom. I'll go down and see if he can move us. Stay here and keep the deadbolt locked. Don't open it for anyone except me." She grabbed a credit card and her passport in case she needed to pay anything additional, before leaving. She waited in the hall for a second to hear Natalia lock the door.

*

"What do you mean you don't have any other rooms?" Christian growled, "Every single room in this building is booked for tonight?"

"Ah, yeah. The annual fiddler convention started today and continues into tomorrow. People from all over the country are here to celebrate," the man said, speaking with a thick, Scottish brogue.

"For fuck's sake," she mumbled.

"What was that? Me old ears aren't as good as they used to be."

"I said that's great," she replied, shaking her head. "Do you have any cots?"

He shook his head. "You know," he said, getting a thought. "You came in pretty late. Our kitchen is closed, but we had a wee bit of Scotch broth, and mince and tatties left from dinner service. I could get a bit of dinner up to you."

"That would be wonderful. Thank you."

He smiled. "Give me about fifteen minutes. I have to wake the missus."

"Oh, don't do that. We'll be fine."

"She'd skin me with a wooden spoon if she knew I let guests go hungry because they came in late. It's no bother." He grabbed a piece of paper. "Now, what room are you in again?"

"Two-thirteen, and please tell her thank you."

He winked and disappeared around the corner to where she presumed was their owner's residence.

Christian walked back to the room. *One more night,* she thought, knocking on the door, and called, "It's me."

*

Natalia was unsure if they would be moved or not, so she waited. Her stomach growled from the minuscule meals served by the airline during their fourteen-hour trip, and her teeth felt like they'd grown fur. She wasn't sure what she wanted more, a hot meal, or clean teeth and a pillow under her head. Looking at the small bed, she decided a stiff drink sounded better. She and Christian had already decided days ago that they wouldn't get physical with each other anymore. This was best for both of them, she knew that. But, how in the hell was she supposed to sleep in that small bed, literally touching Christian, when all she wanted to do was get naked and let the enticing operative burn her to the core with those damn eyes that kept taking her breath away?

Rasping on the door quickly cleared the enchanting haze from her mind. "I'm sleeping on the floor," she huffed in the direction of the bed and headed towards the door.

"Good news and bad news," Christian stated, stepping inside and re-locking the door.

"Okay?"

"We're stuck in here. There's some kind of fiddler convention going on. The hotel is full."

"Are you serious?" Natalia uttered. "Fiddlers?"

"Yes," Christian said, trying not to laugh. She wasn't happy about the situation either. She knew she should've never touched Natalia. Kissing her under that waterfall in Fiji had opened Pandora's Box and she couldn't get the damn thing closed, no matter how hard she tried.

"What's the good news? Are we getting a cot?"

I wish. At this point, the damn thing could fold in half with me in it and I'd be fine with that as long as I didn't have to lie in that bed next to you and pretend I didn't want to be inside of you. "No. They don't have them. Even if they did, it probably wouldn't fit to begin with."

A soft tapping on the door made Natalia jump a foot off the ground.

"What the hell is that?" she questioned, moving behind Christian as she walked towards the door.

"Our dinner."

"What?"

"That was the good news. The old man woke his wife and had her heat us up some leftovers from the restaurant," she said just before she looked through the peephole.

"Christian! It's the middle of the night. How could you let him do that?"

"Sshh!" she hissed. "I didn't *let him* do anything. It was his idea. He said she'd be mad at him if he hadn't fed us."

Natalia shook her head.

Seeing him standing in the hall next to a metal cart with two trays of food on it, Christian pulled the door open.

"Here you are, piping hot," he said, handing her the trays. "Just leave it in the hall when you've finished."

"It smells wonderful. Thank you, and please tell your wife thank you," Christian said before closing and locking the door.

Natalia's stomach growled as she sniffed the air. "What is it?"

"Basically, stew with meat and potatoes, but does it really matter at this point? It's nearly one a.m.," Christian replied, handing her one of the trays, and taking the other for herself as they headed over to the bed, which was the only place to sit in the room. They each kicked off their shoes and leaned back against the headboard with their trays.

Several bites of food were eaten, slowly filling their empty stomachs, before either of them said anything.

"So, what's our game plan from here? I heard the clerk say we were here only tonight," Natalia asked between bites. She silently wished she had some pepper or something to give the bland-tasting food a bit of flavor.

"That's because we're taking the train over to Glasgow in the morning."

"What's there? More castles?" Natalia asked with a hint of sarcasm while setting her tray on the floor, out of the way.

Christian laughed as she got up and placed her tray with Natalia's, adjusting the bowls and plates so that everything fit neatly together, taking up less space.

Natalia had gone into the bathroom to brush her teeth, but she'd left the door open.

"Yes. In fact, there are several castles, but you'll only see a few of them from a distance. You're taking the train to England from there."

"Wait? What?" she mumbled, spitting in the sink and rinsing her mouth. "Are you saying I'll finally get to see my mother tomorrow?"

"Yes," Christian nodded, sliding in next to her to brush her own teeth.

Natalia wiped away a few tears as they slid down her cheeks.

Christian looked away from the woman in the mirror as she finished at the sink and dried her face. She knew what that feeling was like; hoping, praying, and anticipating seeing your mother again. Only, she'd never have that chance. It had been several years, and it rarely bothered her, but she still felt it. Usually, only on days like Mother's Day, her mother's birthday, or her own birthday. She walked over to her bag and pulled out a pair of shorts to change into.

"I'm sorry," Natalia said, grabbing her arm. "I know what it's like for you. I'll never see my father again. I can't imagine both of my parents being gone."

"It's fine. It's been a long time. I'm glad you're finally reuniting with your mother."

"Thanks," Natalia said before going into her bag for a change of clothes as well. All thoughts of getting naked with Christian had long faded from her mind when she slipped under the covers next to her. "I know it's none of my business, but what happened to your parents? Were they sick, or in an accident, or something?"

Christian looked at her. She'd told the story a handful of times in her life but had mostly kept it to herself.

"You don't have to tell me. I understand," Natalia said, moving to turn down the bedside lamp to a soft glow.

"My father worked for Boeing as an engineer when I was a kid," Christian started. "That's why we lived in the states for a while, as well as London and Paris. He was moved around a lot depending on the project he was working on. My parents were living in Paris, and I was going to college in London when they died. My mother had been a schoolteacher all of her adult life, teaching at various schools when we moved around. My father was called to the Seattle, Washington plant for a session of meetings that was scheduled over about a three-week period, so she went with him to go see some of her old schools and teacher friends from when we'd lived there. They were on a commercial plane, on their way home, when it was blown up by a terrorist bomb while in the air over the North Atlantic Ocean."

"Oh, my God," Natalia gasped. "I'm so sorry, Christian."

"It's okay. It's been thirteen years."

"I'm sure you still miss them."

"I do. Many of the passengers' remains were never recovered, so it was difficult at first, but I moved on. My life went on." She paused, remembering her parents' smiling faces.

"I couldn't imagine," Natalia whispered, placing her hand over her own mouth to hide her surprise.

"I was so angry at first. That's actually why I joined MI6. I wanted to catch the bastards who did it, but they were caught and tried before I finished my training two years later. I still continued on my path, and well … here I am today."

Natalia grabbed her hand, wanting to feel some kind of contact between them.

"I know what it's like to suddenly lose a parent because someone deems their life unimportant. It's a harder hit than anything you will ever feel again. Trust me."

"I do … trust you."

Both women stayed silent for what seemed like minutes as the significance of those words set in. They carried more weight than a one-hundred-pound Army rucksack.

"My mom is going to invite you to every family function from now on because you brought me safely to her." Natalia smiled softly. Thinking about everything Christian had endured made her miss her mother twice as much. She tried not to imagine what she might be going through all alone.

"I won't be with you tomorrow … after Glasgow, anyway," Christian sighed.

"What do you mean?" Natalia raised a brow, slightly taken aback.

"Another operative is taking you into England."

"Wait. Why aren't you going with me?" she questioned nervously.

"Those are the orders. I'm probably needed on another mission. This other operative is with MI6. You'll be safe. He will have you with your mother before dinner. I'm sure of it."

Natalia studied her face. Christian's light blue eyes looked darker in the dim light. "So, this …"

"It's our last night together," Christian finished. "You're finally rid of me in about ten hours," she added cheerfully, hoping to quell the sadness she saw on Natalia's face.

"I don't know what to say."

"How about we say nothing at all. Not tonight, anyway. Let's just sleep."

"I want to be close to you," Natalia whispered, wiping a tear from her cheek.

"I know. Me too," Christian said softly, opening her arms for Natalia to curl up against her. She knew she couldn't be intimate again. They were already too close, and she feared she wouldn't be able to walk away if they actually *made love* to each other. Pushing away her desire, she turned out the light and held her close, listening to Natalia's labored breathing as she fell asleep.

Christian stared at the red numbers on the alarm clock. She hadn't thought about her parents much in the last couple of years and certainly hadn't spoken about them. She wondered why she'd done it now? Natalia Luis de Faria Moreno was a mystery to her. She had no idea how the beautiful woman in her arms had managed to slip past her carefully guarded walls. It was something she was completely unaccustomed to, and it both frightened and intrigued her. *I'm not sure I want to know why we are so connected. Saying goodbye to you is going to break my heart no matter what.*

The digital numbers changed to three a.m. just before she finally dozed off, still cuddled with Natalia.

CHAPTER TWENTY

The train station was more modern than the hotel had been, with multiple platforms full of waiting passengers, and new arrivals getting off the long, blue trains. Natalia stayed close to Christian in the crowd as she walked up to a kiosk and printed their boarding passes for direct travel from Edinburgh Waverly to Glasgow Queen Street. Then, she led the way through the terminal to Platform Eleven. The train hadn't arrived yet, and they were scheduled to board in fifteen minutes and depart in thirty.

Feeling her phone vibrate, Christian checked the text message. They were to meet the other operative at the Queen Victoria equestrian statue on the eastern side of George Square.

Not much was said between the women earlier that morning as they pushed their food around the plates during breakfast. Natalia had kept to herself and got ready for the day, and Christian gave her as much space as possible in the small room.

As the train pulled in, Natalia watched the passengers disembark. Christian scanned the crowd. She'd woken up with an uneasy feeling that she just couldn't shake. She knew it was because she'd let Natalia get too close to her.

"Are you ready?" Christian asked as the conductor called for boarding.

Natalia nodded and followed her onto the train. The inside was similar to a subway car with a center aisle and pairs of cushioned seats on both sides that formed long rows. Both women stowed their bags at their feet.

The ScotRail system had direct service, which was non-stop, and service with stops along the way. It ran all over Scotland and down into England as well. There were no refreshments or snacks served on the fifty-five-minute ride from Edinburgh to Glasgow.

Christian settled into her seat as the train lurched forward, easing out of the station, before accelerating to cruising speed. She couldn't help feeling relieved that her mission was almost over. She'd been an MI6 operative for over ten years and had never once let her guard down … until now. As she stared across the train car, through the side window, she knew for a fact that it would never happen again.

*

Natalia stared out the window, watching the old buildings go by, and noting that some of them had to be centuries old, as she thought about the last couple of weeks. Her life had turned into a whirlwind rollercoaster ride from hell. It certainly wasn't all bad, but distracting herself from what was actually going on had become an easy coping mechanism. She wondered if her mother knew any more information about her father's death. Someone had to know something by now. She hated being kept in the dark. She didn't want to think about him being gone, but turning her eyes to the woman beside her created an even greater sense of loss. She wiped away a stray tear and sighed as she stared blankly out the window.

*

The train began to slow as it closed in on the Glasgow Queen Street station. The conductor came over the intercom, asking everyone to stay in their seats until the train came to a full stop.

"Are we meeting the other operative here?" Natalia asked.

"No. We have to walk over to George Square. It's a large park about a block from here," Christian replied, grabbing her bag and standing as the train's brake brought it to a perfect stop alongside the number five platform.

Natalia followed her lead as they exited. The terminal was just as busy as the last one had been with people changing trains, arriving on trains, and waiting to board. The two women had to weave through the crowd towards the restrooms. Natalia went into a stall to relieve herself while Christian stepped into a second one. She quickly retrieved the hairspray can and deodorant from her bag and unscrewed the bottom of each container, before pulling out the parts to her gun and snapping them into place. She checked the clip to make sure it was full before tucking the pistol into the waistband of her pants at the small of her back. Then, she put the containers back in her bag, zipped it closed, and flushed the toilet with her foot.

"Everything okay?" Natalia asked.

"Yes. Let's go," Christian said. She couldn't take any chances. A package changing hands was the most vulnerable time for someone to get ambushed. She needed to be prepared at all costs.

Once outside of the station, their hands softly brushed together as they walked casually down the sidewalk. Christian's head turned slightly to the right, chancing a glance at the woman beside her. Natalia's gray eyes locked onto hers. They were fifty yards from the park, with several people milling about on the sidewalk and cars passing by on the street.

"We're almost there," Christian said, breaking the connection before she let herself close the gap between them and cover Natalia's lips with her own.

"Where is the other operative?" Natalia asked.

"Inside," Christian stated, nodding towards the park in front of them.

Natalia nodded as they crossed the street. She wanted to say more but couldn't form the words. "It keeps getting colder … everywhere we go," she mumbled.

"Yep," Christian replied, zipping her jacket halfway.

The park had four large patches of thick, lush grass, with the rest of the square covered with red concrete. Historical monuments and statues were scattered about, along with potted trees and bushes.

"This is beautiful," Natalia uttered, taking in the large square.

"You should see it at Christmas. It's all lit up."

"Let me guess, you've been here?" Natalia shook her head.

Christian smiled and nodded. She looked towards the eastside, easily spotting the statue of Queen Victoria on a horse. No one was standing near it, but a man with reddish blond hair and a matching five o'clock shadow on his face, was standing close by. He looked like most of the tourists, dressed in jeans and a thin leather jacket to stave off the cold air.

He shifted slightly, bringing his full profile into view.

Christian recognized him as Fergus McDonald, a Scottish man whom she'd worked with on a mission a couple of years ago. She kept walking nonchalantly beside Natalia, doing her best to blend in despite the two of them carrying small, black duffle bags.

"That's him," Christian whispered to Natalia. "Give every man thy ear," she said loud enough for him to hear, as they slowly moved past. Despite knowing him, she had to follow protocol.

"But few thy voice," the man replied.

Christian spun around. "Hamlet?"

He nodded. "Excalibur?"

She did the same. "It's been a few years," she said, shaking his hand.

"I'd say." He smiled. "How have you been, Agent Garnier?"

"Not bad. You?"

"Wait. You two know each other?" Natalia questioned.

"Yes. We worked together a few years ago," Christian answered. She was glad Natalia was going with him. He'd make sure she arrived safely.

"I've heard a lot about you, Ms. De Faria Moreno. I'm Fergus McDonald, an operative agent with MI6," he said. "I've been assigned to take you to a safe house in Manchester."

"Is that where my mother is?" she asked.

"I presume so." He nodded. "We should get going. We're booked on the 12:30 train."

"Can you give us a minute?" Christian asked, pulling Natalia out of earshot. "You'll be safe with him. He'll get you to your mother."

Natalia nodded. "I trust you."

"I've never had to do this," Christian sighed.

"What? Say goodbye?" Natalia replied, looking into her eyes. "We both know it was just sex," she added, looking away to hide the tears welling up. "But, if you're ever in Portugal … come find me."

"I won't," Christian muttered.

"I know," Natalia whispered.

Christian turned and headed off in the opposite direction.

Natalia fell in step with Fergus McDonald at her side as they headed towards the train station. Part of her wanted to run after Christian, but this was for the best. She needed to end this nightmare and get to her mother. She felt a sense of déjà vu as she neared the station, but mostly she was just numb.

She paid no attention at all as Fergus hailed a taxi outside of the train station, and wondered if the cold, solitary feeling would ever go away as she got into the car.

CHAPTER TWENTY-ONE

Christian quickly sent a text from her phone: CHANGEOVER COMPLETED. Then, she tucked her phone into her pocket as she sat down on a bench at the other end of the park.

A few minutes later, she received a text message.

MISSION CLOSED. YOUR EXIT FLIGHT LEAVES IN TWO HOURS. Feeling a small sense of relief mixed with the sadness of knowing she would never see Natalia Luis de Faria Moreno again, she walked out of the park and hailed a taxi.

"Where to miss?" the driver asked.

"Airport," she said, making sure he couldn't see her as she removed the gun and went through the quick process of stowing it away to go through security.

"Which terminal?"

"Air France," she sighed, looking out the window. She should've been looking forward to being home in less than four hours, but a quiet, empty apartment wasn't where she wanted to be. *You have to let her* go, she thought, silently hoping she was given another mission before she had time to unpack the duffle bag full of clothes that weren't hers.

*

Christian was on her balcony, sitting in a chair with her bare feet up on the rail and crossed at the ankle. The aroma of freshly baked baguettes filled the air from the sidewalk café on the first floor of her building. She stared out at the Eiffel Tower reaching towards the sky a few blocks away, a glass of light-bodied red wine dangling from her hand, still awaiting the first sip. She always had a brief period of angst when she came off a mission. Her mind needed time to relax after working on overload twenty-four hours a day. However, the lackluster way she was feeling had nothing to do with her brain unwinding, and she knew it. She'd been home for less than twenty-four hours when her satellite phone finally rang. She hoped it was a new mission that would make her throw all of her concentration towards anything but Natalia Luis de Faria Moreno, but she knew better than that. No, this was the debriefing call where she would have to account for every step of the mission. She was about to relive the entire two weeks all over again.

She set the glass down and answered.

"If it's death from a Saxon's hand that frightens you …" Lancelot said.

"Stay home," Christian answered. *I wish I would have the last time you called me about a mission*, she thought. "I don't understand why we were chased halfway around the world. I thought—"

"This isn't a debriefing call, Agent Garnier," Lancelot hurriedly cut her off. "The mission has been compromised from within. This is the last contact you'll have with me. I'll send further instruction to Avalon. And Christian…trust no one."

"Compromised? Wait!" she exclaimed. "Is the package secure?" Hearing nothing, she asked again, "Is Natalia safe? Is she okay?"

171

The call went completely silent, meaning the line was dead.

PART
2

CHAPTER TWENTY-TWO

"Avalon," Christian whispered, still holding the phone in her hand as she went inside her apartment. She hadn't heard that name in half a dozen years. She wasn't sure Avalon was a safe house anymore. She sat down and recalled the last time she'd heard that name. When she'd first started out with MI6, Lancelot was appointed as her handler. Each handler was a senior agent who managed the missions of at least a half dozen operatives, sometimes more. The two of them didn't know a thing about each other, but they were supposed to trust each other with their lives from the start. The first thing he ever said to her was:

"There is a safe house in Burgundy, France. It's called Avalon. If I am killed, whatever information I have sent to Avalon is all you will have. If I ever tell you to go there, our mission has gone horribly wrong. My life or yours is in grave danger. Trust no one."

She'd only been there one other time when a mission had ended badly, and he thought she was in danger. That was six years ago. Christian rushed inside her studio apartment, stuffed some toiletries and clothes from her dresser into a black, military-style backpack that she dubbed her 'go bag.' Three, fake, up-to-date passports were already in the bag, as well as a few other items that she often used on missions and would surely need if she ever went dark. After that, she pulled a men's dark gray, tailored suit from her closet, neatly folding it so that it wouldn't wrinkle, before adding it to her bag. Lastly, she slipped her handgun into the waistband of her jeans, and pulled on a pair of black, trail running sneakers, and a black t-shirt before removing the battery from her satellite phone and writing down the serial numbers. Then, she grabbed the bag, her car keys, and the phone, and exited the building. Her dark blue, Peugeot 108 was parked in the garage down the street. She hurried along the sidewalk, careful not to bring attention to herself, and wishing she had time to stop for a quick bite as her stomach growled.

Once she reached the car that was the French version of a Fiat or Mini Cooper, she input the numbers she'd written down, into the GPS on the phone, remembering to read them in reverse order. The coordinates quickly popped up. She zoomed in, making sure she was headed in the right direction. Burgundy was the township name next to the waypoint.

Christian had no idea what had gone wrong. She didn't know whether or not Natalia was even involved. All she knew was something bad had happened and she needed to get to Avalon quickly. She started the car, slammed the shifter into first gear, popped the clutch and squealed the tires as the small, two-door sedan took off. According to the GPS, she would be at her destination in two hours.

*

A hundred scenarios went through Christian's head as she pushed the small car to its limit along A6. She thought about the last time she'd been sent to Avalon. She was lucky she'd made it out alive after infiltrating a Russian military base to recover sensitive information from a crashed drone. The informant who had given them the details needed to locate the drone after it's GPS had been disabled, got spooked and turned on Christian once she'd arrived, giving away her cover. Russia supposedly killed him and hunted for the infiltrator. Christian went to Avalon in hiding. However, Avalon was like a mini-MI6 intelligence hub, buzzing with the most state-of-the-art computer equipment. She laid low hoping she hadn't left any trace of herself, but monitored Russian chatter until there was no more talk of the infiltration. Truth of the matter was, they were looking for a Ukrainian man. That was the disguise and passport she'd used to enter Russia after sneaking into Ukraine undetected and crossing the border. She'd followed protocol perfectly. Still, the mishap had nearly cost Christian her life as she raced to get off the base, and more importantly, out of the country before they figured out who she really was.

The car's speedometer was nearly at the last number on the dial when the GPS announced her exit. Christian pressed the brake lightly to slow her speed before swerving off the exit and downshifting.

After several twists and turns through the rolling hills of wine country, past rows and rows of grapevines and a few medieval-looking chateau's, the GPS announced her destination on the left. She turned down the side road that led to a cottage situated well off the main road. It looked like something from a storybook. She vaguely remembered the old, cobblestone building as she pulled around back and cut the engine off.

Getting out of the car with her backpack slung over one shoulder, Christian held up her satellite phone and removed the battery once more. This time, there was a six-letter code: ARTHUR. Using the alphanumeric numbers on her phone's keypad, she assumed the code was 2-7-8-4-8-7.

She walked over to the door of the cottage and entered the numbers on the keypad for the electronic deadbolt. A tiny red light blinked. Thinking for a second, she tried using each letter's placement in the alphabet, she came up with: 1-15 -17-8-18-15. The only numbers on the keypad were 0-9, so she tried 1-5-7-8. Again, the red light blinked. "Damn it," she growled. *This isn't the time for secret codes!*

After grabbing a nearby stick and writing both sets of numbers in the sandy gravel, she sighed and shook her head. Then, she wiped the numbers away with her foot and walked back to the door, entering: 1-2-4-5-7-8. A tiny green light illuminated, and a clicking sound was heard. Christian twisted the handle and the door swung open. She looked around behind her before stepping inside and pushing it closed. She spun the knob to relock the deadbolt, then turned to face the state-of-the-art computer system sitting on a metal framed desk with a glass top, in what should've been the living room of the small house.

The MI6 logo bounced around the large, flat screen monitor like a slow-moving ping pong ball. Christian set her backpack on the floor and did a quick sweep, checking each of the two bedrooms, plus the small kitchen and bathroom, to make sure she was alone. Then, she sat down at the desk and entered her ID number. The screen changed to a dark blue background. A single file named X was on the left side. Christian moved the cursor over the file and double-clicked the mouse, watching intently as an encrypted audio recording opened in a new window. She quickly searched the desk for pen and paper, settling for a broken pencil and a ripped piece of envelope from the trash bin. Then, she pressed play.

"Fourteen days ago, SATCOM codes were stolen from the French government by Sabio Davi de Faria

Moreno. Two days later, he was found dead. The last person to see him alive was his daughter, Natalia Luis de Faria Moreno. We believe he gave the codes to his daughter without her knowing. They are hidden in a necklace. The SATCOM codes are a series of alphanumeric codes that control the satellites operating in each hemisphere. With those codes, someone would have complete control over everything that relies on power and communication in that grid. They could easily shut countries completely down, literally leaving them in the dark and halting the economy.

Cyber Intelligence was trying to reprogram the satellites before the codes got into the hands of whoever was behind all of this, but they are dead in the water until the satellites come back into range in their orbit. You were assigned to close cover of Moreno's daughter to ensure the package didn't change hands until we were able to get the reprogramming completed.

We believe a Moroccan terrorist group was trying to purchase the codes from someone who set up Sabio Moreno, then gave away his identity. They killed him and went after his daughter.

Whoever is behind this has compromised me from the start. MI6 intercepted a message from Interpol, reporting the incident, therefore no other country knows what is going on. You're on your own.

The last facial recognition of Natalia Luis de Faria Moreno was in Rabat, Morocco. The satellites will come back into range in 72 hours. Christian, you must locate and destroy the codes. We cannot be sure Cyber Intel is still trying to reprogram them. Trust no one."

The screen went black, meaning the recording had ended, and more than likely, Lancelot was dead.

When Christian tried to close the file, it had already self-deleted as part of its programming. She leaned back in the chair, reading over the jumble of handwritten notes she'd taken. She had no time to process the scale of the situation. She had a new mission, and for the first time in her career ... she'd have to go dark to complete it.

*

All of the emotions Christian should've been feeling would come later. For now, she was angry. In over 10 years of working as an operative, she'd never let a mission get to her. She'd always done her job, in and out, no questions asked ... until Natalia Moreno. Everything had gone wrong from the start, and she wasn't even the package!

She slammed her hand on the desk, causing the pencil to flip through the air. One thing was certain. "I have to find Natalia," she muttered, reaching for her backpack to check her supplies. She needed to get to work. Whether or not Natalia still had the necklace, was unknown. But, if someone else had it, she could provide a clue as to who it was that took it.

Going through her bag, she made sure she had everything she needed, including money in multiple currencies, and credit cards to match the names on the passports. The hidden handgun that she passed through security with was also in there. The last item was an eye glass case containing a special pair of glasses that were linked to WorldVision, which was a program designed by MI6 and accessed only by high-ranking government intelligence. The lenses projected information from anywhere in the world and were also capable of using an extensive mapping system to show live feed from anywhere in the world using satellite imagery. The program was voice-enabled, allowing only the programmed voice access to the glasses. She slid the black-framed, Armani style glasses on and powered them up, making sure the battery was fully charged. Then, she tucked the case back into the bag and added a small container that looked like a makeup kit, before zipping it closed.

Unsure of where to actually begin, she went to the internet search box on the computer screen, hoping to learn more about Moroccan terrorist groups and arms dealers who may have ties to Portugal. While the computer uploaded the information, she walked over to the world map covering most of the adjacent wall. She put her finger on her location and traced a path to Morocco. She needed to get in undetected.

"I'll go through Spain and take the ferry," she said aloud as she got on her satellite phone and booked a seat on the next flight to Madrid. Lancelot's last words kept repeating in her head. *Trust no one.* She had no idea how far the corruption went, or who was in on it. Going dark was the only option. However, it also meant that she couldn't use any safe houses, or MI6 contacts. She would have to travel like a civilian and stop thinking like an operative.

Back at the desk, the news headlines and internet blogs were a jumbled mess with no real leads. She sighed, knowing she needed government intelligence to find what she was looking for. If she was cut off from MI6, there was only one person she trusted. She dialed a number from memory, hoping it still worked.

The line rang three times before a female voice answered, "Bonjour."

"Bonjour, Colette. C'est Christian Garnier."

The line went dead with a simple click.

"I deserved that," Christian mumbled and redialed.

The woman answered again, this time going off in French about Christian never being around anymore, and she hasn't called her in three years.

"Colette, please. Now, is not the time. I need your help. Can you meet me?"

"Help? With what? Where are you?"

"I can't say over the phone in case the line is not secure. Meet me where we had our first date. I'll be there in two hours."

"Christian … what's going on?"

"Just meet me, Colette. S'il vous plaît!"

"Très bien!"

"Oh, and bring your laptop," Christian added.

Colette growled incoherently before hanging up.

CHAPTER TWENTY-THREE

Christian drove her car towards the nearest train station, ditching it a few blocks away. She put a black ball cap on, pulling it down low as she hoofed it on foot to the station. Within thirty minutes, she was seated on the next train from Burgundy to Lyon. She hoped to look the part of a backpacker who was touring the country, avoiding eye contact as she watched the rolling hills of the countryside disappear through the window. Various conversations went on around her, mostly in French.

She tried to remember the last time she'd seen Colette Babin. They'd first met close to eleven years earlier when Christian entered the academy to become an Interpol officer. Colette was also a new recruit in the same academy class. The two women hit it off right away, becoming friends, then more as the weeks passed by.

When Christian discovered she was eligible to join MI5 because of her dual citizenship, she dropped out of the Interpol academy. However, MI6 recruited her before she could complete the enrollment paperwork for MI5. She'd tried to keep things going with Colette, but once she finished her training, MI6 assigned Christian all over the world, thus keeping them apart indefinitely. They'd remained friends in passing ever since.

Three years, she thought, remembering the last time she'd spoken to Colette. She was back home in Paris, in between missions, and Colette was in the city for the weekend. They'd met for lunch to catch up, promising to stay in contact, but three years had passed.

Christian simply wasn't good with any type of relationship. Even those without sex and feelings. She shook her head.

*

The speeding train rumbled to a stop at the Part-Dieu Railway Station in Lyon, France.

"Excusez-moi!" she said, shuffling through the crowd towards the Lyon Metro station.

She shoved a few Francs from her pocket into the ticket machine and a day pass popped out. She snatched it up and headed towards Line B to board the incoming train. She was barely inside when the doors slammed shut and the train accelerated down the track. She quickly grabbed a nearby pole to keep herself upright.

Checking her watch, she had less than 20 minutes before Colette would arrive to meet with her. Two stations passed by before Christian exited at Saxe-Gambetta to change over to Line D. From there, she only had three stops until Vieux Lyon, her destination. She hadn't rushed onto the next train, but had chosen to stand anyway, leaning against a pole, gripping it tightly as the train picked up speed.

*

Vieux Lyon was the oldest district in the city of Lyon and made up of extensive Renaissance neighborhoods that connected through cobblestone streets and traboules, which were tunnels cut through buildings.

Christian pulled the straps a little tighter on her backpack as she exited the metro station and headed up Rue du Boeuf, a cobblestone pedestrian street that was lined with old buildings from the 16th and 17th century. She came to a stop at the corner of Rue du Boeuf and Place Neuve Saint-Jean, where Café Vieux Lyon was located. She waved at the nearby waiter and took a seat at one of the outside tables, distancing herself from the other patrons.

"Bonjour madame. Voulez vous un café?" he asked.

"Oui. Deux s'il vous plaît," she answered, holding up two fingers.

"Avec des croissants?"

"Oui." She nodded.

When he stepped away, she glanced around. The old café hadn't changed much over the years. They still had the same drab green awning over most of the outdoor tables, and matching floor tiles inside. The few tables outside of the awning, like the one Christian was seated at, had large green umbrellas to match the motif. The surrounding buildings were in need of a coat of paint, but other than that, the late 16th and early 17th century architecture was beautifully crafted and obviously built to withstand time.

She was about to check her watch when the waiter returned with two cups of coffee, a refilling decanter, and a plate of freshly made croissants.

"Merci," she said.

"Somehow, I don't get the feeling you called me here to catch up," a feminine voice stated with a hint of harsh undertone.

Christian looked up at the woman standing across from her. Dressed in a dark blue pantsuit and low heels, Colette Babin looked more like a government agent than she ever did. Her slightly wavy, blonde hair was wrapped up in a loose bun with various tendrils floating freely in the breeze, and her thin, glossy pink lips were pressed firmly together, accentuating already high cheekbones. A single eyebrow arched above the dark glasses that covered her honey-colored eyes.

Christian stood, pulling Colette into a warm hug. "MI6 is compromised. I need your help," she whispered in her ear, before softly kissing her cheek. To anyone around, they looked like old friends, or perhaps mismatched lovers stealing time in the middle of the day.

"How bad is it?" Colette asked as they parted. She took the seat next to her.

"I've gone dark."

"Christian," Colette sighed.

Christian leaned closer. "SATCOM codes went missing from the French government two weeks ago. The man who took them was set up by Moroccan terrorists. He gave the codes to his daughter before he was murdered. I spent the last ten days keeping her safe while MI6 worked to reprogram them. Their plan failed when I handed her over to another MI6 agent 24 hours ago. He has disappeared, believed to be dead, and she was seen entering Morocco yesterday, presumably still with the codes."

"No," she said, matter-of-factly. "I would've known. The world … would've known."

"MI6 intercepted the message to Interpol. No one else knows," Christian replied solemnly.

"You are kidding me!" she growled. "British government thinks they can control France? Have they gone insane? If this has happened, then it is a matter of national security. In fact, it's a worldwide security breach. Do you know what those codes do?" she huffed. "Damn you and the British spy nonsense! They are not in control of France, or the rest of the world, for that matter!"

Christian wondered if she was about to get slapped ... for several reasons, some of which she deserved. "There's nothing you can do about it now, except help me, Colette. You're the only one I can trust. If I don't get those codes before the satellites come back into range, half of the world is going to go dark." Christian grabbed her hand. "Aidez-moi, s'il vous plaît. Je ne peux pas le faire sans toi," she pleaded.

Colette sat quietly for a minute with her lips pursed together. She knew Christian was right. If she contacted Interpol, an entire investigation would take place, starting from the beginning. The process could take weeks ... maybe months. They didn't have that kind of time. They had to trust each other to do their jobs.

"I could lose my job," Colette said, shaking her head. "How are we going to do this?"

Thank God. Christian let out the breath she was holding. "We have to find out who was funding the operation to steal the codes."

"Do you know who stole them?"

"Yes. I have all the details."

Colette pursed her lips and shook her head again. It was too late to be angry. She had work to do. "Give me everything you have. I'll see what I can find. What are you going to do?"

"I'm headed to Morocco. That's the last place the daughter was seen alive," Christian said. She pulled a piece of paper from her pocket that had her satellite phone number, an email address, Sabio Moreno's name and position at the embassy, and the word Morocco, written on it. She also handed her a thumb drive with encryption software.

"This is all you have?"

"Oui."

"Ce n'est pas bon, Christian," she chided.

"Download the software to your Interpol computer before you get back to the building. No one will be able to trace you. It'll bounce back to an MI6 IP address."

"You spies and your gadgets," Colette mumbled.

Christian reached out, placing her hand on Colette's forearm. "Thank you for helping me."

"You can thank me when you've found the codes, mon ami."

Christian stood up, putting her backpack over her shoulders. Then, she bent down, kissing Colette on the cheek. "I'll be in touch," she said before walking away.

Colette shoved the piece of paper into her pocket and headed off in the opposite direction, leaving the croissants and coffee untouched.

CHAPTER TWENTY-FOUR

Colette walked into the ladies' room of a restaurant near where she'd parked her car. Inside one of the stalls, she closed the lid on the toilet and sat down, opening her laptop. It took two minutes for the software program to load, then she packed up and headed back to her office.

Back at the confines of her cubicle, she powered up the computer. "J'espère que cela fonctionne," she mumbled to herself as she illegally bypassed the firewall of the French government, searching for Sabio de Faria Moreno's email account at the embassy. Working for Interpol in International Communications and Information Systems meant she literally hacked international computer systems and databases for a living, searching for terrorist activity, and tracing links.

Once she located Sabio's files on the database, she began scrolling through his inbox and outgoing messages, but they combined to make several thousand emails. She tried using the keyword: SATCOM but found nothing. She glanced at the notes on the paper Christian had given her and changed her keyword search to: Morocco, but again...nothing. She adjusted her search back a few days before Christian believed the codes were stolen, and two emails popped up with the subject: Sovereignty. She clicked on the first one and waited for the email to open in a new window.

Mr. Moreno,

Don't bother reporting this. Once you've opened it, the encrypted bug has notified us. I am already three steps ahead of you. Now, if you don't want any problems, you will cooperate freely.

Two days from now, you have a meeting at Élysée Palace with the council of ministers to go over plans to expand the Portuguese embassy. Inside President Macron's office, you will find a yellow gold pendant with a cloudy stone in the middle that has black and gray swirls in it.

Retrieve the pendant and exit the Palace undetected. I will be in touch.

And Mr. Moreno, Do Not Cross Me…

Colette quickly copied the email and sent it to Christian, along with a note saying she was trying to trace the IP address. Then, she clicked on the second email.

Mr. Moreno,

It seems you did not understand how serious my business partner was. I know you have the pendant. If you do not turn it over within 24hrs, I will be forced to pay you a visit. Mr. Moreno, you do not want me to pay you a visit. Trust Me.

Colette sent the second email to Christian, and another note: Two different IP addresses … heavily encrypted. Will update when I have something.

*

Christian sat in a vacant chair at a busy gate in Terminal 2 at Lyon–Saint Exupéry Airport, waiting to board her flight to Madrid, Spain. Feeling her satellite phone vibrate in her pocket, she pulled it out, reading the forwarded emails from Colette. She would be in Morocco in five hours. Hopefully, Colette had something for her to go on by then. Otherwise, she would be clueless as to where to look for the necklace containing the codes, or Natalia … if she was even still alive. Christian had no way of knowing. Less than 24 hours ago, she was seen boarding a plane to Rabat, Morocco. After that, she disappeared. Thinking about her now only made Christian angry. Angry for letting her guard down throughout the mission. Angry because now it was more than a mission … it was personal. She didn't do *personal*.

Checking her watch, she cleared her mind and stood up, heading to the other end of the terminal to catch her departing flight.

The line wasn't too long, and she slipped easily onto the one-hundred-seater Canada Regional Jet plane.

"Bienvenido a bordo," the flight attendant said, welcoming her aboard, along with the other passengers who were lingering behind her.

"Hola," Christian replied, passing by her and taking her 3B aisle seat.

"¿Estás viajando a casa?" the older woman sitting next to her asked.

"Home," she mumbled, unsure of where that was at the moment, especially since she'd gone dark. For all she knew, her apartment could've been destroyed by now. She simply nodded and opened the magazine from the seatback in front of her.

The plane bounced and jarred a few minutes later as it took flight, making her think of Natalia once again. She bit the inside of her lip, willing herself to concentrate on the mission. *Destroy the package.* But no matter how much she forced Natalia from her mind, she floated right back in. Christian knew she didn't have a lot of time. Once the men who took her got their hands on the necklace and figured out how to retrieve the codes, Natalia would be disposable. *I have to find her.*

*

Once she arrived in Spain, Christian made her way through the immigration line, handing the officer her passport when it was her turn.

"How long will you be staying in Spain, Señora Allison Parker from Los Angeles, California?" he asked, reading the passport.

"Not as long as I'd like, I'm afraid. It's beautiful here," she replied, sounding like an American tourist.

"What brings you here? Are you an actor?"

"I'm a travel blogger. I go where the magazine company sends me."

He nodded and stamped the booklet before handing it back to her. "¡Tenga un día bueno!" he said.

She smiled politely and headed in the direction of the exit before turning the corner and walking back to the arrival terminal. She grabbed a different passport from her bag, stowing the other one in the hidden compartment in the bottom. Then, she got in line to check in and print her boarding pass for her next flight, which was scheduled to leave in an hour.

Removing her phone from her pocket in the security line, she texted Colette the word: UPDATE, and turned it off before she put it in the plastic container, along with her backpack and shoes. The guard waved her through but scanned her bag twice. Then, he nodded for her to step out of line.

"¿Hablas español?" he questioned.

"Sí," she replied.

"¿Puedo ver su pasaporte, por favor?" he asked, holding out his hand.

Christian gave him her passport.

"You are a long way from Sydney, Australia," he muttered.

Trust me. I'm the least of your worries, pal. "I am backpacking through Europe," she said. "My mother and I were supposed to do this together, but she died earlier this year. I decided to go anyway," she lied.

He nodded and handed her passport back. Then, he waved at the other guard who was holding her bag.

Christian retrieved her shoes, backpack, and phone and walked as fast as she could to her gate, checking her watch along the way to make sure the security guards hadn't caused her to miss her flight.

Thankfully, the plane was boarding the last of the passengers when she scurried into the line. Again, she had an aisle seat. This plane was nearly identical to the last, except she had an older man sitting next to her. They were headed to Tarifa, Gibraltar, and the short flight was scheduled to take about an hour and twenty minutes. She wished she could close her eyes but now was not the time.

"Would you care for a beverage?" the flight attendant asked in broken English just after they became airborne.

"Coffee," Christian replied.

The man next to her shook his head no and went back to reading the ratty old paperback between his hands. Christian recognized the stark red cover and raised gold lettering of The Hunt for Red October, by Tom Clancy, a novel her father had also been fond of. She glanced over, taking an extra look at the man. He didn't resemble her father, not in the least, but she'd flown with Raoul Garnier sitting beside her enough times to picture him in the man's place … with the same book in his hand.

Turning her eyes back to the blue sky on the other side of the window, she sighed. She hadn't thought of her father, at least not in that context, in a handful of years. She had no time to analyze why he'd be plaguing her thoughts at the moment. She had more important issues to deal with … like finding Natalia and keeping half of the world from plunging into total darkness.

CHAPTER TWENTY-FIVE

Natalia sat on the floor in the center of a dingy and dusty concrete room. The only light was from the sun pouring in through a window near the ceiling. The air was stagnant and stale. Having been blindfolded, she had no idea where she was. She wasn't even sure what country she was in anymore, and she had no sense of time. Based on the sun, she'd been in the room at least ten hours, maybe twelve. It had to have been well over twenty-four hours since she'd said goodbye to Christian in Glasgow. The loud buzz of a scooter getting closer and closer made her spine straighten. *They're back.*

Two men walked in, closing the door behind them. One tossed a white paper bag on the floor. They were dressed in thin, tan pants and long-sleeved, white shirts, made of the same light material, and sandals. She noticed what appeared to be white embroidery on their collars. Both had black hair and matching full beards, but one appeared somewhat older than the other. They spoke to each other in Arabic, a language Natalia didn't know. She'd seen them once before when she'd first arrived and the blindfold was removed.

One of the men reached down, grabbing Natalia by her upper arm and snatching her to her feet. He yelled at her in Arabic, shaking her at the same time.

Having no idea what he was saying, Natalia shrugged. "You're hurting me," she grimaced as he squeezed her arm harder.

The men looked at each other, said a couple of words, then he threw her to the ground. Natalia's body slammed against the dirty, concrete floor. She rolled to her side, pulling her knees to her chest as she scrambled back against the wall. Heavy tears rolled down her cheeks, mixing with the dirt and dust from the old, abandoned building.

"You will die!" he spat in broken English, obviously the only words he knew.

Natalia trembled with fear as she tightened her arms around her legs. She had no idea who they were or what they wanted. She held her breath until they left the room once more. Then, she allowed herself to relax enough to wipe away the dirty tears. She wondered if these were the men who had killed her father. Did he die there too? A hundred questions raced through her mind. Was her mother okay? Did they have her too? Have they killed her? The more she thought about her parents, the harder it was to breathe as she choked back more tears. She pushed her hair out of her face and over her shoulder, tucking a few loose strands behind her ear. The loud buzz of a nearby scooter grabbed her attention. She listened as it apparently drove off, the sound fading until it was no longer heard. *They're gone ... for now.* She sighed in relief and sniffed the aroma in the air from the food in the forgotten bag as the sun began to slowly fade.

CHAPTER TWENTY-SIX

Christian was happy to feel the plane touchdown. She slung her backpack over her shoulder and pushed her way through the terminal, skirting people with small children and large suitcases, until she reached the exit. Checking her watch, she pulled out her phone and dialed Colette's number.

"Tell me you've found something," she said when the call was answered.

"Oui et non," Colette said. "Where are you?"

"Gibraltar."

"I've traced the IP address from the emails to Morocco, but it's heavily encrypted. Could it be a government server?"

Christian stumbled on the sidewalk. "Government?"

"Oui."

"I don't … I guess. Yes. Hell, it could be anything. We're dealing with terrorists," Christian replied softly, trying not to be overheard. "I'll be in Morocco before dark. I plan on driving to Rabat tonight. I'll call you at first light."

Christian crossed one arm over her midsection with her other resting on it at the elbow and her fist against her mouth, deep in thought. If the Moroccan government was involved, this was way bigger than she anticipated. No wonder Lancelot had been silenced. Her mind drifted to

Natalia, but her reflection was cut short when a taxi driver lurched in front of her, trying to get her attention.

"Taxi … yes," she mumbled. "Yes! I need to go to the ferry," she added, perking up.

"Sure thing, Miss. Do you have any luggage?" he asked, speaking with a heavy British accent.

"No."

"Right this way, then," he said, leading her towards his small car.

The ride to the ferry didn't take long, but the traffic was backed up much further than she'd anticipated because of the cars getting onto the ferry.

"You can drop me here," Christian said, handing him twenty pounds, which more than covered her taxi fare. Then, she tossed her backpack over her shoulders and walked the rest of the way.

The ferry terminal was visible, and less than a half mile away. She moved at a brisk pace, passing all the cars that were still waiting in line. Christian showed her passport and paid the fare for a one-way trip across the strait, before making her way onto the first deck of the ship. From there, she walked up to the passenger area and bought a sandwich before sitting down in an empty seat. Knowing Morocco time was an hour ahead, she quickly changed her watch.

Other passengers gathered around a little at a time until all the seats were taken. As soon as the ferry began to drift away from the dock, the immigration agents began walking around, stamping passports.

"You're a bit of a haul from home," the agent said, looking at her American passport.

"I backpacked my way through Europe and decided I needed to see Casablanca before I went home," she replied with a smile.

"Enjoy your trip," he said, handing her passport back to her.

Christian put it away and began searching on her phone for a hotel in Rabat as she ate. Knowing Moroccan Parliament could be involved, she decided to book a room nearly across the street. Once the transaction was completed, she booked a rental car from the Tangier airport and put away her phone to watch the sunset for the rest of the thirty-five-minute boat ride.

When the ferry was almost to the landing, Christian went to the bathroom, where she entered a stall and removed the containers that hid her gun parts. It took less than thirty seconds for her to reassemble the gun and load it as she listened to two separate conversations. Then, she flushed the toilet, tucked the pistol into the waistband at the back of her jeans, and walked out to the sink. She nodded at the woman next to her, and smiled down at the small child beside her, while she washed her hands. A crowd of people was standing nearby when she exited and noticed one of them had set down a briefcase. Christian picked it up and kept walking, all the way to the other end of the ferry boat, disappearing into another crowd.

*

Taxi drivers leaned against their cars outside of the ferry port, just as they do at airports, waiting for their next passenger. Christian walked along the sidewalk, scoping out the most reliable vehicle. Several drivers walked up to her, but she waved them off, choosing the last guy in the row.

"Do you speak English?" she questioned.

He shrugged.

"How much to go to the airport?" she asked.

He paused, scratching his thick, dark beard, then spit off a number equivalent to twenty dollars.

Christian shook her head and turned to ask someone else, but he quickly cut his fee in half.

Christian nodded in agreement and he waved for her to get into his red Renault Kangoo, which was like a small van. She climbed in, tucking her backpack under the back of her legs, and setting the briefcase beside her. She turned on the GPS on her phone to make sure the driver didn't try anything sneaky. A woman traveling alone was extremely hazardous, especially in Muslim countries.

The driver turned on the radio, blasting some local celebrity musician as he pulled out into traffic, beeping the horn half a dozen times.

Christian thought about Natalia as she grabbed the door handle and checked her seatbelt when he raced around a corner. She had no way of knowing whether or not Natalia was still alive, and that realization caused her chest to ache as it constricted. Feeling anything at all for anyone was completely new to her, and whether she wanted the new sensation or not, now was not the time to decide. She needed a clear head, and she needed to believe Natalia was still alive. She was Christian's only link to the necklace containing the codes.

A little over twenty minutes later, the red taxi pulled up at the airport.

"Arrival," Christian directed.

The driver nodded and pulled through the arrival line, dropping her off outside of one of the main airlines. Christian reached into her bag, pulling out 250 dirhams in bank notes, which was equivalent to a little over $27. She quickly paid him and got out. She emptied some of the contents of the briefcase into the first trashcan she saw, keeping a handful of files and papers, then headed inside to retrieve her rental car.

"How may I help you?" the man at the counter said as she stepped up, speaking in broken English.

Christian gave him the reservation number she'd saved on her phone.

"You have a mini compact rental for two days. Unlimited miles. Yes?"

"Correct."

He typed a few keystrokes, ran her credit card, then made her sign a couple of papers before handing her a key. "It is in space 31D. We have you returning at Salé-Rabat Airport."

Christian nodded and grabbed the key. She had no idea where space 31D was located, but she crossed over to the parking garage, deciding to start there. Luckily, the spaces in the garage were numbered, so it didn't take her long to find space 31D. A tiny, black Fiat 500 was parked in the space. She opened the door and tossed her backpack and the briefcase into the passenger seat. Then, she programmed the address to the hotel in Rabat into her phone's GPS. "Two and a half hours," she growled, reading the estimated trip time. "I should've flown," she mumbled, starting the car and shifting into reverse. She would've arrived much sooner, but she needed to get into the country undetected and flying right into Rabat would've been a bad idea. At least she didn't have to repeat the long drive on her return home.

Shifting gears, she pulled onto A1, where she'd ride for the next 234km. Open land that looked like mini farms with towns in between were situated along the stretch of road on the left. Sand beaches and the Atlantic Ocean were on her right. She was sure the sand was pristine white and the water was turquoise, but it was too dark to see much of anything but the road in front of her.

Her phone rang with Colette's number. "Tell me you have a name," she answered.

"Je sais quoi faire," Colette grumbled. "The IP address the emails were sent from belongs to Emir Al-Khalef. He is a member of the House of Representatives and has an office in the parliament building. He sent the emails from his office computer."

"Can you get into his schedule?"

"His schedule? Why?"

"Can you do it?" Christian snapped.

"Oui."

"Put a man named Tarik Behari, an Algerian diplomat that is there to discuss foreign relations, on his schedule for a meeting tomorrow morning."

"Who is that?"

"The less you know, the better."

"I'm already in over my head," Colette replied. "I can't help you if you don't let me."

"I'm going in undercover. Just make sure the meeting is on his schedule. Text me with the time, and don't forget to put Tarik Behari in the security system."

"I'll get you in there, but there's one other thing, Christian. I found a back door once I got into the server. Emir Al-Khalef copied someone else on the emails sent to Sabio Moreno, but the firewall on that server is unlike anything I've ever seen. However, in searching through Emir Al-Khalef's email, I found he responded to an email from a different server which had a much weaker firewall. That same server had also sent emails to Sabio Moreno.

"What do we know about this new server? Can you trace the IP address?"

"I already did. It's in Scotland. It belongs to Fergus McDonald. Does that name mean anything?"

Christian ran off the road and quickly swerved back on, nearly causing the small car to flip over. *Oh my God.* "No ... this can't be. It's not ..." she muttered. "Son of a bitch! I fucking handed her right to him!"

"Christian?" Colette called. "What's going on? Do you know him?"

"He's MI6!" she snapped. "I have to go. I'll call you in the morning. Text me the meeting time," Christian said before ending the call. "Goddamn it!" she yelled, slamming her hand on the steering wheel. "I have trusted that piece of shit with my life, and he betrayed me. He betrayed all of us!" Seething with anger, she could barely see the road in front of her. She couldn't believe one of their own was corrupt to begin with, but it being someone she knew, someone she trusted ... blew her mind. Knowing Fergus was a part of this the entire time, working with crooked politicians and terrorists, made her blood boil, but knowing he had Natalia ... that made her see red.

She was a little further down the road before she started thinking rationally again. "I should've gone to the UK instead of Avalon. If Fergus killed Lancelot, I may have been able to see what he was trying to access on the computer," she mumbled. "Knowing protocol though, Lancelot would've destroyed everything."

CHAPTER TWENTY-SEVEN

Natalia tried to sleep on the dirty, cold floor, but nightmares plagued her mind as she shivered. The only light in the room was from a lantern left behind by the men who were holding her captive. Next to it sat the empty paper bag from the takeout food they'd given her earlier. She wasn't sure what she'd eaten, but starving to death wasn't the way she wanted to die. If they were going to kill her, they'd have to be bold enough to do it. She wasn't doing it for them.

Unable to take the cool air anymore, she sat up and slipped on the jacket she'd been using as a pillow, and laid back down, curled on her side with her head in the crook of her arm.

She'd almost fallen asleep once more, hoping to stave off the horrendous dreams, when the distinct sound of a car door brought her to full attention. She sat up and quickly scurried into the corner with her knees pulled to her chest. She inhaled shallow, rapid breaths, and her heart pounded against her chest cavity.

Heavy footsteps grew closer. Then, the door creaked as it opened. Natalia looked up to see the MI6 agent who had brought her to the building to begin with. It made her sick knowing he worked with Christian and was a part of whatever this was.

"I guess I have to do this myself," he said, shaking his head.

"Where are those men?"

"Miss them already?" he laughed, walking closer. "There's no use in holding out, Lass," he sneered, changing his tone as he grabbed her jacket collar and pulled her to her feet. "Christian Garnier is dead, just like your father. No one is looking for you."

Natalia barely had time to react as he snatched the necklace from around her neck and pushed her away. She watched him walk over and place it on the small, white table against the side wall.

"I know the codes are in here. Show me how to get them, and I'll let you go."

"What codes?" she growled, seething with anger as tears welled up in her eyes. *Christian's dead?!*

"Don't play dumb with me!" he yelled.

"I don't know what you're talking about," she said through her tears. She didn't care anymore. If he killed her, then so be it. If Christian really was gone, she had no hope in anyone finding her anyway.

"I suggest you figure it out by morning," he grumbled before leaving the room.

Natalia slid down the wall until her butt hit the floor. She hadn't realized he'd come alone until the sound of the car was out of earshot. She honestly had no idea what he was talking about. She knew nothing about any codes. Was this why her father was killed? Had Fergus, the MI6 agent, killed him? She was too confused to think. More tears rolled down her face, forming a puddle where she sat.

Eventually, Natalia cried herself into a fitful sleep, tossing and thrashing around on the cold, concrete floor.

CHAPTER TWENTY-EIGHT

The hotel looked like it had in the internet pictures, although Christian was far from caring how many stars it had. At this point, she needed a place to lay her head for a few hours of sleep before the meeting with Emir Al-Khalef, which based on Colette's text, was scheduled for nine-thirty in the morning.

"Ms. Carrie Lowell, thank you for staying with us. Will it be just the one night?" the man at the desk asked.

"Is it possible to make it two? I have some business that may take longer than expected."

He typed a few keys on the computer and smiled. "We have the same room available, so I will change you to two nights."

"Thank you."

"Here is your room key. You are in 121," he added, explaining how to get to her room from the lobby. "Put this pass on the dashboard of your car for parking."

Christian grabbed the paper and the key card, and headed outside to her room around the corner. Thankfully, all the rooms had exterior doors, so no one would see her coming and going through the lobby. Once she located #121, she slid the key card and swung the door open. The plain room had white walls and dark brown carpet. The only furniture was a makeshift desk made out of a table and a rickety chair, and a pair of double beds with tan and white linens.

"It's not a palace, but it'll do," she sighed, tossing her backpack and the briefcase onto one of the beds. Within minutes, her head hit the pillow of the other one and she was out like a light.

*

Three hours later, Christian awoke in a fit, snatching and kicking at the covers she hadn't realized she'd pulled on. "Damn it," she grumbled, getting up out of the bed to use the bathroom and check the time. She didn't have any new messages or missed calls, meaning Colette had probably stopped for the night as well. "I should sleep," she whispered, but every time she closed her eyes, she saw Natalia smiling and staring back at her as she walked away with Fergus McDonald. She steadied her breathing and focused on clearing her mind. She needed more than three hours of restless sleep.

*

The sun had barely risen, casting the capital city of Rabat in an orange glow from the marina to the King's Palace. Christian stood near the window, watching the colors change as she waited for Colette to pick up the phone. She'd woken early, having very little luck getting back to sleep, and began working on her planned meeting at the parliament building across the street. She'd also torn open the bottom of the briefcase from the inside, creating a secret compartment that was hidden once she put the papers and files back inside.

"Bonjour mon ami," Colette said.

"Bonjour," Christian replied. "Have you ever worked with WorldVision?"

"No. Interpol officers aren't spies, Christian."

Sighing, Christian closed the blinds and moved across the small room. "I will be able to upload anything I see to you, as well as record and send conversations, and you'll be able to message me without anyone knowing. It's all done through a very expensive pair of glasses."

"Spies and their toys," Colette uttered.

Christian ignored the jab. "You already know I'm going into the meeting with Emir Al-Khalef as Tarik Behari. I will email you a link that is going to give you access to his phone. You'll need to search his text messages, incoming and outgoing calls, emails, anything pertaining to the codes or Natalia. Also, scroll through his photos. Text me everything you find once you get in."

"Es-tu sûr de ça?" Colette questioned.

"Yes, I'm sure. The software will work. Crois-moi s'il te plait."

"Okay," Colette muttered. "Christian … be careful."

"I'll be in touch soon. Stay in front of your computer and make sure you have interrupted internet access," Christian added before ending the call.

She walked over to the bathroom, looking in the mirror one last time, before beginning the transformation that would turn her into Tarik Behari. It had been a while, maybe even two years, since she last had to change her identity for a mission. She, like all MI6 Operatives, was trained to use a Hollywood make-up kit with everything from prosthetics to human hair.

She began by applying a cream that would protect her skin from the glue and wax. Then, she added a thin layer of prosthetic skin that stretched from her cheeks down to her jaw on both sides, meeting at her chin. She smoothed it out, then applied a make-up like paint to her entire face, concealing the prosthetic skin and giving her an even skin tone.

Checking the mirror, she was surprised to see how different she already looked. "Now for the hair," she mumbled as she dug through the case, searching for the clippings of black, human hair. She pulled out a handful, sprayed it with glue, then applied it to her face in the shape of a mustache and goatee. Once the glue set, she combed through the hair with wax to make sure it looked as if it were naturally growing and facing in the same direction. After that, she put some stiffening gel in her curly hair and slicked it back. "As-salāmu ʿalaykum, Tarik Behari," she said, staring at the person in the mirror, who looked nothing like herself. Her own piercing blue eyes were the only thing reminding her that she was still there.

She sprayed her throat with a clear, mint flavored liquid from the kit. Her vocal cords reacted, causing her voice to deepen a couple of octaves. She knew it was only temporary and would wear off in an hour, but she needed to play the part as best she could.

Moving across the room, she glanced through the window at the parliament building. Her meeting was in thirty minutes. She quickly dressed in her dark gray, three-piece suit and black wingtip shoes. Then, she tied a black, Windsor knot tie around her neck, stuffing it behind her button-down vest, before putting on her WorldVision glasses. She checked her pockets to make sure she had her phone and room key one last time before grabbing the briefcase, heading out the door and crossing the street.

*

The inside of the parliament building reminded Christian of a church with red carpet, carved wood paneling, high ceilings, and long halls. She passed easily through security and made her way towards the House of Representative's secretary, which was down another hallway off to the side.

"I'm Tarik Behari. I have an appointment with Emir Al-Khalef at nine-thirty," she said, happy her voice still sounded deeper.

"Right this way," the woman replied after checking her computer. "Mr. Al-Khalef will be with you shortly."

"Do you have a restroom?"

"Down the hall on the left," the woman said, pointing.

Christian nodded and headed off towards the men's room. Luckily, no one was inside. She quickly removed the hidden compartment in the bottom of the briefcase and retrieved her loaded gun. She knew she'd have to walk through a metal detector, but her briefcase would simply be opened and searched, not scanned. She tucked the gun into the back waistband of her pants and left the room.

Back at the other end of the hall, she sat on the wooden bench. Each representative had his own office and assistant in the large building. She sat still but took in her surroundings as she waited. There wasn't much to see besides the red carpet and wood panel walls. When the door in front of her opened, she looked up to see a woman waving her inside.

"I'm Mr. Al-Khalef's assistant. His office is right this way," she said, leading Christian through another room and to a closed door. She knocked softly, and a man opened the door. "Mr. Al-Khalef ... Mr. Tarik Behari."

He nodded and flicked his wrist. Christian stepped into the small room, reaching into her suit pocket as the door closed behind her. Emir Al-Khalef was only about ten years older than her, but he looked much older with his balding head and scruffy, miniscule facial hair. He was also fifty pounds overweight. He was wearing a dark brown suit with a crème-colored shirt and a tan tie. His black eyes concentrated on the cell phone in his hand as a light sheen of sweat glistened on his head.

As they walked away from the door, Christian bumped into the preoccupied man, knocking his phone from his hand. He cursed as Christian bent to pick it up, simultaneously pressing a clear sticker with a built-in scanner to the back of it.

"Thank you," he said as she handed back his phone. "Please, have a seat. I must say, I am surprised to see a member of Algerian diplomacy. What can I do for you, Mr. Behari?"

"That is why I am here. I've come to negotiate an agreement."

"On what exactly?" he asked, quickly reaching for his phone when it vibrated, indicating a message of some sort.

Colette sent a message to Christian, which scrolled across her glasses: I'M IN. SEARCHING HIS MESSAGES NOW.

"Foreign relations," she said, pulling a fake file from her briefcase to stall time.

"I wasn't aware we had any agreements to negotiate on. Surely, I'm not the person for that anyhow."

"Oh … I believe you are," she said as Colette sent another message: HE HAS SEVERAL TEXTS FROM THE SAME NUMBER. TRYING TO TRACE IT NOW.

TEXTS AS FOLLOWS: *Not talking; She's going to die within the hour; We will get codes another way.* Christian stiffened in her seat. "In fact, I know you're the exact person."

"If this has to do with Western Sahara … I'm not at liberty to negotiate anything," he said nervously. "Who sent you here?"

Christian was aware of the strained relationship between Morocco and Algeria because of Western Sahara and the Polisario Front, a liberal movement by the Sahrawi rebels to get Morocco out of there. She wondered if his nervousness had anything to do with that since that was why he thought she was there. Her cover had worked out wonderfully. She adjusted her glasses, pressing the button on the side to record. They vibrated so softly, she barely felt it, indicating they were recording.

"Actually," she said, "I'm here to talk about the codes."

"What?" he mumbled, looking dumbfounded.

"I know you have them, and I want them."

"What codes? I don't know what you're referring to," he said, puffing his chest out.

Another message scrolled across Christian's glasses. PICTURES OF A WIFE AND 3 CHILDREN ON THE PHONE. STILL DIGGING. NO MORE TEXTS.

"I'm sure your wife and children will help you figure out what I'm talking about. There are three of them … yes?"

"I don't have the codes! You leave my family out of this!"

"Emir …" Christian shook her head. "Take me to the necklace and the codes, or I will shame you for the traitor you are and have your family killed for all to see."

Emir rubbed his sweaty head and slammed his fist on the desk. Then, he nodded and wrote an address on a piece of paper. Christian picked up the paper, getting a good look through the lenses as she touched the arm of the glasses, taking a picture and sending it directly to Colette with a simple swipe of her finger along the side of the frame.

"I don't know where this is. You have to take me there," she said.

"Take you?" he shook his head no. "I can't leave."

"You can, and you will." She held up her phone. "I guess your wife and children mean less to you than your job…"

"Wait!"

Christian checked her watch as Emir wiped his sweaty head with his hand. *Two hours left.* She shook her head. "Emir, you're wasting my time," she growled.

"It's across town."

"I don't care," she seethed, giving him a displeased look as she pulled out her gun.

"Okay. Okay. We'll go," he muttered, fumbling with his briefcase to get his car keys.

Christian nodded and stood as she put her gun away while waiting for him to lead the way to the lot where his vehicle was parked.

*

Colette copied the address from the email into the Interpol GPS system. A picture of a blue and white abandoned building in the Kasbah district came up. She took a screenshot of the latest satellite images that were taken in that area as it passed over and sent them to

Christian. Then, she went back to the program she was using to trace the phone number Emir's texts had been coming from. It was an unregistered burner phone, which meant she wasn't going to have much luck. She could try to see what cell tower it was pinging, but that didn't matter since they now had an actual address.

I'm doing everything I can, Christian," she whispered. "You're running out of time."

CHAPTER TWENTY-NINE

Natalia sat on the floor with her back to the cold concrete wall and her knees tucked under her chin. She cringed when she heard a car pull up outside.

"I'm only going to do this one more time, Lass!" Fergus yelled, slamming through the door. "Give me the codes!"

"I don't know what you are talking about," she cried. "I don't have any codes."

"The codes your father stole for me and decided to keep for himself. I know he gave them to you."

"The only thing he gave me was the necklace, and you already have it," she explained, wiping her tears.

Fergus snatched the side table over to the center of the room and grabbed her by the arm, propelling her up against it and to her feet. "Find the goddamn codes or I'll kill you," he said in a low, menacing tone.

She had no idea what he was referring to. Was this why her father was killed? Did he really steal some secret codes? Her chest deflated as the image of her perfect father began to go up in flames behind her heavy eyes. *Papai* ... A lone tear slid down her already wet cheek.

Fergus smacked the table with his hand, making the necklace bounce up. Natalia jerked back in fear, before noticing the necklace had landed in the direct sunlight, causing the rays to shine on the swirls and form a pattern on the white table underneath. She picked up the necklace,

215

holding it a few inches above the table in the sun. Small, black letters and numbers began to form. Unsure of what she was doing, Fergus moved closer. Seeing the lettering, he quickly snatched it from her hand and shoved her back down to the ground.

Using his cell phone light, which was much brighter and easier to contain than the sun's rays, he held the necklace in one hand and shined the light with the other, adjusting the positioning until he could clearly read a pattern of letters and numbers forming the codes on the white tabletop.

"Son of a bitch!" he yelled with a happier tone.

Natalia was unsure what his next plan was as he quickly sent a text message on his phone, then went back to the codes. She remained as quiet and still as possible. Now that he had the codes, he no longer had a need for her. Was she next? She inhaled and exhaled slowly, trying to remain calm and limber. She wished she knew how to surprise attack someone and take them down the way Christian had done. She wished Christian was there. Thinking of her and knowing Fergus had killed her too, along with her father, only made her want to cry again. *No.* She told herself.

*

Christian looked at the images Colette had sent. The building was in the Kasbah district, and from the looks of the blue and white structures surrounded by a concrete wall up ahead, they were getting closer.

"Faster, Emir," she growled, tossing her stolen briefcase out the window.

He shifted gears, increasing his speed as he whipped his car in and out of traffic. When his phone lit up with a new message, he glanced at the screen but kept his face towards the road in front of him so she wouldn't notice.

A few seconds later, a text scrolled across Christian's glasses: I HAVE THE CODES.

"The Scottish man has the codes. He'll kill the girl now. He has what he wants," Emir stated.

"How much further?" she questioned through clenched teeth, ignoring his comment.

"It's the building right up here," he said, turning down a side road. She saw a similar car parked further up, outside of one of the blue and white buildings.

As the car moved closer, Christian held her pistol up and pulled the trigger, shooting Emir clean through the side of his head. The car slowed as his foot slipped off the accelerator, then stalled and rolled to a stop. She got out, holding her gun at her side as she shuffled along the wall, careful not to make any noise as she made her way around back to the wooden door. She tried the knob, but it was locked. She knocked, hoping whoever was in there would think it was Emir.

"Come on in," Fergus called.

Christian's skin crawled. She gripped her gun and stood back, kicking the door as hard as she could. The lock broke and the door swung open.

"Help!" Natalia cried, hoping the newcomer would save her. Fergus was standing halfway behind her, holding a gun to her throat.

"Let her go!"

"Excalibur? Is that you?" he laughed. "Nice disguise. I see MI6 taught you well. I'm not surprised you came for the girl," he taunted. "I kept her alive just so we could see each other again."

"You son of a bitch!" Christian yelled. She looked around the room, spotting the necklace on the nearby table.

"You're too late. I have the codes," he said with a grin.

"Why? Why do all this?"

"The same reason anyone betrays their country … money, my friend."

"Fergus, you're making a huge mistake. I can help you," Christian said.

"You're such a poster child for MI6. They should give you a medal or some fancy corner office, really," he laughed. "You know, your precious Lancelot tried to stop me too, just before I shot the poor bastard."

"You make me sick, you fucking coward traitor!" Christian growled.

"Easy now. You wouldn't want me to hurt the little lass … now, would you?" Fergus smiled like a Cheshire cat.

Christian moved her aim from his direction to the necklace in a split second and he reacted, moving his gun away from Natalia. She readjusted and fired, piercing his forehead. Then, she fired two more shots into the necklace, shattering it into teeny tiny pieces as he crumbled to the floor in a heap.

Natalia hurried away from the dead man as blood seeped from the hole above his right eye. "Who are you?" she whispered, terrified this new man would kill her, too.

Christian tucked her gun into the back of her waistband and reached up, turning off the recorder on the glasses, before pulling the prosthetic skin from her face to reveal herself.

Natalia gasped in shock. "Christian!" she cried, rushing into her arms as tears streamed down her face. "I thought I would never see you again."

"I couldn't let that happen," Christian said, kissing her softly as she held her close. "Come on, we have to get out of here," she added, backing away and grabbing Natalia's hand.

"Where are we going?"

"The one place no one will ever think to look for you," Christian stated as they got into the car Fergus had been driving because Emir's body was slumped over the steering wheel of the other one.

*

Back at the hotel, Christian quickly gathered her things while Natalia showered the grime off her body. "We need to keep moving," she said when Natalia appeared in the doorway, dressed in Christian's clothes, which were a size too big. "How are you feeling?"

"I'm okay. Hungry … but, okay," she replied.

Christian stepped closer and wrapped her in a hug. Natalia closed her eyes and listened to Christian's heartbeat as she held her.

"Come on. We'll eat at the airport. We have to go," Christian said, pulling away and grabbing her bag.

Christian drove Fergus's car over to the parliament building, then walked back across the street where Natalia waited in her rental car.

CHAPTER THIRTY

Christian stared through the windshield at the stars in the sky as she drove. Nothing had gone as planned in the last three weeks. Her life was always controlled, with every mission calculated from beginning to end ... until she met the woman beside her. Christian let out a slow breath as her eyes moved from the sky to the mass of wavy hair on her shoulder where Natalia's head lay. Completely exhausted, she'd fallen asleep minutes after they got onto the desolate highway.

Noticing Natalia stir against her in the seat, more than likely reliving a hellish nightmare from the last seventy-two hours, Christian reached over and ran her hand along the arm of the slumbering woman, wishing she could pull her close. She hadn't said much during the entire day as they'd traveled from Rabat by plane on three separate flights lasting more than eight hours, before landing in Finland and switching to a rental car.

Seeing white lights in the distance, Christian knew they were getting close to the border. She pulled over on the side of the road and pulled out her make-up kit. Then, she reached over, gently shaking Natalia. "You have to wake up...just for a bit," she said softly.

Natalia stiffened but quickly relaxed when she opened her eyes and saw Christian beside her. "What time is it?"

"12:44AM. We're about to cross the border. I need you to pretend to be asleep but get up groggily when I wake you. You won't have to say much. If I nod my head, say, 'Da'. If I shake my head, say, 'Net'. Make sure to say them with confidence. Okay?"

"Da and net. Yes. Where the hell are we?" she questioned, looking around at the darkness.

"The middle of nowhere."

Natalia shivered and reached over, turning the heat up a little higher in the car. Blankets of white snow covered everything around them. Every time she closed her eyes, she was back in that damp, cold, dingy room, but as soon as she opened them, Christian was there by her side, allowing her to breathe a sigh of relief. She couldn't find the words to say to thank her because 'thank you' didn't seem like enough. And … she didn't want it to be either.

*

It took less than twenty minutes for Christian to go through the same routine of applying prosthetic skin and a full beard of facial hair, similar to what she'd done earlier in the day for her meeting at the Moroccan Parliament building. However, this time she hadn't taken as much care to perfect her disguise. It was the middle of the night, and she needed to look less dapper.

Before spraying her throat with the concoction that would temporarily change her voice, she looked over at Natalia, who was stunned at the transformation.

"That's phenomenal," she uttered.

Christian smiled thinly. "How are you feeling?" she asked, reaching over and squeezing her hand.

"I'm okay. I'll be better when you are you again. The beard reminds me of one of the men who was keeping me in that room. I don't like it."

Christian nodded and sprayed her throat. Then, she put the kit away and pulled two passports out of her bag, before getting back on the road.

*

The border guards had thick, dark-colored beards and wore heavy, combat-style clothing to ward off the cold weather and profound snow. Christian pulled the small car up alongside the booth as the men stepped out in front of her.

"It's a little late for border crossing," one of them said in Russian.

"Da," she said with a nod, handing him their passports. "I'm Dr. Dmitri Sarkov and this is my wife, Mischa Sarkova. You'll have to excuse her acrimony. We were on a much needed trip away when I got an emergency call from a patient. She's only twenty-six weeks, and she's gone into labor with her firstborn. I'm rushing back to see if I can stop it before she loses the child," she continued, also speaking Russian.

"Where at?"

"Lesogorsky," she lied.

The man read over both passports, noticing they shared a Lesogorsky address. Then, he went back into the booth while the other guard kept his place in front of the car. Using his computer, the guard looked up Dr. Dmitri Sarkov. The name came up in the system as a male OBGYN in Lesogorsky. However, there was no picture listed. Stepping out of the booth, he handed the passports back to Christian and nodded to the guard in front of the car. "Welcome home," he said, looking at Natalia a little longer than he should have.

"Da," she growled, folding her arms.

The man grinned and backed away as the gate opened.

Christian let out a deep breath as she passed through and kept on going towards the urban locality known as Svetogorsk in the Leningrad Oblast. It was situated on the bank of the Vuoksi River in Northwest Russia, 20 km from Finland.

"Are we seriously in Russia?" Natalia questioned, looking back at the distant border in the side mirror. The lights were almost completely out of sight.

"Yes," Christian replied.

"Are you sure this is the best place to go?"

"Yes," Christian replied.

Are—"

"Trust me," Christian sighed, grabbing her hand. She rubbed her thumb across the back of Natalia's soft skin. "No one will know you are here. I know these agents well."

"Didn't you know the operative who held me hostage, too?"

Natalia hadn't meant the words to be harsh, but Christian took them as such. Natalia had every right to question her. Christian had handed her over to a traitor who nearly killed her, and she was sure she would never let it go.

"I'm sorry. I shouldn't have said that," Natalia uttered.

"No. You're right. I knew Fergus McDonald. We worked on a mission together about four years ago. You have every right not to trust anyone in MI6, but I assure you, we're not all corrupt. I have no idea what changed Fergus, or why he decided to work for a terrorist group. I haven't seen him since that mission. However," Christian paused, turning down a side road once she entered the town. She kept her eyes glued to her mirrors, looking for a tail.

"The two agents we are about to meet are nothing like Fergus. In fact, they're not operatives. They're agents. I can't tell you anything else. It's way above my pay grade. What I do know is, they will keep you safe. I'd trust them with my own life," she finished, taking a couple more turns.

"Are you sure you know where you're going?" Natalia questioned, feeling as if they might be lost.

Christian ignored her as she checked the mirrors again. There was no sign of anyone following them. She quickly made a U-turn and cut down another side street that led to a neighborhood full of small houses with small yards. She pulled into one of the driveways and cut the engine off. The house in front of them was brown with a green door and white window trim. It had a detached, single car garage next to it, painted in the same colors. Together, the two buildings looked like a gingerbread house.

"Come on," Christian said, opening her door. She placed her hand on the gun in the waistband of her pants, more out of peace of mind than anything else, but it was also a habit.

"Dmitri," a man said, speaking in Russian. The lines in his face and deep set of his beady, brown eyes made him look at least fifteen years older than Christian. He had dark hair, thinning into a widow's peak, and a thick salt and pepper beard that he kept short and clean. He appeared every bit as Russian as the guards at the border.

Christian rushed Natalia into the house and closed the door. The man stood behind it, staring through the peep hole at the dark street. As soon as the coast was clear, Christian peeled the fake skin and facial hair from her face.

"You looked handsome, but I like you better like this," a woman said in Russian, causing Christian to smile at her. "You had a long trip. Are you hungry?" she asked, looking at Natalia. She was about the same age as the man, but the lines on her face appeared somewhat softer. She had shoulder-length, chestnut colored hair that curled outward at the bottom, and big brown eyes.

"Natalia, this is Adrik Volkov and his wife, Lera Volkova," Christian said, then switched to Russian. "Adrik, Lera, thank you for doing this. I don't want to cause any trouble for you."

"Nonsense," Lera said, waving for them to sit on the couch.

Natalia had no idea what they were all saying, but when Christian sat down, she moved with her. The living room of the house was small, with a sofa, two side chairs, and a coffee table. A TV hung above the fireplace. There was a hallway on the side that led to the kitchen and dining room, which combined, were no bigger than the living area. A half bath was next to the staircase that led up to the two bedrooms and additional bathroom.

"Does she speak Russian?" Adrik asked.

Christian shook her head.

He sighed as he scratched his thin beard. "Have you heard anything from London?"

"Come. I make coffee," Lera said in English as she patted Natalia on the arm.

Christian nodded and watched them walk down the hall. "No. I changed my sim card in my phone when I went dark. I'm off the grid at the moment. What about you? Has there been chatter?"

Adrik shook his head. "You are probably in contact way more than we are. However, I did see this," he said, handing her his phone.

Christian scrolled through the funeral notice regarding Lancelot's upcoming service in three days. She shook her head as she handed it back to him. "I don't know how far this goes. I have to keep digging. I'm booked on a flight out of St. Petersburg ..." She checked her watch, it was nearing one a.m. "At noon," she continued.

"You should leave with the heavy morning traffic, so you blend in. The girl will be fine with us. We'll keep her safe. Four people know where we are, and three of them are in this house. If Fergus McDonald accessed our assignment here, the UK has much bigger problems than SAT codes."

"Thank you," Christian said.

"Keep me informed on what's going on. I'll let you know if I pick up any chatter through my contacts," he said as Lera and Natalia walked back into the room.

"We should get you situated," Lera said. "I know you were traveling all day."

"Yes, and I have to leave again soon," Christian stated.

"What?" Natalia stared at her.

"Come, Lera. I'll fill you in. The room upstairs to the right is all yours," Adrik said.

Christian nodded and waited for them to get up the staircase. Then, she grabbed Natalia's hand and motioned for her to sit down. "MI6 was compromised. I have to go. That's all I can tell you. I'm sorry."

"Compromised? No shit! One of your operatives tried to kill me!"

"I know that," Christian sighed. "I need to find out who else is involved."

"What about my mother?"

"I'm going to find her, too."

"Then, I'm going with you. I'm done with all of these damn spy games, Christian."

"Natalia, I can't do what I need to do with you in tow. You have to stay here. When it is safe, Adrik and Lera will make sure you are on the first flight back to Portugal."

"When are you leaving?" Natalia sighed, unhappy with the situation.

"In the morning," Christian answered. "Go on up and get some sleep. You're safe here. I promise."

"What about you? You look exhausted, Christian."

"I'll be fine down here."

"Where? On the couch?" Natalia questioned, shaking her head.

Christian didn't need to be coerced. As soon as Natalia stood and held her hand out, she grabbed it, letting the smaller woman pull her to her feet. Together, they headed up the narrow staircase.

*

Natalia was fast asleep by the time Christian walked out of the bathroom and into their shared bedroom. She eased into bed, careful not to disturb her. She thought about the last four weeks as she lied awake, listening to the even breathing of the slumbering woman next to her. Both of their lives had changed so drastically, she wondered if either of them would ever go back to normal. Honestly, she wondered what normal was anymore. She bounced from mission to mission with little downtime in between, but she loved every minute of it. The thrill of not knowing what was next was an adrenaline rush like no other. The only other thing in the world to ever make her feel so alive was the woman lying next to her, and that scared Christian to death. She sighed inwardly and rolled towards the window, away from Natalia, as she closed her eyes.

*

A couple hours later, Christian awoke to Natalia thrashing around. She rolled over, trying to comfort the woman through her nightmare. Natalia's face was covered with wet tears as she cried in her sleep.

"Wake up," Christian whispered. "It's only a dream."

Natalia murmured, but Christian couldn't understand her. She wrapped her arms around Natalia, pulling her against her chest. "It's okay. I'm here. I'm right here," she whispered in her ear. "Listen to my voice. Come back to me, Natalia."

Slowly, Natalia calmed down. She stopped thrashing and crying, and her breathing returned to normal. Christian watched her eyes gradually open in the soft moonlight cascading in through the window.

"Christian?" she whispered, almost questioning her vision.

"I'm here," Christian said, releasing her hold.

"No ... don't let go ... please," she begged.

"I won't." Christian swallowed the lump in her throat. "Are you okay?"

Natalia nodded against her chest. "It was so real. He was hurting you. I ... I watched you die," she whimpered.

"Who?"

"The guy who had me …"

"Fergus?"

"Yes."

Christian let out a deep breath. "I'm right here, alive. Feel me," she said, putting Natalia's hand on her face. "I'm alive."

Natalia sat up, their faces inches apart as she looked into Christian's eyes. "I've never felt so much pain and agony. I couldn't do anything to help you. I just … I just watched," she mumbled as a tear rolled down her cheek.

"It wasn't real," Christian whispered. "I'm alive. This is real. Right here, right now," she said, wiping the tears from her face as she pressed her lips to Natalia's in a warm, soft kiss.

Natalia deepened the kiss, opening her mouth to Christian and moaning as their tongues touched.

Christian held her breath, reveling in the kiss as long as she could. She tried pulling away, as cool air began to fill the space between them, chilling their heated skin, but Natalia pulled her close once more.

"Make love to me, Christian," she whispered.

Unable to say no, she closed the space between them, pushing Natalia to her back as their lips met once more. The arousing kiss was slow and languid, waking every cell in Natalia's body. Their tongues moved together in a devilishly slow tango. Christian pulled Natalia's bottom lip between her teeth, nipping and licking it before diving back in for another deep kiss.

Natalia's hands ran down Christian's sides and up her back, tugging her shirt with them. Christian broke the kiss, pulling away enough to shed her t-shirt and shorts, and help Natalia out of her own clothing.

Their bodies moved against each other, enjoying the nude, soft feeling of skin to skin. Christian ran her mouth over Natalia's chest above her breasts and slid her hand down her flat stomach to the outside of her thigh. Working her way lower, she dragged her lips over her stomach, licking the circle of her naval as she followed the path of her hand.

Natalia's breath hitched in her chest as Christian's mouth skimmed over her thigh and down to her knee. Christian paused, leaning back enough to make eye contact with the woman under her. Then, she continued her leisurely descent to Natalia's ankle before moving to the other leg and working her way back up excruciatingly slow.

"I need you," Natalia whispered breathlessly.

Christian kept her eyes on Natalia's as her mouth crept up Natalia's leg. Her tongue snaked out across her thigh, slipping dangerously close to her center, before moving up to her hip. Christian's hands stayed on the bed, flanking Natalia's torso as her mouth continued its northern path over her stomach and up between her breasts, finally landing on her lips once again in a searing kiss.

Natalia wrapped her arms around Christian with one hand tangled in her short curls and the other running up and down the corded muscles of her back. Christian's thigh slipped between Natalia's, causing Natalia's wet center to connect with it while Natalia's thigh slipped between Christian's legs, pushing against her wetness. Joined together, they moved as one, rubbing back and forth in sync with their kissing. Despite the house being cold from the freezing temperatures outside, their bodies were heated and covered in a light sheen of sweat.

The feeling of Christian on top of her, rocking in a slow, steady motion, nearly drove Natalia over the edge.

She wanted to burn that feeling into her memory in hopes she'd never forget it.

Christian broke the kiss, sliding her lips down to Natalia's neck to the soft spot behind her ear.

"You feel so good," Natalia murmured, running her hands up and down Christian's back.

Christian applied more pressure to Natalia's center as her thigh moved against it, causing her to moan. She forgot about the agents sleeping next door as she ran her tongue along the outside of Natalia's ear, then kissed her way back down her neck. Pushing up on her elbows, she continued her kisses across Natalia's chest. Inching lower, she sucked one brown nipple between her lips, flicking its tip with her tongue. Natalia arched her back, urging Christian to suck her other nipple as she whimpered with pleasure.

Moving back up, Christian claimed Natalia's mouth in another heated kiss. Natalia's hips lifted in search of Christian's hand as it slipped between her legs, but Christian only grazed the inside of her thigh before shifting to Natalia's side.

Natalia followed, settling herself face to face with Christian, both on their sides. Their sensual kissing continued like it was the oxygen they needed to breathe. Leaning back slightly, Natalia put space between their chests and dragged her hand up, cupping one of Christian's breasts. Christian hissed against her mouth as Natalia rolled her nipple between her finger and thumb.

Christian pressed her thigh between Natalia's legs once more. Warm wetness coated her skin as she slid her hand over Natalia's back to the dip at her waist. Feeling Natalia moving against her made Christian's center throb. She adjusted her leg, spreading Natalia's thighs as she skimmed her hand over her stomach, inching lower until her fingers passed through the wet folds.

"Mmmm," Natalia growled, urging her hips forward as she spread her legs further.

Christian paused her movement and reached up, and grabbing Natalia's hand, she pushed it down between her own legs, pressing her fingers into the wetness. She bit her bottom lip hard as Natalia began to slowly stroke her. Moving her hand back between Natalia's legs, she made a lazy path through her folds, careful not to graze her swollen center or dip inside.

The snow clouds outside finally drifted away, allowing the full moon to shine through the slits of the blinds, casting the room in moonlit stripes. Natalia's eyes locked onto Christian's before their lips met in a breathless kiss. Their bodies rocked together in a slow and steady rhythm, neither in a hurry to end the passion burning between them.

Christian ran her tongue around the edge of Natalia's lips. Mimicking the same motion with her fingers, she teased her mouth and throbbing center before going back in for another deep kiss as her fingers passed over her swollen center. Natalia groaned against her mouth and her body trembled from the pleasure. Copying Christian's movement, she worked her fingers in delicate circles before stroking her in the same manner.

Both women pulled away from the kiss, panting as their bodies neared the edge of climax.

"Cum with me," Christian whispered in Natalia's ear as she pushed her fingers deep inside of her.

"Oh God," Natalia groaned, slipping her fingers inside of Christian, matching her stroke for stroke.

Their thrusting hips matched the motion of their plunging fingers, causing the old, metal-framed bed to creak a steady cadence. Neither woman paid any attention to the sound as they traded breathless, panting kisses.

Natalia's body stiffened first as she tightened around Christian's fingers, squeezing her deep inside when she began to climax. The feeling of Natalia pulsing against her fingers sent Christian over the edge. A million shards of color flashed behind her closed eyes as she rode the enormous wave of pleasure.

Nearly a full minute passed before both women rolled limply to their backs, pulling their fingers free of the clutches that were just grasping them. A light sheen of sweat covered their naked bodies, glistening in the moonlight that was peeking through the blinds.

Christian stared out the window while her body slowly relaxed. *What am I doing?* she thought, knowing the answer.

Natalia shifted to her side, propping herself up on her elbow, slightly against Christian. She gently ran her hand over Christian's chest between her breasts.

Lulling her head to the side, Christian searched Natalia's face before locking eyes with her. "This is wrong on so many levels," she sighed, "but I can't make myself not feel," Christian whispered, running her hand over Natalia's cheek.

Natalia closed her eyes for a long second, nuzzling against the soft palm caressing her skin before meeting Christian's gaze once more. "I'm in love with you," she said softly.

Christian moved her hand to the back of Natalia's neck, pulling her down as their lips met in a sultry kiss. Then, without parting their lips, she rolled Natalia onto her back with Christian on top of her. Natalia wrapped her arms around Christian's shoulders.

Christian kissed her as if Natalia was the very air she breathed. Rocking back and forth, she grazed their hips together in a teasing motion. Natalia moaned against her mouth and spread her legs wider for Christian to grind against her.

Pulling out of the lascivious kiss, Christian skimmed her lips down Natalia's neck, sucking her nipples before easing further south across her flat stomach.

Natalia gasped as Christian's mouth inched lower. She threw her head back and gripped the sheets as Christian's tongue snaked out, licking her wet, pulsing center in one long, wide stroke from the bottom to the top and back down again. "Oh God," she cried out.

Christian reached up, clasping her hands with Natalia's on both sides of her hips as she swirled her tongue in circles, dipping the tip inside of her on each pass. Natalia could barely control her hips as they jerked and bucked. Each breath she took was a gulping gasp. Her heart thumped like a drum, sending scorching hot blood racing through her veins with every beat as she rode the razor-thin edge of arousal.

Christian feasted on her like a hungry animal, licking, sucking, and biting as Natalia's entire body writhed under her, completely engrossed in the raw desire pulsing through her body.

"Oh God! Yes!" Natalia shouted as her body finally let go, giving in as the animalistic orgasm consumed her.

Christian pulled her drenched mouth away, rubbing the wetness onto Natalia's quivering thigh before sliding up next to her. She wrapped her arms around the limp woman and pulled her close as she came down from the euphoric high, slowly catching her breath along the way. Exhausted, Natalia fell fast asleep with her head tucked under Christian's chin and her arm draped across her stomach.

"I love you," Christian whispered to the slumbering woman. "I know I shouldn't, but I can't help it."

CHAPTER THIRTY-ONE

The sun rose just before five a.m., shining bright rays of light through the slits in the blinds, and directly onto Christian's face. She quickly woke, having only slept a couple of hours, and slipped out of the bed, careful not to wake the slumbering woman next to her.

"Did you sleep?" Adrik asked, speaking English with a thick Russian accent. His eyes peered at Christian over the top of a dark blue coffee mug as she walked quietly into the kitchen. She was dressed once again in her jeans, a black sweatshirt, and sneakers.

"Like a baby," she replied, knowing the paper-thin walls of the old house gave away everything she and Natalia had done. The aroma of the percolating coffee smelled like heaven. Searching around for a mug of her own, she asked, "Did you sleep okay? I know it probably wasn't easy having us here."

He nodded. "Sounded like it was a lot easier for the two of you to be here."

Christian raised a brow but didn't say anything.

"Are you sure that's wise?" he asked, finally pointing to the cabinet beside the sink where the mugs were stored.

Christian poured steaming hot coffee into a red mug with the Russian flag printed on the side, reminding her of something she'd find in an airport gift shop.

"Cream and sugar are in those canisters," Adrik said. "The coffee here is like mud."

"I remember," she replied, adding a tablespoon of each to her cup. She thought about his question. Was it wise? Of course not. But neither was his choice to take them in, especially knowing she'd gone dark. Having the two of them there could compromise all of the work he and Lera had done for their assignment. Christian leaned against the counter across from his position at the tiny kitchen table and took a long sip. "Honestly, I don't know what's wise anymore," she sighed. "A month ago, I was working a mission in Madrid. I had a purpose. I had a handler. I had a life. I did my job. I went home. I've been running for my life ever since, doing everything I can to keep this woman … a stranger until four weeks ago, safe from God knows who. My handler is dead. I have no idea what the mission even is anymore, or who is in charge because I've gone dark, completely turning my back on the agency. So … is it wise? Who the fuck knows, but I can't make myself not care for her. I'm done trying. All I can do now is figure out whoever is behind all of this so that he can be stopped and she can finally go home safely."

"The agency hasn't turned its back on you. That I assure you. You're doing the right thing, Christian. Based on what you've told me, she's innocent in all of this. I just don't want—"

"I need to get on the road," Christian said, cutting him off. "Thank you again for taking her in. I'll be in touch when she has the green light to travel." She finished her coffee and set the mug in the sink beside her. Then, she walked over, holding her hand out.

Adrik gave a small nod as he shook her hand.

Without another word, Christian turned and left the room. The soft click of the front door echoed in the small house, followed a minute later by the sound of a car engine.

"She blows in and out like the Santa Ana winds, bringing the heat, fanning the wildfires, and leaving everything burned in her wake," Natalia mumbled from the doorway of the kitchen.

Adrik looked up at the sleepy young woman. She was wearing a t-shirt and sweatpants that were a size too big. Her wavy, dark hair was slightly disheveled. He waved to the seat across from him. "Coffee?" he asked.

Natalia nodded.

He stood and walked over to the counter. "The life of an operative is never easy," he began as he reached for a mug. "She won't stop until the mission is completed. That's ingrained in all of us," he continued, filling the solid black mug. "I know you care for her. That's ... it's something we do not do. The agency doesn't give us the freedom to get close to anyone." He handed her the mug, then sat back down. "However, she's obviously gotten close to you," he added, shaking his head.

"Why is that such a problem?" she questioned harshly.

"Because you are the mission," he sighed.

"I don't know what really happened, or why it happened. My life has been turned upside down. I've been shot at, kidnapped, shuffled around the world ... and I still don't understand any of it. But what I do know is I trust Christian. She will come back to me, and when she does, I'll be waiting for her," she snapped before leaving the room, taking her coffee mug with her.

"She's in love," Lera said in Russian. She'd been in the living room, listening in, and Natalia had just missed her as she headed back up the stairs.

"She's going to get her heart broken," he replied.

"You don't know that. It sounded pretty mutual to me last night." She gave him a stern look. "People do actually fall in love; in case you've forgotten."

"People … not MI6 operatives."

Lera shook her head.

"I believe it is better to love whom one cannot have," he stated.

"Better … probably," she replied. "It's certainly safer. But Christian knows what she's doing, or she wouldn't have done it. She's a very good operative … one of the best you and I have ever seen. Give her more credit, and leave that girl up there alone," she said, pointing up at the ceiling. "She's been through hell."

Adrik finished his coffee without saying anything else. He was sure Christian was making a mistake, but he knew Lera was right. He also knew not to argue with her. He and Lera were about as far away from in love as you could get. They had been on a deep undercover assignment in Russia for almost three years now; living together as a married Russian couple and working regular jobs. Christian had been partnered up with them almost two years ago when she was in the country working and their missions' crossed paths. She didn't know a great deal about why they were there, no one did except their handler, but she knew they were MI6 agents who were deep undercover, and trustworthy.

"You're sleeping on the couch tonight. You snore like a locomotive," Lera added as she began the prep work for breakfast. Natalia had no idea they were pretending to be a married couple, so as long as she was there, they'd have to play house.

Adrik rolled his eyes and shook his head. "There couldn't have been much snoring because all I heard was—"

Lera cleared her throat, having heard the squeak of the stairs as Natalia descended them.

"I hate to be a bother," she said, walking into the kitchen with her empty mug.

"Oh, you're no bother, dear," Lera replied in English with a thick Russian accent as she gave Adrik the side eye over Natalia's shoulder. "You want more coffee? Adrik, get the girl some coffee."

His grumpy pout was hidden behind his thick beard as he moved to go refill her mug.

"I've got it," Natalia said. "You took me in when you didn't have to. The least I can do is help myself. May I help you with breakfast?"

Lera waved her off and went back to what she was doing.

Natalia poured herself another cup of coffee and sat down at the table across from Adrik, who was reading what appeared to be a newspaper. She turned her attention to the window where flakes of snow slowly floated past, adding to the white blanket of powder covering the ground.

*

Christian was halfway through her seven-hour flight to Lyon, France when her mind drifted back to that morning, when she'd woken with Natalia curled up against her.

After slipping out of bed and dressing quickly, Christian had walked back over to the bed. Natalia was sleeping peacefully when Christian bent down, kissing her cheek with a feather light touch. Then, she backed away, taking one last look, and burning the image of the beautiful woman into her mind before grabbing her backpack and quietly leaving the room.

Her phone beeped with a text message, pulling Christian from her thoughts. It was Colette. HAVE NEW INFO. WILL RENDEZVOUS AS SCHEDULED. "New info?" Christian said aloud, wondering what she'd found as she checked the GPS on her phone. The plane still had another thousand kilometers to go.

Turning her attention to the window, she was happy to be out of miserably cold and snowy Russia, especially after a hairy, two-hour drive to St. Petersburg on icy roads, but leaving Natalia behind had been difficult. She trusted Adrik and Lera to keep her safe, but she'd also trusted Fergus McDonald. It still blew her mind that he'd turned on the agency. She'd heard stories of agents becoming corrupt but had never witnessed it firsthand. The fact that he was now dead was a double-edged sword. He couldn't do anymore infiltrating for whatever terrorist group he was working for, but at the same time, she was unable to get that information out of him.

"Would you care for lunch service, miss?" the flight attendant asked, stopping next to her first-class seat. "We have a vegetable tray, a fruit and cheese tray, or a turkey sandwich, or you may upgrade to our premium dish which is a chicken cordon bleu quesadilla."

"I'll have the upgrade," Christian said, pulling a couple of Euros from her pocket to pay the extra charge.

The attendant smiled, lingering a bit too long after handing Christian her lunch. She simply ignored the young woman as she went to work filling her empty belly, one bite at a time.

*

The next time the flight attendant bothered Christian it was to wake her because the plane was landing. Christian was surprised she'd fallen asleep, but happy to have gotten some much needed rest.

"You looked sad in your sleep," the young woman said.

Feeling a little disturbed that the flight attendant had watched her sleep, Christian simply nodded.

"Do you live in Lyon?" she asked, smiling like a schoolgirl with a crush.

"No," Christian answered honestly.

"Shame. I was hoping to see you again."

"I'm just passing through," Christian replied before ignoring her as she readied herself and her bag for the landing. When she looked back up, the woman was gone.

She watched through the window as the ground came closer and closer. *Natalia would have a death grip on my hand right now*, she thought, making her smile. The plane touched down with barely a bump and slowed to a crawl before taxiing around to the gate.

As soon as she was off the plane, Christian made her way through customs, claiming nothing, then headed outside where a slew of taxis were lined along the curb, waiting to take new arrivals wherever they wanted to go.

"Combien coûte aller au Vieux Lyon?" she asked.

The driver leaning against the car uncrossed his arms and stepped closer. She spoke perfectly, so he knew she wasn't a tourist he could rip off. "Trente cinq Euros," he said.

Christian nodded and opened the back door of the small car. "La rue du Palais de Justice du Vieux Lyon s'il vous plaît," she said, telling him she was going to the courthouse. Then, she pulled the worn, black ball cap from her backpack and slipped it on her head, tucking it low.

He nodded and pulled out into traffic. It was after seven p.m., but there was still close to two hours of daylight left, and an hour before her scheduled meeting with Colette at the same café where they'd met before.

Christian glanced through the window at Lyon-Bron, a smaller domestic airport, as they passed by, then switched her view to the large blue Ikea store on the opposite side of the A32. The driver made mention of the traffic, but she ignored him, wishing she'd rented a car. When they crossed the Rhône River, she perked up a little, knowing they were getting closer. The driver skirted alongside the river in heavy traffic, then crossed the Saône River, which dumped him into Vieux Lyon. Then, he drove along the river once again before turning on the street beside the courthouse.

"Voici bon, merci," she said.

The driver pulled over to the curb and came to a stop. Christian pulled forty Euros from her pocket, handing the banknotes to him before getting out. He drove away, slipping back into the traffic as she headed off on foot in the opposite direction. The café was a block up and two blocks over. She reached it within two minutes walking at a relaxed, but steady pace.

"Bonsoir," the waiter said, nodding in Christian's direction as she sat down at one of the outdoor tables.

"Bonsoir," she replied, adding, "deux cafés s'il vous plaît."

"Annuler la commande," Colette said, stopping the waiter from placing the order.

Christian raised a brow, surprised and a little peeved the woman had snuck up on her. *I must be more tired than I thought.* She put her backpack over her shoulder and followed Colette when she began walking away. "What was that about?"

"Too many people," Colette mumbled. "Get in," she added, pointing to a black Fiat.

Christian slid into the passenger seat and tucked her backpack on the floor between her feet as the tiny car sped away. "Slow down before you kill us or bring attention to us … or both!"

"Nous devons nous dépêcher," Colette said, shifting gears.

"Hurry? Where are we going?"

"Paris."

"Paris? What?"

"Oui," Colette replied, keeping her eyes on the road.

"Wait! Pull over!"

"There's no time, Christian!"

"What did you find out?"

"A man named Farooq Ashraf Massoud funded the operation to steal the SATCOM codes."

"How did you find this?"

"I've been tracing every email from Emir Al-Kahlef's accounts ever since you got me into his phone. He had several email exchanges with someone who had a highly encrypted server. I finally broke through and traced the IP address to this Farooq guy. Then, I connected several of the phone calls to him as well. He's a very rich Algerian with ties to Western Sahara ... the Polisario Front to be exact."

"Are you serious?" Christian muttered in shock.

"Oui. Ça a empiré," she sighed. "As soon as I started digging, he became more and more imbedded. I found offshore bank accounts with transfers from him to Al-Khalef and Al-Khalef to Fergus McDonald. It's all connected."

"Damn it. Was he planning to start an actual war over Western Sahara?"

"My thoughts exactly."

"Where is this Farooq person?" Christian asked.

"Paris! He's a hard partier ... loves women. He's supposed to be at Le Souterrain tonight before midnight. If you miss him, he's liable to disappear off the grid."

"Does this thing go any faster?" Christian huffed.

"Five minutes ago, you wanted to slow down and pull over! Laisse-moi tranquille!" Colette growled.

Christian rolled her eyes and crossed her arms. She could do nothing but wait as they drove for the next hour and a half.

*

"How is the girl?" Colette asked, ending the silence in the car an hour later.

"Safe ... at the moment."

"You're in love with her, aren't you?"

"No."

"You're a good spy, but a shitty liar, Christian."

"We're almost there. You should stay in the car in case my place is being watched."

Colette shook her head. Christian never was one to talk about anything real, especially emotions.

CHAPTER THIRTY-TWO

"He's into women ... not men, Christian," Colette said as Christian opened her closet full of jeans, shirts, and pantsuits.

"I know that! Just wait in the living room, and don't open the door for anyone," she growled. "I told you to stay in the car."

"Passer à autre chose," Colette replied, walking back out to the small living area. Peeking through the closed curtains, she fixed her eyes on the lights of the Eiffel Tower, glistening in the distance.

*

With Colette out of her way, Christian pulled a box down from the top of the closet and removed the lid. Inside she retrieved a disguise she hadn't worn in at least four, maybe five years. On the top was a long, silky, black wig, which she took out, running her hand through the fake hair before placing it on her bed. Under that, was a swanky, short, black dress that left little to the imagination. She laid it next to the wig and removed the black, six-inch stiletto heels from the bottom of the box. "I hope you still fit," she said, looking at the contents sprawled on her bed.

After removing her clothes, Christian rushed around the bathroom, shaving her legs, applying make-up and tantalizing perfume, before slicking her hair back with gel so that she could glue the wig in place. She walked back into the bedroom and grabbed the right shoe from her bed. Holding it in one hand, she used her other hand to tug on the long, skinny heel. It slipped loose, revealing a razor-sharp six-inch blade hidden underneath. She checked the tip, knowing it was carved into a perfect point and ready to go. Then, she pushed the heel back over the blade and began the transformation into the French Femme Fatale ... better known as Eva Dubois.

*

Colette heard the bedroom door click open and turned around. Christian Garnier had gone into that room, but the sexy, sultry woman in front of her was certainly not the same person. "Merde! You look dressed to kill! Who are you? And what have you done with Christian?"

Christian raised a brow and shook her head.

"I'd forgotten how nice your ... assets were," Colette said, leering at her. "Then again, I'd never seen you like this."

"You'll most likely never see it again, so roll your tongue back up. We have work to do." Christian crossed the room to where her backpack sat. "I'll be wearing my WorldVision glasses, so you'll need to be on your laptop and linked in. Once I'm inside, send me his picture. I'll record everything like I did in Morocco," she said.

"Oui." Colette nodded. "Are you protected? You'll be alone, and I'm sure he has people with him."

"I'll be fine. Just make sure I get into the club."

"There's no list that I was able to find, so you'll have to work with what you have," Colette replied, indicating her disguise. "Do I even want to know where your gun is?"

"It's in my room."

"What?!"

"Exactly where would you like me to put it? In my ass or my vagina?" Christian asked, standing with her arms crossed, tapping one of her stiletto heels on the floor.

Colette shook her head. "Are you going to arrest him and hand him over to Interpol?"

Christian shook her head. "There's no protocol to follow. I'm dark … remember?"

"I'm worried," Colette sighed, not liking this plan at all. "Maybe you should call someone."

"I did. You. Now, let's go."

*

The club had a line of people outside when Christian walked up, swaying her hips and working her legs enough to get the bouncer's attention. Colette had dropped her off at the corner, then circled around to the back of the building. She turned off the car and powered up her laptop. Once she was linked to the glasses she texted: I'M IN.

Christian pushed the button to show Colette a live picture, so she'd know she was inside of the club. She went to the bar and casually looked around as she waited for the photo. The dimly lit club had three levels, and the third level had VIP ropes blocking it off. *I bet that's where you are.*

"Martini rouge s'il vous plait," Christian said, softening her voice slightly. "Où se trouvent les toilettes?" she asked when the drink was handed to her. The bartender pointed towards the back, past the entrance to the third level. She nodded, smiled, and paid the bill with the few Euros she had stuffed down between her pushed up breasts, which were squeezed together to form cleavage she didn't really have.

Christian meandered through the crowd, pouring a little of the drink out here and there without anyone noticing so that it wasn't full and sloshing any longer. She didn't drink much to begin with and certainly wasn't going to drink something in a dark club that could have easily been spiked. She sighed in relief as the picture finally came through. She went to the bathroom, hoping the light was bright enough for her to see the image. As she passed by the third level stairs, she made sure to move slowly, sashaying her body enough to accentuate the fake curves the disguise had created on her lithe frame. She had to admit, she liked the way her legs looked with the heels keeping her calves tight.

The lights in the restroom were much brighter, allowing her to see the photo. Farooq Ashraf Massoud had thick, dark hair, a thin mustache and large ears that matched his square face. His eyes were dark and beady, and he had a medium build. She touched the arm of her glasses to push the button that cleared the picture from her view, then she walked out of the bathroom with her half empty glass.

"Excusez-moi," a man said, stepping in front of Christian. "Rencontre mon ami."

Christian smiled and shrugged innocently. "Anglais?" she said, pretending she didn't speak French.

"Anglais? Oui." He nodded. "Bashir. And you are?" he asked, holding out his hand.

"Eva," she replied, taking his hand.

"Come. Meet my friend," he said, leading her up the stairs.

Christian glanced around, looking for the man in the photo, but Bashir led her straight to him. Farooq Ashraf Massoud was sitting in a large leather chair, with two women dressed similar to Christian, flanking him and sitting on the arms of the chair. He cocked his head to the side, taking Christian in from the bottom to the top. He raised a brow and grinned, then patted the women's butts as if to shoo them away.

Christian moved closer, claiming a seat on the arm of the chair and crossing her legs so that her dress slid dangerously high on her thigh.

"And you are?" he asked in English with a thick accent as his hand passed over her leg.

Christian leaned over, giving him a good look at her cleavage as she whispered in his ear, "Eva."

"I am Farooq," he said, resting his hand at the edge of her dress, teasingly sliding a finger underneath it. "Tell me. What is a beautiful woman such as yourself doing in the club this late at night?"

"The same thing you are," she replied huskily as she uncrossed, and then re-crossed her legs, trapping his hand between them in a move of pure seduction.

"You are asking for trouble," he mumbled.

"Am I?"

"Are you a bad girl … Eva?" he asked, moving his trapped hand against her crotch.

"I can be as bad as you want me to be … or I can be very, very good."

He watched her tongue snake out, licking her painted lips. Then, he grabbed her hand, placing it on his hardness. She squeezed, then thrust her hand back and forth, jerking him.

He stilled her hand and nodded at Bashir. "Let's go to my private room. I want you all to myself," he said, standing and tugging her up against his side.

Bashir led the way as they walked to the back of the third level, and down a short hallway. The walls, floor, and ceiling were all painted black, making it look like a maze in a haunted house. The brushed-chrome knob jutting out was the only indication a door was even there. Bashir turned the knob and held the door open. Farooq nodded for Christian to enter first. He followed, closing and locking the door behind himself.

The room was small, maybe six by ten, with a long, black, leather sofa against the far wall, and a wet bar along the left side. A side door led to a small bathroom.

"Would you like a drink?" he asked.

Christian locked eyes with him and shook her head no.

Her hips swayed and the muscles of her legs contracted as she moved closer, nearly up against him face to face. "Shall we sit?" she asked.

He leaned in, kissing her neck and groping her pushed up breasts. Christian backed away and reached up, adjusting her glasses and turning them on as she sat down on the couch. He watched her for a second, before joining her.

"What is it that you do, Farooq?" she asked, running her hand up his thigh.

"That's not why you're here."

"I can't know anything about you?" she pouted, sliding her hand back towards his knee. "What if I want to see you again?"

"I will find you if and when I want to make your acquaintance."

"I didn't know there were rules."

"Now you do."

Christian moved her hand back up, rubbing his hardness over and over. "Where are you from? I'm not sure of your accent."

"Algeria," he said, stilling her hand. "I didn't bring you in here to ask me questions and jack me off, Eva."

Christian climbed on top of him, hiking her dress up around her waist as she straddled his lap. She ran her hands up and down his chest and began unbuttoning his shirt as she rocked her hips back and forth against him. The thick patch of dark curly hair covering his chest was revealed as she opened his shirt. Running her fingers through the hair, she located his nipples, pinching and pulling them as she grinded against his hardness poking up at her.

"Do you want to fuck me?" she asked, biting and sucking his ear.

"Yes," he moaned.

"Hard?"

"Yes."

She pushed herself harder against his bulge as he began to pant. Reaching down and squeezing him, she could tell he was about to explode. "Tell me about the codes."

"Huh?"

She squeezed him harder. "The codes, Farooq. You paid a lot of money to Emir Al-Khalef for some codes."

"How do you know this?" he stumbled, trying to sit up, but she had him pinned with his pecker in her hand.

"Tell me!" she growled, tugging him.

"Okay. Okay," he panted. "Who are you?"

"Your worst nightmare," she growled in a low tone. "Now tell me about Emir Al-Khalef …"

"Morocco took Western Sahara from the Sahrawi People … my people," he grunted as she continued to squeeze him.

"Keep going."

"Emir was a traitor to his country. I used his hatred to help me get the satellite codes."

"Who else is involved?"

He shrugged.

"Who else, Farooq?" she yelled.

"I don't know. Emir put together the plan on his end. He was supposed to deliver the codes to me himself. He said he knew a guy who could help us."

Fergus McDonald. Christian shook her head. "What were you planning to do with them?"

He swallowed hard, fighting back the pain.

"Answer me!"

"Take the war to Morocco where it belongs. Western Sahara will never be theirs. With those codes, the Polisario Front will win once and for all, and I will be a martyr to my people!" he yelled as he grabbed her, trying to throw her off of him.

Christian kept a death grip on his penis as she reached down, removing her stiletto with her other hand. In one swift motion, she let go of him, removed the heel cover, and shoved the six-inch blade through the front of his throat. Blood spewed, and Farooq thrashed around for a few seconds, before going completely limp. His bulging eyes stared straight at her.

She turned off the recorder on her glasses and climbed off him, heading directly to the bathroom. Blood spatter covered her arms like tiny red freckles. Avoiding her own eyes in the mirror, she pumped soap into her hands. A pool of red filled the sink, lightening to near pink as it mixed with water and swirled down the drain. Once her arms and hands were clean, Christian rinsed off the knife and slid the stiletto cover back over it.

Back in the room, she grabbed the liquor with the highest proof, dousing Farooq's body and the couch, as well as the carpet in the room. She found a pack of matches in his jacket pocket and lit several, tossing them where she'd poured the booze. Bright orange flames flashed immediately, covering the dead man, the couch, and the carpet all around it. Christian moved towards the door and waited for the smoke to fill the room as the flames licked the wall behind the couch. When she could no longer breathe, she beat on the door, knowing Bashir was outside. "Help! Help!" she screamed. When she heard him trying to get in, she turned the lock and rushed out of the room, knocking him to the ground. He jumped up and ran into the room, trying to get to Farooq, but the flames were too hot. Half of the room was engulfed, and Farooq's limp body was in the center of the fire. The fire alarm began screeching loudly and the house lights came on as people trampled each other to get out of the over capacity building.

*

"Qu'est-ce qui est arrivé?!" Colette exclaimed as Christian slid into the passenger seat of the car.

"Drive!" Christian yelled. "Aller! Aller!"

Colette started the car and squealed the tires as she took off down the street, opposite the fire trucks screaming towards the burning building. "Why is the club on fire?"

Christian didn't answer. She stared in the side mirror as she removed the wig that was glued to her skin.

"Réponds-moi maintenant. Christian, did you start the fire?"

"It doesn't matter. The least you know, the better. Head back to my apartment. I need to pick up a few things, then you can drop me at the airport."

"Aéroport? Where are you going? It's the middle of the night."

"Where is your laptop?" Christian asked, ignoring her.

"In the backseat. I copied everything to the same thumb drive from when you were in Morocco. It's sitting in the cup holder."

Christian felt around in the dark.

Colette reached down and handed it to her. "Spies and their secrets," she mumbled.

*

It took less than ten minutes for them to arrive back at Christian's apartment. She quickly washed the make-up off her face and wet her hair, trying to towel out as much of the stiff gel as she could. Then, she changed into jeans, a t-shirt, and sneakers, and packed a few things into her hanging bag. On the way out, she grabbed her backpack and took one last look around.

"Do you even have a flight reservation? It's the middle of the night. There aren't many flights departing," Colette said when she got back into the car, looking like her old self once again.

"Je vais bien mon ami," Christian reassured, checking her watch. Her flight was the last scheduled flight out for the night. She was tired ... exhausted really, but she was almost finished with what had become the most difficult mission in her career.

CHAPTER THIRTY-THREE

The hour and a half flight to London was uneventful. Having booked at the last minute, then arriving just before the final boarding call, Christian had wound up in coach class, and a center seat to boot. As soon as the plane was on the ground, she waited patiently for the long line of passengers in front of her to exit. Then, she slipped her backpack over her shoulders and grabbed her hanging bag from the overhead bin.

London Heathrow Airport was desolate at 12:15A.M. The only people working were the cleaning crew, emptying the trash and polishing the floors. Christian yawned twice as she walked at a brisk pace, past the crowd standing in baggage claim, and directly to the Underground Terminal. Three other people were standing on the platform when the train arrived. Christian stepped inside and took a seat facing inward so that she could see the two people, as well as the doors.

The subway ride out to Hatton Cross Station only took a few minutes. Christian stepped off when the train came to a stop. Then, she took the stairs up to the surface and paid her fare before exiting the station. A Black Taxi, Mercedes van was waiting by the curb.

"Good evening, miss," the driver said, holding the rear passenger door open. "Where to?"

"Tudor Hotel in Vauxhall, please," she said.

He nodded and climbed into the driver's seat in front of her.

Thirty minutes later, they crossed the River Thames. Christian looked out the window at the lights of Westminster across the water as they arrived in Vauxhall. She had fond memories of London. Born in Westminster, she lived in a flat there with her parents for the first six years of her life, before relocating to the states, and then Paris, returning to Westminster years later to attend Kings College.

"Tudor Hotel, miss," the driver said, clearing the stroll down memory lane from Christian's head as the van rolled to a stop in front of the large, river front building.

Leaning forward, she handed him fifty pounds worth of bank notes and helped herself out of the vehicle. It sped away as she ascended the steps.

"Good evening ... or shall I say good morning, to you, miss?" the door man said with a smile.

"A little of both, I suppose," she replied in an American accent, also smiling as she stepped inside.

The lobby of the hotel was the epitome of modern elegance with its contemporary style. Glass tables and fine leather upholstered chairs sat on top of polished, marble floors. Granite statues flanked the elevator doors. The front desk was solid black, and shiny enough to see yourself in a mirrored image when you stood in front of it.

"Welcome to Tudor Hotel," a young woman said with a big smile.

Christian nodded, handing her a passport with the name Olivia Sanford on it, and her picture. "I'm checking in."

"I'll have you processed straight away. I'm sure you're knackered after that long trip across the pond," the woman said.

Christian's eyes hovered over the woman's snug-fitting black dress. A gold nametag was just above her right breast with the name *Talia* on it. Checking her watch, she nearly gasped when she saw that it was close to two a.m.

"Here you are, room 512," Talia said, handing her a key card.

"Thanks," Christian replied, taking the card and heading towards the elevator.

*

Inside the studio room, Christian found the same modern-style décor. A queen-sized bed jutted from the back wall, with a couch, two chairs, and a coffee table to the right of it, and floor to ceiling windows beyond that. A wall-to-wall wet bar was to the left, complete with a refrigerator, a microwave, and a granite countertop with a small sink in the middle. A single door off to the side led to the closet and bathroom, where a large glass shower and soaking tub were located. The polished tile floors glistened in the bright white lighting.

After setting her backpack down and hanging her other bag in the closet, Christian walked back over to the wet bar, where a welcome note was sitting, along with a basket of fresh muffins in various flavors. She grabbed one banana nut and one blueberry muffin, then opened the refrigerator, nearly fist-pumping the air when she saw that it was stocked with bottled water.

"Dinner is served," she mumbled, walking across the room. Her eyes bounced between the pristine white, high thread-count linens and duvet on the bed, and the crème-colored couch. Shrugging, she opted for the bed and kicked off her shoes before sitting down with her back against the headboard. She couldn't remember the last meal she'd eaten, or the last time she'd done anything remotely normal.

Her mind drifted back to Natalia as she ate. "She'd be hoping I'd make a mess on the bed so she could laugh at me," Christian muttered, shaking her head. "It'll all be over soon. I promise you," she whispered, feeling a dull ache in her chest.

With her makeshift meal finished, she took a quick shower, brushed her teeth, and climbed into bed nude. She was fast asleep from pure exhaustion by the time her head hit the pillow.

*

At six a.m. Christian woke. Her internal alarm somehow always knew what time zone she was in and when to wake her. She got out of bed, stretching her arms above her head as she walked over to the window. There was already hustle and bustle in the street below, with the sun having been up for a little over an hour. She quickly dressed in jeans and a polo shirt and headed down to the restaurant for a cup of coffee. Not knowing when she'd eat again, she slapped a few strips of bacon between a croissant, making a sandwich for herself. Then, she grabbed a banana and a newspaper and went back up to her room.

As she drank her coffee and ate her breakfast, she perused the paper, looking for the obituary section.

Lawrence Dunnigan, better known as Larry to his friends and family, passed away recently. He worked behind the scenes for British Parliament for close to twenty-five years and was an avid Shakespearean. He leaves behind an ex-wife, Mildred Dunnigan, and no children. Services will be today at noon at St. Benedict Cathedral in Twickenham.

She'd never known Senior Agent Dunnigan's first name or seen him face to face for that matter. But to her, he was Lancelot, the great knight to King Arthur, and a damn good agent, whom she'd trusted with her life.

Christian tossed the banana peel into the trash and stared at her satellite phone, wanting so badly to call Adrik, even if it was just for a second to check on Natalia, but she couldn't. She had to keep her safe and off the grid until this mission was closed. She checked her watch. It was nearing 7:30.

With nothing to do for another hour and a half, she changed into shorts, a hoodie jacket with only a sports bra underneath, and a pair of sneakers, and headed out for a run along the bank of the River Thames, something she hadn't done since she was a student at Kings College.

*

Christian listened to the staccato of her sneakers on the pavement, and steady pace of her breathing as she passed by the Lambeth Bridge and back of St. Thomas Hospital. Barges and other ships littered the waterway, docked in various places as well as motoring along.

Her pace never faltered when she reached the Westminster Bridge. She took the stairs two at a time, then took the bridge across the river, carefully weaving in and out of the pedestrians who were also crossing. Beads of sweat began rising on her forehead as she shuffled down the stairs on the opposite side of the bridge, turning left onto Abingdon Street and passing by Westminster Palace, and then Victoria Tower Gardens.

She was keeping her usual pace as she crossed the Lambeth Bridge and headed back towards her hotel. The two-and-a-half-mile rectangle was shorter than her typical runs, but it still felt good to get out and stretch her legs, especially after being cooped up on airplanes for several hours over the past few days.

When she returned to her room, Christian took a quick shower, allowing the hot spray to soothe her body. Then, she dressed in jeans, sneakers, and a black polo shirt, hoping to fit in with the locals and tourists milling about, and stuffed a small thumb drive into her front pocket before leaving once more.

CHAPTER THIRTY-FOUR

It had been twenty-four hours since Christian had left Natalia sound asleep in a house with strangers, in a small, Russian village. After what she'd endured in Morocco, staying with Adrik and Lera was a cake walk, albeit an odd one. She couldn't quite figure them out. They'd talk to her in English and then have a go at each other in Russian. She wasn't sure if they were arguing or talking dirty. Instead of paying much attention to the two of them, she tried focusing her mind and energy on her mother and what she must be going through. Christian said she'd find her, and Natalia believed her.

"You cook?" Lera asked from the kitchen doorway.

Natalia was curled up in a chair by the window, staring out at the snow while a Russian show that Adrik had left on the TV, played in the background. "I know how, yes. My mother taught me when I was young. I'm afraid I don't do much cooking these days, though," she sighed.

"You miss her, yes?"

Unsure if she was referring to her mother or Christian. Maybe both. Natalia simply said, "Yes."

"Everything will be okay in the end. If it is not okay, then it is not the end."

Natalia nodded, wiping away a lone tear.

"Come. We make doughnuts," Lera said, scrunching her face in thought as she threw the dish towel over her shoulder and turned around.

Natalia shrugged and followed her. She had nothing better to do, and no idea how long she was going to be stuck there. She watched as Lera went through the cabinets and drawers, getting out the pots and pans she'd need. Then, she went through the pantry and refrigerator, pulling out all the ingredients.

"You look nervous," Lera mumbled, looking over at her.

"A little," Natalia replied.

"Vampires live in Transylvania, not Russia. I won't bite you," Lera joked dryly, causing Natalia to smile and laugh softly.

CHAPTER THIRTY-FIVE

Christian walked a couple of blocks from her hotel and up the steps of a large, modern building with a concrete and glass exterior. She touched the pads of all the fingers on her right hand to the tinted glass door. A green light flashed and she pulled the knob, opening the door. Once she was inside, she walked through a metal detector and a full body scanner. Then, she stuck her face up to what looked like a tablet screen on the wall. It scanned the retinas of her eyes and flashed a blue star in the middle, before going black again. Three men, dressed in black suits, operated the machines, while a fourth waved her through to the next room where another man in a white lab coat swabbed the inside of her mouth for a DNA analysis. He then disappeared through a side door.

A semi-circular reception desk was in the middle of the space, with yet another suited man sitting behind it. Three chairs were against the wall to the left, and another door was to the right. There was nothing else in the room.

"Please have a seat," the man said.

Feeling like a guinea pig that had just visited the vet's office, Christian was on edge. She hadn't been inside the MI6 building for several years. Operatives were mostly unknown to other agents, and almost never seen at headquarters.

After a few minutes, the man behind the desk picked up the phone receiver and listened for a few seconds. Then,

266

he hung it up. "Assistant Director Hibbert will be with you in a few minutes," he said, peering over the desk at Christian.

She nodded. Newman Hibbert was the assistant director of operations who managed the handler agents and their operatives. She'd never met him personally.

The side door opened and another suited man waved for her to follow him. They walked down a hallway, past two different rooms full of cubicles that looked like something out of the late 1990s, then another room full of filing cabinets, and finally came to a stop outside of an office with Newman Hibbert's name on the metal plate. The man knocked, then opened the door.

"Excalibur," the man behind the desk said, standing with his hand out to greet her. "Come in. Have a seat."

Christian did as she was told, with the door closing behind her.

"I apologize for making you wait so long. We have to follow protocol when an operative comes in to ensure they are really the person whom we believe them to be," he said. "Anyhow, I'm surprised to see you, especially after finding out you'd gone dark. However, I had a feeling I'd be seeing you at some point."

"Sir, what I'm about to tell you is disastrous for the agency," she said.

"Go on." He nodded.

"Obviously you are aware of Lancelot's death, which is why you've been expecting me. However, what you do not know is Special Agent Fergus McDonald killed him after compromising mission A06217X."

"That's preposterous!"

"If you'll let me explain, I have the proof with me."

He waved his hand for her to keep going.

267

"McDonald was working for a small terrorist organization run out of Morocco but headed by the Polisario Front in Western Sahara. Everyone involved is deceased. The package has been destroyed, and Natalia Luis de Faria Moreno is safely hidden," she said, pulling the thumb drive from her pocket. She set it on the desk and slid it over to him, nodding towards his computer.

ADO Hibbert exhaled a heavy breath as he picked it up and stuck it into the USB port on the side of his laptop. The first video that came up was Emir Al-Khalef admitting to everything and driving Christian to the location. The second video showed Fergus McDonald with the necklace, talking about how he killed Lancelot, as well as Sabio Davi de Faria Moreno, and compromised the mission from within. The last video was Farooq Ashraf Massoud, also implicating himself as the money behind the operation, while giving his motive for stealing French government property to start a war. When the final video cut off, Hibbert removed the thumb drive and put it in his desk drawer.

"I had a feeling you'd go dark when Lancelot died. He was able to upload the entire mission file to me before he self-destructed his computer. He knew someone had gotten into his system and was working diligently to figure out who it was. They seemed to be right on top of you every step of the way. Obviously, it was Fergus McDonald." He shook his head in disgust. "I'm glad you came in. You had no idea how far this went in the agency and could've easily remained dark. What I'd really like to know is how you accomplished all of this … while dark," he said, folding his hands together.

"I had help … yes. But I can't reveal my source."

ADO Hibbert smiled. "Tell Colette Babin she has a job at MI6 if she wants one."

Christian stared at him. She knew once the agency found out Lancelot was dead, they would be monitoring anything to do with his current mission. They'd obviously caught on when Colette had logged onto World Vision with an Interpol IP address.

Seeing the crease form in her brow as she put the pieces together, ADO Hibbert continued, "I trusted you to complete your mission. I knew you'd go after whoever did this. You're a great operative, Special Agent Garnier."

"Thank you, Sir," she said.

"I'm serious about Babin."

Christian smiled. "She'd never do it. She hates spies."

He laughed.

"There is one more thing," Christian stated. "I have been unable to track down Ana Cintia de Luis Moreno."

"Fortunately, Lancelot had her hidden in a safe house in Spain. He had an operative sitting on her when he sent you for the package. As soon as Sabio was murdered, the operative moved her. Fergus McDonald had never worked with Lancelot and didn't know any of his deep safe house locations. She's safe, and now that this mess is over, she'll be able to return home immediately. Sabio Davi de Faria Moreno's body has been held until his next of kin can claim it, so she'll be able to lay him to rest properly."

"If you can get word to her through the operative, have him give her this number to call her daughter as soon as possible," Christian said, handing him a piece of paper.

"If that is all, you are dismissed. Your new handler will be in contact momentarily. Here is the new sim card for your phone."

Christian slipped the card into her pocket and shook his hand before leaving the room. The suited man who had escorted her in, once again led her in the opposite direction, all the way to the front door, which quickly closed behind her.

*

The inside of St. Benedict Cathedral was beautifully decorated. The walls were off-white with bright white trim, which reflected the 100-year-old, arched, stained-glass windows, and the nave was carpeted in a color that looked like red wine. The pews were all dark teak wood, with the lower level facing the sanctuary, and the upper level turned in, facing the nave on both sides. The outer edge of each row on both levels had ornate carvings dating back to the 19th century. The wall behind the sanctuary matched the pews, and the carpet was the same as what covered the nave. Three massive chandeliers hung above the nave, and the wide, arched ceiling above the sanctuary and choir pews had a single chandelier matching the others. A large gold cross sat on a narrow table at the back of the sanctuary, with two candlesticks on either side of it.

The choir, dressed in black cassocks with white surplices over them, were in the middle of Amazing Grace when Christian walked into the cathedral, dressed in a black pantsuit with a light gray, button down shirt. Half of the pews on the lower level were full. Wanting to go unnoticed, she took the stairs to the empty second level and chose a second-row pew near the front. Looking down, she saw the casket sitting on a stand in front of the sanctuary on the trestle. It was draped in a white pall that had a dark red line down the middle, and a gold cross in the center.

She wasn't Episcopalian, like Lancelot had been, or even Catholic for that matter, but she still felt the need to cross herself. She took her right hand, placing it against her forehead, then the center of her chest, followed by the right and left sides of her chest.

As the song ended, Christian noticed the priest. He was vested in a white alb with an off-white chasuble over it that had three appliquéd crosses in gold lamé down the front, making a simple yet elegant statement to the otherwise solid white vestments that were worn for weddings and funerals within the Anglican Church.

"O God, whose mercies cannot be numbered," the priest said, opening with a prayer. "Accept our prayers on behalf of thy servant Lawrence Dunnigan and grant him an entrance into the land of light and joy, in the fellowship of thy saints; through Jesus Christ thy Son our Lord, who liveth and reigneth with thee and the Holy Spirit, one God, now and forever. Amen."

"Amen," replied the congregation before taking their seats.

Christian sat down, vaguely listening as the priest went on, beginning the liturgy with a reading from the Old Testament. She was raised without much religion, as her parents weren't married in a church and thus, didn't follow any religion themselves. She'd learned a long time ago about God, heaven and hell through her parents, but they'd mostly reflected on right and wrong and do unto others. She'd become somewhat Buddhist while living in China but hadn't stayed true to that religion and culture over the years.

The priest moved on, reading Psalm 23. "The Lord is my shepherd; I shall not want. He maketh me to lie down in green pastures; he leadeth me beside the still waters. He restoreth my soul; he leadeth me in the paths of righteousness for Lawrence's Burial. Yea, though I walk through the valley of the shadow of death, I will fear no evil; for thou art with me; thy rod and thy staff, they comfort me."

Christian turned her attention once again to the priest as his words brought back the memorial service that was held for the plane crash victims in the terrorist attack that killed her parents. Most of the bodies were never recovered, including her parents, so a mass memorial service had been held by a local church. She'd sat in one of the front pews, listening to a man she'd never met, talk about the Lord and resurrection. He'd known nothing of her parents, yet he'd included their names as he'd read down a list of passengers and crew members. One of the last things he read during the service was that same Psalm. She remembered specifically the line: 'Though I walk through the valley of the shadow of death, I will fear no evil.' She wrote that line on the wall in her dorm room at the MI6 training academy, using it as fuel to keep her going, and a reminder of why she was there, with hopes she'd never forget.

The sound of footsteps nearby, brought Christian out of her cloud of memories. She turned her head to the left in time to see a man approaching. He was dressed in a dark suit and tie, and had gray hair with patches of white on the sides, thick eyebrows over brown eyes, and no facial hair. She watched as he quietly sat down next to her.

"They're about to do the Eucharist," he said, speaking with a pronounced English accent.

Christian nodded slightly. "I won't be staying."

"I'm not a fan of funerals either," he added, holding his hand out. "I'm Merlin, by the way."

Christian's hand froze against his.

"This is the last time you'll see me face to face." He pulled his hand free, leaving a small piece of paper in her hand.

Christian barely had time to turn her attention back to the funeral, before the man, *Merlin*, vanished like a ghost. She knew without looking at the paper that the number to call in for her next mission was on it. She stood, looked down at the casket one last time, crossed herself, then walked away. On her way out of the cathedral, she read the numbers and slipped the paper into the holy water font.

The ink washed away and the paper disintegrated in the amount of seconds it took Christian to walk outside and get into the Black Taxi idling by the curb.

CHAPTER THIRTY-SIX

Natalia curled her legs under her as she dipped her day-old doughnut into her coffee. Snowflakes continued to fall outside, creating a cloudlike blanket over the minuscule front yard. Her tired eyes began to close, but the sound of a phone ringing grabbed her attention. It wasn't Lera or Adrik's phone. She quickly ran to her room. The burner phone Christian had left her was ringing.

"Christian?!" she answered excitedly.

"Natalia …?"

"Mamãe?"

"Sim! Minha filha doce! I'm so happy to hear your voice," her mother said, crying.

"Oh, Mamãe. I love you and miss you so much."

"Nita, your Papai …"

"I know," Natalia sighed, wiping her own tears. "I'm so sorry."

"I don't even know how. Why," her mother cried.

Natalia closed her eyes and shook her head. It broke her heart to hear the pain in her mother's voice. "Where are you?"

"London. I'm getting on a plane. I need to go. I love you, Minha filha doce. I'll see you soon."

The line went dead before Natalia could say anything else. She stared at the black screen on the phone, feeling like she'd just had the worst dream of her life. When she turned to walk out of the room, she nearly ran into Adrik.

"It's time for you to go home," he said, handing her a plane ticket.

EPILOGUE

Natalia felt the heat from the sun, warming her skin as she stepped out onto the balcony of her apartment. The blue, cloudless sky was full of sunshine, making her smile for the first time in weeks.

It had been over a month since she'd last seen or heard from Christian. Her life had somewhat gone back to normal after she and her mother laid her father to rest four weeks ago. The last two months felt like a nightmare that haunted her day in and day out. Having the funeral for her father was like losing him all over again, and every time she closed her eyes at night, Christian appeared in her dreams. She'd tried to go back to work; back to her *life*. In the beginning, she felt lost, and a little scared. She found herself looking over her shoulder, waiting for someone who was trying to hurt her, but the anxiety was slowly fading away. After finding out about her father being killed and she being kidnapped, which was the story that was told, minus MI6, her company gave her the promotion she was working so hard to get when she'd gone on her birthday vacation to begin with. She was weeks away from taking the test to get her PHD.

"Papai, you would be proud," she said to the sky. On a whim, she decided to go to the beach to celebrate. She packed a day bag and prepared to leave.

Christian Garnier was standing a foot away, about to knock as the door opened. "I'm sorry it took me so long," she said.

Natalia dropped her bag to the floor and threw her arms around Christian's neck. Christian picked her up as their lips met in a ferocious kiss. Natalia wrapped her legs around Christian's waist as she kicked the door shut behind them. Then, Christian walked across the apartment, carrying her.

"I knew you would come back to me. I love you," Natalia said, breathlessly.

"I love you, too," Christian replied with a smile as she lay her back on the bed, simultaneously crawling on top of her.

About the Author

Graysen Morgen is the bestselling author of several bestselling lesbian fiction titles. After spending most of her lifetime in the Florida sun where she was born and raised, she now resides in the Midwest. She enjoys reading, writing, coaching rugby, boating, fishing, watching sports, snowy days, and spending as much time as possible with her family.

You can contact Graysen at graysenmorgen@aol.com; like her fan page on Facebook.com/graysenmorgen; follow her on Twitter: @graysenmorgen and Instagram: @graysenmorgen

Other Titles Available From Triplicity Publishing

Stargazing by Kathy L. Salt. Lissa stared open-mouthed at the GIF that played over and over on the screen in front of her. Heat flushed to her face, igniting her skin. Her heart started pounding in her chest. *Stupid internet, it should really come with a warning label.* She's never been interested in relationships or sex and as the years have gone by she has retreated more and more into her work. Everything changes when she meets Star, a porn actress with a heart of gold and a troubled childhood. *They say that opposites attract, but how much of that is true? What chance do they have when one of them is a virgin and the other one star in pornography?*

A New Beginning by KD Rye. There's a quietness, an empty space, that surrounds your life after losing someone you love. Autumn lives in that empty space, day after day, following the same routine, in unresolved angst. She doesn't know how to keep her head above water until the arrival of May, a mysterious dream-like girl who just moved in. Autumn finds refuge in their quickly defined friendship. As her mother falls deeper into depression, Autumn doesn't see a way out of her current situation, until May shows her that anything is possible. However, nothing is what it seems and Autumn has to decipher if the relationship she has built with May is real.

I Belong with Her by Domina Alexandra. Tajel Pierce loves the thrill of being a paramedic. Every call she goes on gives her a rush. She makes no time for a personal life. No one can ruin her love for her career. Then there is Arianna Castaldi, who just transferred to her new paramedic position in a whole new state. All she needs is a new start without any distractions. Arianna and Tajel's relationship doesn't start off perfect. Embarrassed of the one night stand Arianna believes she had with Tajel, she wants to pretend they never met and make their relationship strictly business. The only choice they have to keep from strangling each other is to go from denying their feelings to accepting them as they work through intense 911 calls.

Awakened by Fate by Lynn Lawler. Jackie is a woman living life according to her own rules. She's married, but it's the unspoken, open kind. She can have as many female lovers as she likes; she just can't talk about them. After a bizarre encounter turns her world upside down, things slowly begin to change. She finds herself in desperation as she searches for answers. What she discovers is nothing is delivered in a neatly wrapped box. Now that everything has been brought out into the open, she finds she can't run away from her truth anymore. With her new life, comes new responsibilities and a different outcome than what she was expecting. Jackie isn't alone in the story. She meets several new people who help her along her journey.

Nautical Delights by S. L. Gape. Lady Elizabeth Barrington has spent her entire life trying to please her family; constantly opting for a quiet life, she utilises her profession as a doctor to keep out of her families' clutches; bar the annual two-week Caribbean private cruise, where there is simply no budge. Confined to two weeks on board the Iconica super yacht, she intends on keeping her head down and enjoying as much of the holiday as she can, whilst keeping her family at arm's length. Until a crew member catches her eye.

Whispers of the Heart by KA Moll. Days after completing her fellowship in pediatric ophthalmology, thirty-five-year-old Aki Williams travels from her home in Los Angeles to a small town in Illinois, interviewing for a job that she doesn't want. What she does want is to meet her biological sister, Jack Camdon, a sister whom she didn't know existed until she dreamt of her. Three years ago on Sunday, forty-three-year-old professor of archaeology, Carsyn Lyndon, lost her parents and her wife in a tragic accident. Since then, she's suffered from PTSD and loneliness. She's kind-hearted and handsome but dates no one. When she meets Aki at her four-year-old Godson's birthday party, they're incredibly attracted to one another, and those feelings intensify during a family camping trip— a particularly interesting development for Aki since prior to that she'd never considered that she might be a lesbian.

Worlds Apart by S.L. Gape. Hollywood A-lister Heidi Spencer-Brady is everything you'd expect of an Idol. Loved by all, the British Beauty is graceful, talented, humble and so far removed from the 'typical' LA scene. When her husband's infidelity with his new 'leading lady' is leaked, Dawn, Heidi's best friend and manager, goes all out to protect her. She arranges for Heidi to go back to the UK and stay on her cousins farm they had visited as children, much to the disappointment of the animal fearing Heidi.

Castor Valley (Law & Order Series Book 2) by Graysen Morgen. Jessie Henry is torn when she reads about the capture of the Doyle brothers, two young men who were part of her old gang. Unable to let them hang for a crime she's sure they didn't commit, Jessie leaves her wife and the Town of Boone Creek behind, and sets out on a journey back to the one place she thought she'd never see again, *Castor Valley*. Ellie Henry watches the love of her life leave, not knowing if she will ever return. When she gets an odd telegram, nearly a week later, she fears Jessie is in trouble. With no other choice, she goes to the one person who can help her.

Close Enough to Touch by Cade Brogan. Joanna Grey injects the deadly poison into the chamber of the syringe—time after time. She's murdered before and she'll do it again. She's intelligent, educated, and beautiful. Rylee Hayes is a respected homicide detective. Her best friends are her grandparents, her coonhound, and her partner—in that order. Kenzie Bigham is the single mom of a thirteen-year-old, a church secretary, and a woman who's struggled much of her adult life with her own sexuality. Their paths will cross when Rylee's new investigation involves members of Kenzie's congregation. Will Rylee have what it takes to meet the challenge of a serial killer who's proven herself to be a more than worthy opponent?

Fight to the Top by S. L. Gape. Georgia is a forty year old, single, Area Director from Manchester, UK who is all work and definitely no play. Having no time to socialise or spend time with her family she prides herself on being fit and well-polished. Erika is an Area Director for the same company, but in the United States. Whilst she is concentrating so heavily on the promotion she has been fighting for, she's starting to feel like her life outside of work is falling apart. The two women are exceptionally different, and worlds apart. Both of their lives are turned upside down when their jobs are snatched from under their noses, and they are suddenly faced with being thrown together by their bosses for one last major project...in Texas.

***Boone Creek (Law & Order Series book 1*)** by Graysen Morgen. Jessie Henry is looking for a new life. She's unknown in the town of Boone Creek when she arrives, and wants to keep it that way. When she's offered the job of Town Marshal, she takes it, believing that protecting others and upholding the law is the penance for her past. Ellie Fray is a widowed, shopkeeper. She generally keeps to herself, but the mysterious new Town Marshal both intrigues and infuriates her. She believes the last thing the town needs is someone stirring up trouble with the outlaws who have taken over.

Witness by Joan L. Anderson. Becca and Kate have lived together for eight years, and have always spent their vacation in a tropical paradise, lying on a beach. This year, Becca wanted to try something different: a seven day, 65-mile hike in the beautiful Cascade Mountains of Washington state. Their peaceful vacation turns to horror when they stumble upon a brutal murder taking place in the back country.

Too Soon by S.L. Gape. Brooke is a twenty-nine year old detective from Oxford, who has her life pretty much planned out until her boss and partner of nine years, Maria, tells her their relationship is over. When Brooke finds out the truth, that Maria cheated on her with their best friend Paula, she decides to get her life back on track by getting away for six weeks in Anglesey, North Wales. Chloe, a thirty three year old artist and art director, owns a log cabin on Anglesey where she spends each weekend painting and surfing. After returning from a surf, she stumbles upon the somewhat uptight and enigmatic Brooke.

Blue Ice Landing by KA Moll. Coy is a beautiful blonde with a southern accent and a successful practice as a physician assistant. She has a comfortable home, good friends, and a loving family. She's also a widow, carrying a burden of responsibility for her wife's untimely death. Coby is a woman with secrets. She's estranged from her family, a recovering alcoholic, and alone because she's convinced that she's unlovable. When she loses her job as a heavy equipment operator, she'll accept one that'll force her to step way outside her comfort zone. When Coy quits her job to accept a position in Antarctica, her path will cross with Coby's. Their attraction to one another will be immediate, and despite their differences, it won't be long before they fall in love. But for these two, with all their baggage, will love be enough?

Never Quit (Never Series book 2) by Graysen Morgen. Two years after stepping away from the action as a Coast Guard Rescue Swimmer to become an instructor, Finley finds herself in charge of the most difficult class of cadets she's ever faced, while also juggling the taxing demands of having a home life with her partner Nicole, and their fifteen year old daughter. Jordy Ross gave up everything, dropping out of college, and leaving her family behind, to join the Coast Guard and become a rescue swimmer cadet. The extreme training tests her fitness level, pushing her mentally and physically further than she's ever been in her life, but it's the aggressive competition between her and another female cadet that proves to be the most challenging.

For a Moment's Indiscretion by KA Moll. With ten years of marriage under their belt, Zane and Jaina are coasting. The little things they used to do for one another have fallen by the wayside. They've gotten busy with life. They've forgotten to nurture their love and relationship. Even soul mates can stumble on hard times and have marital difficulties. Enter Amelia, a new faculty member in Jaina's building. She's new in town, young, and very pretty. When an argument with Zane causes Jaina to storm out angry, she reaches out to Amelia. Of course, she seizes the opportunity. And for a moment of indiscretion, Jaina could lose everything.

Never Let Go (Never Series book 1) by Graysen Morgen. For Coast Guard Rescue Swimmer, Finley Morris, life is good. She loves her job, is well respected by her peers, and has been given an opportunity to take her career to the next level. The only thing missing is the love of her life, who walked out, taking their daughter with her, seven years earlier. When Finley gets a call from her ex, saying their teenage daughter is coming to spend the summer with her, she's floored. While spending more time with her daughter, whom she doesn't get to see often, and learning to be a full-time parent, Finley quickly realizes she has not, and will never, let go of what is important.

Pursuit by Joan L. Anderson. Claire is a workaholic attorney who flies to Paris to lick her wounds after being dumped by her girlfriend of seventeen years. On the plane she chats with the young woman sitting next to her, and when they land the woman is inexplicably detained in Customs. Claire is surprised when she later runs into the woman in the city. They agree to meet for breakfast the next morning, but when the woman doesn't show up Claire goes to her hotel and makes a horrifying discovery. She soon finds herself ensnared in a web of intrigue and international terrorism, becoming the target of a high stakes game of cat and mouse through the streets of Paris.

Wrecked by Sydney Canyon. To most people, the *Duchess* is a myth formed by old pirates tales, but to Reid Cavanaugh, a Caribbean island bum and one of the best divers and treasure hunters in the world, it's a real, seventeenth century pirate ship—the holy grail of underwater treasure hunting. Reid uses the same cunning tactics she always has before setting out to find the lost ship. However, she is forced to bring her business partner's daughter along as collateral this time because he doesn't trust her. Neither woman is thrilled, but being cooped up on a small dive boat for days, forces them to get know each other quickly.

Arson by Austen Thorne. Madison Drake is a detective for the Stetson Beach Police Department. The last thing she wants to do is show a new detective the ropes, especially when a fire investigation becomes arson to cover up a murder. Madison butts heads with Tara, her trainee, deals with sarcasm from Nic, her ex-girlfriend who is a patrol officer, and finds calm in the chaos of police work with Jamie, her best friend who is the county medical examiner. Arson is the first of many in a series of novella episodes surrounding the fictional Stetson Beach Police Department and Detective Madison Drake.

Change of Heart by KA Moll. Courtney Holloman is a woman at the top of her game. She's successful, wealthy, and a highly sought after Washington lobbyist. She has money, her job, booze, and nothing else. In quiet moments, against her will, her mind drifts back to her days in high school and to all that she gave up. Jack Camdon is a complex woman, and yet not at all. She is also a woman who has never moved beyond the sudden and unexplained departure of her high school sweetheart, her lover, and her soul mate. When circumstances bring Courtney back to town two decades later, their paths will cross. Will it be too late?

Mommies (Bridal Series book 3) **by Graysen Morgen.** Britton and her wife Daphne have been married for a year and a half and are happy with their life, until Britton's mother hounds her to find out why her sister Bridget hasn't decided to have children yet. This prompts Daphne to bring up the big subject of having kids of their own with Britton. Britton hadn't really thought much about having kids, but her love for Daphne makes her see life and their future together in a whole new way when they decide to become mommies.

Haunting Love **by K.A. Moll.** Anna Crestwood was raised in the strict beliefs of a religious sect nestled in the foothills of the Smoky Mountains. She's a lesbian with a ton of baggage—fearful, guilty, and alone. Very few things would compel her to leave the familiar. The job offer of a lifetime is one of them. Gabe Garst is a police officer. She's also a powerful medium. Her work with juvenile delinquents and ghosts is all that keeps her going. Inside she's dead, certain that her capacity to love is buried six feet under. Anna and Gabe's paths cross. Their attraction is immediate, but they hold back until all hope seems lost.

Rapture & Rogue by Sydney Canyon. Taren Rauley is happy and in a good relationship, until the one person she thought she'd never see again comes back into her life. She struggles to keep the past from colliding with the present as old feelings she thought were dead and gone, begin to haunt her. In college, Gianna Revisi was a mastermind, ring-leading, crime boss. Now, she has a great life and spends her time running Rapture and Rogue, the two establishments she built from the ground up. The last person she ever expects to see walk into one of them, is the girl who walked out on her, breaking her heart five years ago.

Second Chance by Sydney Canyon. After an attack on her convoy, Marine Corps Staff Sergeant, Darien Hollister, must learn to live without her sight. When an experimental procedure allows her to see again, Darien is torn, knowing someone had to die in order for this to happen.

She embarks on a journey to personally thank the donor's family, but is too stunned to tell them the truth. Mixed emotions stir inside of her as she slowly gets to the know the people that feel like so much more than strangers to her. When the truth finally comes out, Darien walks away, taking the second chance that she's been given to go back to the only life she's ever known, but she's not the only one with a second chance at life.

Meant to Be by Graysen Morgen. Brandt is about to walk down the aisle with her girlfriend, when an unexpected chain of events turns her world upside down, causing her to question the last three years of her life. A chance encounter sparks a mix of rage and excitement that she has never felt before. Summer is living life and following her dreams, all the while, harboring a huge secret that could ruin her career. She believes that some things are better kept in the dark, until she has her third run-in with a woman she had hoped to never see again, and gives into temptation. Brandt and Summer start believing everything happens for a reason as they learn the true meaning of meant to be.

Coming Home by Graysen Morgen. After tragedy derails TJ Abernathy's life, she packs up her three year old son and heads back to Pennsylvania to live with her grandmother on the family farm. TJ picks back up where she left off eight years earlier, tending to the fruit and nut tree orchard, while learning her grandmother's secret trade. Soon, TJ's high school sweetheart and the same girl who broke her heart, comes back into her life, threatening to steal it away once again. As the weeks turn into months and tragedy strikes again, TJ realizes coming home was the best thing she could've ever done.

Special Assignment by Austen Thorne. Secret Service Agent Parker Meeks has her hands full when she gets her new assignment, protecting a Congressman's teenage daughter, who has had threats made on her life and been whisked away to a Christian boarding school under an alias to finish out her senior year. Parker is fine with the assignment, until she finds out she has to go undercover as a Canon Priest. The last thing Parker expects to find is a beautiful, art history teacher, who is intrigued by her in more ways than one.

Miracle at Christmas by Sydney Canyon. A Modern Twist on the Classic Scrooge Story. Dylan is a power-hungry lawyer who pushed away everything good in her life to become the best defense attorney in the, often winning the worst cases and keeping anyone with enough money out of jail. She's visited on Christmas Eve by her deceased law partner, who threatens her with a life in hell like his own, if she doesn't change her path. During the course of the night, she is taken on a journey through her past, present, and future with three very different spirits.

Bella Vita by Sydney Canyon. Brady is the First Officer of the crew on the Bella Vita, a luxury charter yacht in the Caribbean. She enjoys the laidback island lifestyle, and is accustomed to high profile guests, but when a U.S. Senator charters the yacht as a gift to his beautiful twin daughters who have just graduated from college and a few of their friends, she literally has her hands full.

Brides (Bridal Series book 2) by Graysen Morgen. Britton Prescott is dating the love of her life, Daphne Attwood, after a few tumultuous events that happened to unravel at her sister's wedding reception, seven months earlier. She's happy with the way things are, but immense pressure from her family and friends to take the next step, nearly sends her back to the single life. The idea of a long engagement and simple wedding are thrown out the window, as both families take over, rushing Britton and Daphne to the altar in a matter of weeks.

Cypress Lake by Graysen Morgen. The small town of Cypress Lake is rocked when one murder after another happens. Dani Ricketts, the Chief Deputy for the Cypress Lake Sheriff's Office, realizes the murders are linked. She's surprised when the girl that broke her heart in high school has not only returned home, but she's also Dani's only suspect. Kristen Malone has come back to Cypress Lake to put the past behind her so that she can move on with her life. Seeing Dani Ricketts again throws her off-guard, nearly derailing her plans to finally rid herself and her family of Cypress Lake.

Crashing Waves by Graysen Morgen. After a tragic accident, Pro Surfer, Rory Eden, spends her days hiding in the surf and snowboard manufacturing company that she built from the ground up, while living her life as a shell of the person that she once was. Rory's world is turned upside down when a young surfer pursues her, asking for the one thing she can't do. Adler Troy and Dr. Cason Macauley from Graysen Morgen's bestselling novel: *Falling Snow*, make an appearance in this romantic adventure about life, love, and letting go.

Bridesmaid of Honor (Bridal Series book 1) by Graysen Morgen. Britton Prescott's best friend is getting married and she's the maid of honor. As if that isn't enough to deal with, Britton's sister announces she's getting married in the same month and her maid of honor is her best friend Daphne, the same woman who has tormented Britton for years. Britton has to suck it up and play nice, instead of scratching her eyes out, because she and Daphne are in both weddings. Everyone is counting on them to behave like adults.

Falling Snow by Graysen Morgen. Dr. Cason Macauley, a high-speed trauma surgeon from Denver meets Adler Troy, a professional snowboarder and sparks fly. The last thing Cason wants is a relationship and Adler doesn't realize what's right in front of her until it's gone, but will it be too late?

Fate vs. Destiny by Graysen Morgen. Logan Greer devotes her life to investigating plane crashes for the National Transportation Safety Board. Brooke McCabe is an investigator with the Federal Aviation Association who literally flies by the seat of her pants. When Logan gets tangled in head games with both women will she choose fate or destiny?

Just Me by Graysen Morgen. Wild child Ian Wiley has to grow up and take the reins of the hundred year old family business when tragedy strikes. Cassidy Harland is a little surprised that she came within an inch of picking up a gorgeous stranger in a bar and is shocked to find out that stranger is the new head of her company.

Love Loss Revenge by Graysen Morgen. Rian Casey is an FBI Agent working the biggest case of her career and madly in love with her girlfriend. Her world is turned upside when tragedy strikes. Heartbroken, she tries to rebuild her life. When she discovers the truth behind what really happened that awful night she decides justice isn't good enough, and vows revenge on everyone involved.

Natural Instinct by Graysen Morgen. Chandler Scott is a Marine Biologist who keeps her private life private. Corey Joslen is intrigued by Chandler from the moment she meets her. Chandler is forced to finally open her life up to Corey. It backfires in Corey's face and sends her running. Will either woman learn to trust her natural instinct?

Secluded Heart by Graysen Morgen. Chase Leery is an overworked cardiac surgeon with a group of best friends that have an opinion and a reason for everything. When she meets a new artist named Remy Sheridan at her best friend's art gallery she is captivated by the reclusive woman. When Chase finds out why Remy is so sheltered will she put her career on the line to help her or is it too difficult to love someone with a secluded heart?

In Love, at War by Graysen Morgen. Charley Hayes is in the Army Air Force and stationed at Ford Island in Pearl Harbor. She is the commanding officer of her own female-only service squadron and doing the one thing she loves most, repairing airplanes. Life is good for Charley, until the day she finds herself falling in love while fighting for her life as her country is thrown haphazardly into World War II. Can she survive being in love and at war?

Fast Pitch by Graysen Morgen. Graham Cahill is a senior in college and the catcher and captain of the softball team. Despite being an all-star pitcher, Bailey Michaels is young and arrogant. Graham and Bailey are forced to get to know each other off the field in order to learn to work together on the field. Will the extra time pay off or will it drive a nail through the team?

Submerged by Graysen Morgen. Assistant District Attorney Layne Carmichael had no idea that the sexy woman she took home from a local bar for a one night stand would turn out to be someone she would be prosecuting months later. Scooter is a Naval Officer on a submarine who changes women like she changes uniforms. When she is accused of a heinous crime she is shocked to see her latest conquest sitting across from her as the prosecuting attorney.

Vow of Solitude by Austen Thorne. Detective Jordan Denali is in a fight for her life against the ghosts from her past and a Serial Killer taunting her with his every move. She lives a life of solitude and plans to keep it that way. When Callie Marceau, a curious Medical Examiner, decides she wants in on the biggest case of her career, as well as, Jordan's life, Jordan is powerless to stop her.

Igniting Temptation by Sydney Canyon. Mackenzie Trotter is the Head of Pediatrics at the local hospital. Her life takes a rather unexpected turn when she meets a flirtatious, beautiful fire fighter. Both women soon discover it doesn't take much to ignite temptation.

One Night by Sydney Canyon. While on a business trip, Caylen Jarrett spends an amazing night with a beautiful stripper. Months later, she is shocked and confused when that same woman re-enters her life. The fact that this stranger could destroy her career doesn't bother her. C.J. is more terrified of the feelings this woman stirs in her. Could she have fallen in love in one night and not even known it?

Fine by Sydney Canyon. Collin Anderson hides behind a façade, pretending everything is fine. Her workaholic wife and best friend are both oblivious as she goes on an emotional journey, battling a potentially hereditary disease that her mother has been diagnosed with. The only person who knows what is really going on, is Collin's doctor. The same doctor, who is an acquaintance that she's always been attracted to, and who has a partner of her own.

Shadow's Eyes by Sydney Canyon. Tyler McCain is the owner of a large ranch that breeds and sells different types of horses. She isn't exactly thrilled when a Hollywood movie producer shows up wanting to film his latest movie on her property. Reegan Delsol is an up and coming actress who has everything going for her when she lands the lead role in a new film, but there one small problem that could blow the entire picture.

Light Reading: A Collection of Novellas by Sydney Canyon. Four of Sydney Canyon's novellas together in one book, including the bestsellers Shadow's Eyes and One Night.

Visit us at www.tri-pub.com